Dear Clara

Dear Clara

SHELLY E. POWELL

SWEETWATER BOOKS
An imprint of Cedar Fort, Inc.
Springville, Utah

ISBN 13: 978-1-4621-3833-3

Published by Sweetwater Books, an imprint of Cedar Fort, Inc.
2373 W. 700 S., Springville, UT 84663
Distributed by Cedar Fort, Inc., www.cedarfort.com

Library of Congress Control Number: 2020925042

Cover design by Shawnda T. Craig
Cover design © 2021 Cedar Fort, Inc.
Edited and typeset by Valene Wood

Printed in the United States of America

10 9 8 7 6 5 4 3 2 1

Printed on acid-free paper

To Jacob, whose letters charmed me from the beginning

Prologue

A letter is a dangerous thing, Clara thought, *alive with words, yet deceptively still, a sentiment made solid, yet helplessly bare.*

The power of that thought squeezed her hand and rose up her arm like a coiling snake as she gripped her pen.

Calm down. It's just a letter.

She took a steadying breath. Not just a letter. A love letter, her first, to a man she could barely recall ever meeting. She could write anything, any secret, any confession, and give the paper a life of its own, or rather, she would breathe her life into it. Even so, its life would begin anew when *he* read it.

To think he will read it! And think about me! The coiling sensation made its way to her chest and tightened. She didn't know if she could do it, if she could make herself so vulnerable. *What will he do with it?* She could write her heart on that paper and offer it to him, a feat both exhilarating and liberating, but committing her heart to paper would do nothing to protect it.

Hopes and dreams could be wrapped and sealed like a gift, but she could never ensure he would value them. Her letter was a risk.

Or a promise, she countered, *full of possibilities.* A promise she would give their love a chance.

Clara applied her pen and let the words fly from the ink with a will of their own. At last, her thoughts flowed, line after line, stroke after stroke, poetic yet blunt in their honesty. Though it had taken her days, perhaps weeks, to discern her heart, she knew she needed to confess the love that had taken hold there. Otherwise, she risked a lifetime of regret.

With the next dip of her pen, her hand shook with unsteadied nerves, aware that her message was too unrestrained for a lady, and a stray drop of ink fell and seeped into the corner of the letter. She flinched and imagined her own blood had dripped there. Was her heart already so fragile, pricked by a mere thought?

Yes, a letter is a dangerous thing.

Chapter 1

Clara Everton knew she was a competent dancer, but her partner had commented on it so many times, she began to doubt it.
Wasn't there anything else he could say?

"You really are an exquisite dancer, Miss Everton."

"You are too kind, sir," she repeated, having given up on varying
her responses just as she had given up on London balls.

The music ended abruptly, and Clara, out of breath, bowed to her
partner and escaped from the dance floor.

It was a mistake to come tonight, she thought. She didn't care for
any of it anymore, not the extravagant dress, not the rich food, and
definitely not the men, who were either too irksome to tolerate or
not sensible enough to fall in love with her. With a whole season in
London nearly at an end, and not a single viable suitor to show for it,
the luster had worn off and in the wake of all the grandeur trailed a
predictability that wore on her senses. She just wanted to go home.

She wanted to laugh with her father and draw under the oak tree
by the pond. She wanted to kick off her slippers and run through the
grass, and oh, how she wanted to ride her own horse again! But more
than anything, she wanted to be where she belonged, where she felt
most like herself. Milton Manor—home. It was the fresh breeze that
kept the stuffiness of the ballroom at bay. With a deep breath, she
remembered she just had to make it through tonight. Then it was only
a few days' time before she would be sleeping in her own bed again.
Unfortunately, the night was young.

Clara chose a place along the wall to pause and fan herself. Her white muslin gown was clingy with sweat, and it felt good to rest. Tugging at her waist, she straightened her ribbon, blue to match her eyes, and noticed a long strand of hair fall loose from her upswept curls. She twisted it in her finger, noticing how the candlelight brought out the bronze highlights from the chestnut brown, and brushed it back. She tried to blend into the surrounding scenery, but it was pointless to hope that she could evade the watchful eye of her aunt, Louisa.

Louisa was her father's sister and lived with them in Milton. It was all due to Louisa's persuasion that Clara's father had finally consented to a season in London. The expense might have been a small deterrent in previous years, but Clara suspected her father just didn't want to see her grow up. At twenty years old, Clara was out in society, but opportunities for socializing had been limited to small assemblies and local dinner parties. She had never spent more than a week in London until now.

Clara sometimes thought it would have been better to keep it that way. London teemed with an energy and expectation she doubted she could ever keep pace with. So much wealth, so many outings, all calculated to advance ever upward among London's elite. But where did that leave Clara, the daughter of a disinherited lady and a poor man with no title?

True, Clara's mother had been disinherited when she fell in love with George Everton, who was merely the son of a country doctor, but a year after the marriage, Clara's father inherited his great uncle's estate and thereby made peace with his wife's family. The young couple left their modest cottage for Milton Manor, and Clara was raised in comfort while still learning the hard work and self-sufficiency her father had grown up with. She was an elegant, oddly skilled young woman, but no one in London was impressed that she dressed without help and could make her own bread.

Clara continued to fan herself as she thought about such distinctions and wondered how much time she had before Louisa found her. It turned out to be very little.

"Well, my dear?" asked Louisa as her slightly plump figure strode over, skirts bunched in one hand.

"Yes, Aunt?" Clara asked, knowing perfectly well what her aunt wanted to hear.

"Your dance partner! That was Mr. Garrett! From what I hear, he has a very elegant estate and a comfortable living. Every girl in this room is hoping he will dance with her, if I'm not mistaken." Little beads of sweat bordered Louisa's hairline and glistened as much as her jewelry, evidence she had walked several laps around the ballroom to examine the eligible gentleman on Clara's behalf.

Clara looked around the room and continued to fan herself. "Is that so?" She knew her aunt expected more of a reaction, but Clara was focused on the blister forming on her heel.

"Well, did he ask for another dance? How was the conversation? Did he pay you any special compliment?"

The corners of Clara's mouth rose playfully. "I think he liked my dancing. In fact, it was the only topic we discussed."

Louisa huffed. "Don't tease me, my dear! I need to know everything. This is your last chance!"

"My last chance for what, exactly?" Clara folded her fan and let it hang from her wrist. "It seems unlikely that he or any other man here is going to make me an offer of marriage tonight and even less likely that I would accept."

Clara thought about how her season had gone differently than planned. She knew what the expectations were. She had to be on the hunt for a husband without looking like she was. Her aunt had been quite vocal about it for the past several weeks, but Clara could never be prevailed upon to simper and flutter like other ambitious girls. With bait like that, what kind of husband would she attract? Certainly not the kind she wanted.

Truthfully, Clara wasn't sure she was ready for matrimony. She had once been captivated by the idea of having an admirer, someone interesting and handsome who danced well and generously complimented her, but the only man she'd met who fit that description had left town before ever calling on her. Interesting, handsome gentlemen were apparently scarce. So why show any interest beyond dancing?

To Clara's dismay, Louisa had noticed this change of attitude. "Why, Clara, why?" she exclaimed. "Why can't you let these men, just one of these men, know you are interested?"

"Because I am not interested in any of them," Clara insisted, refusing to admit her regret over a certain gentleman's absence.

Louisa sometimes hinted to Clara that the men were interested in her but were too intimidated by her graceful beauty and confident air. Other times, Louisa accused Clara of being too aloof or, in more extreme situations, of giving men the outright impression she completely disliked them. Louisa had once exclaimed, "What is a man to think, Clara? Your words say *good evening* but your eyes say *I detest you!*"

Clara endured such criticisms as best she could while inwardly fretting over whether they were true. None of it was intentional, but discerning who she liked and who she didn't was complicated enough without her aunt watching her every move.

"Let's go find Mr. Garrett again," Louisa proposed, taking Clara by the arm. "Perhaps he will ask you to dance again."

Clara planted her feet as Louisa tugged. "Please, Aunt Louisa. I think I've danced enough this season, and I must confess, I've enjoyed the art more than the men." She gestured toward a wall lined with portraits.

To Clara, the paintings and architecture in London were more memorable than the men she had met there, but more than anything, she had relished her own time to create. Sitting by a window with paper and pencil in hand drawing townhomes across the street or carriages awaiting their patrons was one of her great pleasures. Sometimes she sketched her own hand or a tiny flower that grew between a crack in the stones. She especially loved that little flower, its delicate purple petals standing out against the cold grey. Clara remembered the effort she put into that sketch, discerning the best way to portray the flower's brave efforts to boast its colors in its hard, artificial surroundings. Drawing took concentration and effort, but it was within her reach and much easier to understand than the politics of a ballroom.

Louisa acted as if she hadn't heard anything Clara had just said. Instead, she pointed to a fellow a few paces away and asked, "What about that one? Sir Hampton?"

"He stepped on my feet at least five times when we danced." Clara bent down and rubbed her foot.

Not to be deterred, Louisa pointed to another man and asked, "Well, what did you think of him? Mr. Lacey?"

"I don't need to think of him," she smiled. "He thought enough of himself for the both of us."

"That one?" Louisa persisted.

"We haven't been introduced yet, but I'd prefer it remain that way. Every time I pass by, I hear him belch."

Louisa looked down and pinched the top of her nose. "You are not giving any of them a chance, Clara!"

Why bother if my heart isn't in it? Clara had long ago decided that if she married, it would be for love. She knew such an attitude was foreign to Louisa, so rather than explain, she waved her fan and expressed her intent to find a less crowded room. This time, Louisa didn't protest.

Clara wandered through the throngs until she came to a smaller room surprisingly empty of people that had a large oil painting of the sea hanging between two windows. It reminded her of trips she had taken with her parents before her mother died. The artist had captured the movement of the waves and the setting of the sun that shone lavender grey above the water. It held a certain peace and solitude that Clara hadn't felt since coming to London, a reminder that there was more to life than balls.

For the moment, no one was paying her any attention, so she leaned in closer to examine the artist's strokes. Her peace, however, was soon interrupted by the approach of heavy footsteps from behind.

"It is a beautiful painting," a deep voice said.

"It is, indeed." Clara kept her eyes on the canvas, hoping to keep the exchange brief.

The gentleman continued, "I have often wondered what an artist thinks about while painting, but right now, I am more interested in the lovely young woman admiring the painting. How are you, Miss Everton?"

At the sound of her name, recognition struck, and her breathing stopped.

"Mr. Shaw! I did not expect to see you this evening." Clara began to fidget with her glove and suddenly didn't know what to do with her hands. She turned to face him, taking in his rust-colored hair, which was an appealing mess of curl and wave, and realized she couldn't remember what he had just asked her. He didn't seem to mind, though, as he spread his lips wide. *Oh, that smile!* she sang to herself. The blood rushed to her cheeks, and she hoped Louisa was nowhere in sight.

Clara fixed her gaze on that smile and remembered the first time Mr. Shaw bestowed it on her. It was at a dinner party her first week in London. She had met mostly old acquaintances of her Uncle William and Aunt Rose, the relatives on her mother's side with whom she and Louisa were staying in town, but then Mr. Shaw arrived and livened up the whole scene. Judging from the shuffling of the hosts and servants that night, his presence had been a surprise, but for Clara, it had been a pleasant one. There was something different about Mr. Shaw. He was interesting to talk with and decidedly the most handsome, and he must have liked her too because it wasn't long before he singled her out and dominated her attention. She tried not to communicate any of those unspoken displays of dislike that Louisa had referred to, and somehow, that night, things came easier with Mr. Shaw.

Later, Clara overheard him telling her uncle that he would soon be leaving town to tend to some personal affairs. It was unusual for him to leave in the middle of the season, but it couldn't be helped, he explained. Her uncle asked Mr. Shaw how long he would be gone. Mr. Shaw didn't know, but it was likely to be a longer stay.

"Thank goodness for that," Aunt Rose remarked to her husband later that evening, to which he readily agreed.

Clara didn't know why they should be so thankful. As far as she was concerned, it was terrible timing. Her main consolation had been in imagining that he must have also felt the regret of being pulled away before they could form an attachment. The rest of the season floundered after that.

Yet, in that small room before the painting of the sea, Mr. Shaw's smoldering grin had a way of reducing past weeks to mere moments.

"I'm very pleased to see you again, Miss Everton." He cocked an eyebrow and made Clara forget all about the painting. "I did not know whether you would still be in town." His smile was enough to show how pleased he was to see her.

"Well, yes . . ." Clara searched for something more to say. "But I leave for home in just three days."

"Only three days?"

Her blush deepened at the disappointment in his voice.

"Nothing to do but make the most of it then," he said, offering his arm and leading her to the next dance.

With Mr. Shaw as her partner, Clara no longer doubted she was a competent dancer. She matched his steps and took his hand with confidence, appreciating his strong grip and the way his gaze fixed on her.

She imagined the conversation she would have later that night with her aunts. Wouldn't Louisa be happy! As much as Clara proclaimed not to be that interested in men, she had to admit that having a charming man to dance with made the ball much more enjoyable.

When the dance ended, Mr. Shaw escorted Clara to an out of the way corner and began whispering about the people around them, ladies whose headdresses molted feathers, men whose faces reddened from cravats tied too tightly, and so on. Clara never would have laughed or cared to notice such things had Mr. Shaw not managed to couple each salty statement with a sweetly crafted observation of her superior qualities.

At one point, when Clara bit her lip to contain her laughter, she noticed Louisa watching them from across the room with narrowed eyes and tightened lips. Clara's merriment caught on that glare like fabric on a pin.

When Clara let Mr. Shaw lead her to the dance floor for the second time that night, she saw Aunt Rose and Uncle William join Louisa. The trio began whispering, and soon Louisa was patting her face with her handkerchief. Clara cringed at the way her relatives scowled in her direction, making little effort to hide the fact that they were discussing her and Mr. Shaw. She tried to focus on the dance, but that snagging feeling kept coming. After all that pestering, why wouldn't Louisa be happier to see her with someone? Clara gritted her teeth and determined to enjoy the rest of the dance.

The violins stretched their final chords before ending in one brisk note. As the couples dispersed, Clara let her hand linger in Mr. Shaw's. She had almost forgotten about her relatives until Louisa sidled over and linked arms with her.

"I beg your pardon," Louisa apologized to Mr. Shaw, "but I must steal my niece for a moment. This is her last ball for the season, after all, and I have been missing her company."

"Aunt Louisa—" Clara tried to quickly come up with an excuse or promise to find her later, but Aunt Rose approached from the other side.

"Goodness, Clara, you must be exhausted after all that dancing! Allow me to help you get some refreshment." As Rose spoke, she slipped her arm through Clara's other arm, making it impossible to break free.

With no time to gauge his reaction, she gave Mr. Shaw an apologetic look over her shoulder as her aunts led her away.

"What is this about?" Clara asked in a strained whisper, but they kept walking and smiling at guests until they were standing in the same small room with the painting of the sea. All that grey and lavender now looked very dull.

"Child," Aunt Rose began, her face full of concern, "you must be cautious around Mr. Shaw."

Clara didn't understand. What was their objection to Mr. Shaw? She was about to ask when her uncle joined them.

"Well, Clara. How are you this evening?" he asked.

"Uncle," Clara stated with a hint of accusation.

"Yes, I suppose you want to know why we pulled you away." Clara always appreciated how her uncle didn't mince words.

"This is not the place, William," Rose whispered.

He lowered his voice and leaned closer to his wife. "If that man is going to ask her to dance again, she needs to know what he is. We can't let him make a fool of her." He paused and looked at Clara. "My child—"

Clara lowered her eyes. Didn't they trust her?

"Forgive me. Of course, you're not a child," he said. "You're *eligible*. Mr. Shaw is no doubt a pleasant man with a decent inheritance. If he had shown interest in you last year, I would not have had such qualms about it, but as it happens, his character has shown quite another side this year."

"What do you mean?"

"What I mean is that over the past several months, he has squandered more money than you can imagine. He is unrestrained in showing attention to several ladies at once, getting their hopes up for nothing. Rumor has it he has been hiding from creditors and will want to make an advantageous marriage to save him from debts he acquired over the summer."

"If that is the case, why would he pay me any attention at all? I've not so much money to my name as to be tempting to him if that is his purpose."

"Ah, there you have it!" He lightly poked her arm. "You don't have the kind of money he is looking for in a marriage, so you are nothing more than a diversion to him right now."

Clara stiffened at the insult.

"Let me explain," he insisted. "He has already proposed to at least one young lady that I'm aware of. I'm told the girl accepted, but what continues to shock me is that he has not honored the proposal. He merely lost interest and left this poor girl without a clue as to why he jilted her."

Even Clara had to admit the news was shocking. "Why would he do that? And how do you know all this?"

Uncle William shrugged his shoulders. "Common knowledge. News like that has a way of spreading, you know." He paused and looked around. "Clara, your father trusts us to watch over you, which is all we are trying to do. Keep a wary eye out, my dear." He patted her hand and walked away.

The news lingered in the thickness of air between her and her aunts.

"Trust us, Clara." Rose patted her other hand.

Clara did trust her relatives, but she had to make her own conclusions about Mr. Shaw. Rumors were not always true. She had spent enough time in London to know the *ton* could be vicious. She wanted to give Mr. Shaw a chance just as much as her aunts wanted her to be careful. Perhaps she should rein in her feelings a bit, but she also saw the wisdom in not being too hasty to judge Mr. Shaw either way. He might have reformed, even if the rumors were true. What Clara really wanted was more time to get to know him.

After giving each aunt a brisk hug, Clara went in search of Mr. Shaw with the intent to quietly observe him from the cover of the crowds. Everywhere, clusters of men and women stood chatting. She circled her way through to the card room and refreshments room but with no luck. It was only when the music started again that she noticed Mr. Shaw on the dance floor with a pretty, coquettish girl maybe a year or two younger than herself. What could they be discussing that was making them smile so much? Clara couldn't take her eyes off them as they spun, circled, and clasped hands, occasionally leaning close to whisper and laugh.

When the music stopped, Mr. Shaw's penetrating eyes cut through the crowds and connected with Clara's. She didn't know her face could burn so quickly. Eager to flee, she turned away too sharply and bumped right into Uncle William. She teetered, but his arm shot out to steady her. Had he not been there at that precise moment, Clara might have spent the rest of the night in the carriage waiting for the ball to end. As it was, Uncle William didn't allow for that and began introducing her to a young gentleman as if nothing awkward had just happened.

"Clara, I'd like to introduce you to Mr. James Thayne of Felton Park. His father has been a good friend of mine these past several years."

Clara hardly had time to compose herself before she took note of the man before her. Mr. Thayne wasn't striking, but he had richly dark brown hair, a natural smile, and handsome hazel eyes.

More introductions ensued, which meant hearing several names she would forget, and the dullness of the evening weighed on her once again.

After exchanging a few pleasantries about how they were enjoying the evening, Mr. Thayne asked Clara to dance. She accepted with the hope that Mr. Shaw would be watching. As Clara danced with her new partner, she searched the crowds for Mr. Shaw's face. Whether her partner noticed how distracted she was, she couldn't say, but he soon gave up on making conversation. When the dance was over, she curtsied and wandered off.

Finally, guests began to trickle out, and it was time to go. Clara normally would have been relieved, but Mr. Shaw was not normally at the balls she attended. Instead, she felt like someone had taken away her cake after only one bite.

As Clara went to find her shawl, she kept her eyes open, hoping there might be one last chance to speak to Mr. Shaw, but he was nowhere to be seen. Once she had her shawl, she shook it out to wrap around herself, and just as before, his familiar voice from behind made her pause.

"May I?"

"Oh, thank you, Mr. Shaw." Clara tried to keep her voice steady as she let him help her.

"I tried to find you again, you know," he said meaningfully, letting his hand rest on her shoulder longer than necessary.

"Oh?" Clara had difficulty focusing on anything beyond his touch.

Coming round to face her, he said, "I know you are leaving for home soon, and I never had the opportunity to call on you in town. So . . ." he trailed off and grinned nervously. "May I write to you?"

"Write to me?" Clara was confused. His request seemed very forward. She had never heard of a gentleman writing to a single lady unless they were engaged or related.

"Well, yes," he admitted. "I'd like to become better acquainted with you, and after I send you a letter, I was hoping you would send one to me." All hints of embarrassment fled. Only confidence remained, which annoyed Clara, but she had to admit it was drawing her in. "And . . ." He leaned in and lowered his voice. "The next time you are in town, I won't let anything keep me away."

Clara felt silly for nearly losing her balance with him standing that close to her. She tried to formulate a clever response, but before she had the chance, he bowed low, rose quickly with that roguish grin on his face, and walked away leaving Clara breathless.

Chapter 2

Clara stepped off the carriage feeling like she could finally breathe again. Everywhere she looked grew something green. Long, deep draughts of air brought hints of honeysuckle and fresh rain to her lungs.

Stepping out next, Louisa exclaimed, "I'd forgotten how nice the country air smells!"

"At least we can agree on *that*," Clara added, wrapping her arm around Louisa's shoulder.

During the long drive from London to Milton, Clara's patience had been brutally tested. Louisa had talked of nothing but men and strategies to turn one of them into Clara's husband. Being confined to such close quarters left Clara without refuge, and in a rebellious moment, she declared that after reviewing all the men in town, Mr. Shaw was looking better than ever, questionable reputation and all. Louisa merely huffed in reply and turned toward the carriage window. Now that Clara was standing in front of her own house again, she felt much more generous toward her aunt. Milton Manor's calming influence was already taking effect.

Their man, John Rolley, came out to gather trunks and bags as Louisa directed him, while Clara, eager to stretch her legs, walked to the carriage horses and rubbed their fuzzy necks. Taking her own horse, Rabbit, for a ride would be a priority now that she was home, but before anything else, her father came first. It was his love and acceptance that always drew Clara home.

She looked up at his bedchamber window, noting how the ivy had grown thicker in her absence, and watched the main doors for signs of him coming out to welcome her.

Clara continued to breathe deeply as she looked around. Milton Manor had always been known as a charming, respectable estate, but to Clara, its value lay in the memories it held. Every nook, every room and hallway held some childhood secret. It was where she remembered her mother best and where she was still creating memories with her father. It was a place that had proven itself against many storms. Weathered but firm, it was the one place where she felt completely safe. Though nothing to boast of to the highest of gentry, it was home.

Before long, a grey-haired gentleman of average height and build stepped through the main doors and into the sunlight with arms held wide.

"Father!" Clara beamed and ran to embrace him.

"Ah, my precious Clara!" He paused, eyes dancing as he took her in. "It is still you, isn't it? You look so elegant, and though I know you are all grown, I would be willing to wager you are at least three inches taller than when I last saw you."

"It could be these horrible shoes." Clara laughed and pulled up her hem just enough to show her father the heeled shoes she had purchased in town on a whim. She regretted the purchase her first night wearing them, but all her favorite slippers had since worn out, leaving her with only the most uncomfortable of options. She never wanted to wear them again. She kicked them off, not caring what became of them, and walked up to the house in her stockings.

Walking inside was like putting on her favorite pelisse, warm and familiar and made to fit. Clara's muscles unwound as the smells of ginger and cinnamon wafted from the kitchen. No one in London could cook like Olivia, their maid-of-all-work.

When Clara reached her bedchamber, her smile faltered. It was the same room, complete with her beloved writing desk, yet somehow simpler than she remembered. She closed her eyes and shook off the discomfort. It was only her eyes adjusting after all those nights in sparkling ballrooms. She dropped her shawl on a nearby chair and fell onto her bed, satisfied that at least that felt familiar.

For a while, she laid resting, grateful there were no social engagements or rattling carriage wheels to disrupt her thoughts. The only sounds were of wind in the leaves outside and her own breathing within, each blending into the quiet and clearing the way for reflection.

What had it all been for? All that time in London. Hundreds of pounds spent and hours wasted on the borrowed hope that she might make a match. Here she was, months later, in the same place she had started.

No matter, she tried to reassure herself. *I'm home.*

Before long, she heard her father and Louisa going down to dinner. Hastening to catch up, she threw on a gown that was comfortable and plain compared to the heavily laced variety she had been expected to wear in town. Satisfied with her simple appearance, Clara descended the stairs, breathing slow and deep as if she were still recovering from a stifling ballroom.

When she entered the dining room, she kissed her father's cheek and sat across from Louisa. The conversation naturally revolved around her first season. Clara answered all her father's questions, how she liked town, how Rose and William were getting on, and what drawings she had completed. Clara didn't mind these kinds of questions, but she knew what was coming. Her aunt cleared her throat, and Clara's shoulders sank.

"Well, I might as well say it. No luck with the men." Louisa placed her cup on the table with a thud, causing a few drips to spill over.

Clara looked at her father to see his reaction. His face seemed to say *what a pity,* but she was not sure whether he meant the part about the men, the spilled liquid, or the fact that her aunt was embarrassing her.

"I can't understand it!" Louisa declared. She scowled and sat back with her arms crossed.

Clara considered correcting her aunt. There was one man she had attracted, but his name couldn't come up without gleaning a glare from Louisa.

"Well I'm glad to hear it!" Clara's father added with certainty. "I'm not quite ready to part with my Clara."

"Really, George, you could be a little more encouraging."

"Men are scoundrels," Clara's father replied coolly, adjusting his serviette. Turning to Clara, he said, "I hope you can forgive me, daughter, but I can't help but see them all as unworthy of you."

Clara reached out and squeezed his hand, wondering what he would think of Mr. Shaw.

Louisa still had much more to say on the subject. "She needs to marry one day! At least she has had a season now. She should have had one years ago, but you were always too distracted to plan it. We have no time to waste." Louisa began mumbling to herself. "I suppose there will be dining invitations and assemblies in these parts soon enough. We will just have to make the best of it until next season. Of course, this gives us time to economize and plan for a new wardrobe and . . . "

"Please, let's not talk about next season," Clara pleaded.

"Did you not enjoy yourself, my dear?" Louisa brought a hand to her chest as if wounded by the thought.

"Certainly, I did, Aunt!" Clara filled her voice with affection. She did not want Louisa to think her ungrateful. "I enjoyed the art, and of course, I enjoyed your company. I couldn't have navigated my way through society without you." Seeing Louisa nod and sit a little straighter, Clara added slowly, "But I'm not in a rush to go back."

"Not in a rush? Not in a rush!" Louisa exclaimed. "Be that as it may, there's no need to delay our efforts. You must think seriously about marriage. You're attractive and eligible, and if you wait too long, all the good ones will be taken!"

"Well, I only need one good one, don't I? Perhaps I'll let him seek me out for a while. I'm tired of looking." Clara hadn't expected the pressure she'd felt in London to follow her home.

Louisa rambled on. "Of course, there is always Stallings."

"Oh, no!" Clara would be firm on this point. "Not Stallings."

Stallings was the home of Mrs. Hatfield, an elderly widow with a temper as pleasant as her rheumatism. Her grandson, Mr. Platt, had taken residence there last year. As far as Clara could tell, Mr. Platt's only occupation was watching his grandmother's health decline. A few weeks before Clara had left for London, Mr. Platt had begun to express a preference for her company, always leaning too close, pinning her with his stare, and making vague references to wanting time alone with her. She had tried to discourage him, but Louisa continued to see great merit in his status as the only obvious bachelor in the vicinity.

"Mr. Platt is a respectable gentleman, and I'm certain he is fond of you."

"Being fond of me is not enough to outweigh the fact that he is too old for me and smells like burnt oil. Besides," Clara added, "the way he looks at me doesn't seem very gentlemanly."

Louisa massaged her brow. "George, help me!"

"All men are scoundrels," he repeated between bites of roast.

"I don't know why I bother," Louisa muttered to herself. "A whole season wasted."

Clara bit her lip as her aunt spoke the words she had already spoken to herself. To hear them aloud stung bitterly, and she was no longer hungry for the food on her plate. Blinking back tears, Clara looked up. "I'm sorry you feel that way. I never meant to disappoint you. Please excuse me." She rose from her chair and was in the hallway in seconds.

"Clara!" Her father's voice echoed after her. "Oh, my precious girl!"

Clara slowed her pace. She loved it when he called her his precious girl. Except for a trembling lip, she stood still at the bottom of the stairs and waited for him. His steps were unhurried as he leaned on a cane for support.

Clara couldn't remember ever seeing that cane before.

He gestured to a tufted bench that leaned against the stairwell, and together they sat. She looked up at portraits of her parents on the wall opposite that had been painted shortly after they were married. Her father had always been handsome but now had more lines in his face and grey in his hair. Her mother, however, remained unchanged in Clara's memory, ever youthful as she was in the portrait. Clara could see herself in each of them, her father's slim nose and curve of mouth, her mother's chestnut hair and blue eyes, but when Clara looked in the glass at her own reflection, all she saw was an unfinished girl.

She lowered her eyes. "Are you disappointed I didn't find a husband, Father?"

He put his arm around her. "Of course not. Whatever gave you that idea?"

"I don't know. I just returned from my first London season with nothing to boast of, at least not by most ladies' standards." Clara rubbed her arm and looked off to the side.

"Are your standards the same as most ladies?"

She returned her gaze to her father. "No." At least she was certain of that. Her standards were and always would be her own, never to be decided by others. Her father had taught her that.

"Good," he replied firmly.

"But is Louisa right? About marriage, I mean."

Clara's father opened his mouth to speak but then stopped. A few seconds passed, and he asked, "Did you meet anyone in London you earnestly wanted to marry?"

She flushed with embarrassment. "I . . . I don't think so. At least, I didn't become well enough acquainted with anyone to really know."

Her father raised a questioning eyebrow but didn't say anything.

She added, "Louisa seems to think marriage is my only option."

"Ah, well . . ." he paused, "Your aunt does hold to that rather pervasive opinion, but if you are truly to understand her, you will need to ask her why she feels so strongly about it."

"Will she tell me?" Clara asked.

"In her own time, perhaps."

Her father looked her in the eye. "I want you to know, Clara, that even if your loving aunt, along with all the meddlesome gossips in England, believe that marriage is your only option, know that it is not. You are clever. You have talents and skills. I have tried to teach you what I know and so has your aunt. You can use that knowledge to make your own path whether or not you choose to marry. Marriage may be your only option if you wish to be a wealthy gentlewoman, but that is nothing if you do not have something worthwhile to live for."

Clara leaned into her father and buried her face in his shoulder.

"I am very proud of you, my girl," he said softly as he wrapped an arm around her.

Clara had no words, just tears.

"No matter what Louisa believes about the urgency of finding you a husband, you do not need anyone to make you more than you already are. I do not even think it possible."

Clara hugged her father as hard as she could.

He pulled her back a little and looked her in the eye. "Still, I want to see you happy, Clara. Take this piece of advice from an old man."

"You are not that old, Father—"

"Listen carefully." His tone was earnest. "No one can make you happy. You have to choose happiness. It's never easy, but you best find it when you choose to live for someone else." He was silent a minute before adding, "All the luxury in the world means nothing if you don't love the people you are with."

Clara laid awake a long time that night. Her thoughts were full of London parties, Louisa's disappointment, and Mr. Shaw's smiles. At some point, such thoughts carried her to a lucid sleep, and she found herself wondering how long it would be before Mr. Shaw fulfilled his promise to write to her.

Before long, however, Clara sat up with a start. Her heart was knocking and her head was throbbing. Had something happened? It took a moment to remember she was home in her own bed again. A glance at the window revealed a moonless sky thick enough to stir with a spoon. She laid back on her pillow wanting to sleep, but her blood was coursing too quickly. What could have woken her so suddenly? Her answer came in a rumble of thunder as rain started snapping at her window. Sleep was not likely to come again soon.

Clara propped herself on the edge of her bed and rubbed her eyes. She was tempted to call for Olivia to bring a warm drink, but she didn't have the heart to disturb her at this hour. Instead, she decided to walk down the hall to her father's study to find something to read by candlelight until she grew tired again.

Using the last of the embers from the fire, she carefully lit a candle and slipped through her bedchamber door. The storm had chilled the air in the hallway, making her wish for her shawl. She tiptoed around the creaky spots on the floor so as not to wake up Louisa or her father, but when she reached the study at the end of the hall, she could hear their voices and a small fire crackling. What time was it? The door was open two or three inches, so Clara, full of questions, blew out her candle and leaned close to make out their words.

She first recognized Louisa's lowered tone. "When are you planning on telling her? She is going to find out eventually." Footsteps sounded on the floorboards inside the study as Louisa's figure passed in and out of the small space open to Clara's view.

"I don't want to worry her," was her father's calm response. She could see his feet atop a cushioned ottoman.

"Worry her? What do you think will happen if she learns about this after you die? At least now, she can make plans."

"Ah, Louisa, but that is just it. I do not want this to influence her decisions."

"George, that's absurd! Did you ever consider the possibility that telling her could protect her? She should know, and it should inform her decisions."

"Clara is stronger than you think."

"I have no doubt she is a strong girl, even if you do indulge her too much, but the world is cold. She needs a plan. For goodness sake, I need a plan!"

"Louisa, I am sorry to put you in this position. I see that it is hard on you, but please. She is my daughter. I think it is better this way. There is no need to upset her prematurely. Clara will always rise above her challenges."

"George, that is a lovely sentiment, but why not just tell her?" Louisa sounded exasperated.

Clara's father leaned forward just enough for her to make out the back of his head. Was he shaking it?

Louisa stepped right in front of him, exhaling and pinching the top of her nose. "For her sake, I hope she is as strong as you are stubborn. I'm off to bed, and you would do well to get some rest too."

Clara heard bustling with cups and saucers on a tray and realized Louisa was heading for the door. At that moment, a great clap of thunder shook the house and sent Clara scrambling for a nearby curtain. She barely covered herself in time before Louisa entered the hallway.

Clara waited and listened as Louisa's footsteps grew closer and then faded away. Hidden behind the heavy fabric and dusty shadows, Clara's guilt for listening in on the conversation wrestled with her curiosity. She couldn't imagine what this secret could be about, but it clearly revolved around her. Even more incredible was that her father and Louisa were keeping secrets from her. If the two of them disagreed on whether she should know something, it must be important. Yet, as much as she respected her father, she agreed with Louisa. She would rather err on the side of knowing too much. She had half a mind to walk right in and ask her father all about it, but something about standing in the dark in her nightdress during a thunderstorm weakened her resolve.

Instead, Clara walked back to her room having completely forgotten about finding a book. Her mind was jumping on several possible secrets and reasons for keeping them, but one stood out among the rest. Was her father dying? What a dreadful thought! He did seem thinner and slower than usual and had bouts of coughing, but surely he would tell her if his health was in danger. She was only speculating after all.

Clara returned to bed fully expecting to lay awake for the rest of the night, but her tiredness had caught up with her. As she lowered her head to the pillow and pulled her blankets close, she quickly fell into strange dreams.

Chapter 3

Clara woke the next morning with memories of pelting rain, hushed tones, and midnight secrets floating around like fog. Which were real and which came from dreams? A look through the window revealed wet drizzles and grey light overcasting the landscape. She reluctantly concluded that the whispered conversation between her father and Louisa was real. But why the late hour? Why the secrecy?

When Clara walked downstairs to breakfast, she had every intention of confronting her father and Louisa, but, arriving later than she realized, she missed her opportunity. Her father had already pulled out his newspaper, his one morning indulgence. As was his habit, instead of eating right away, he would read for at least fifteen minutes, completely absorbed. Also true to habit were Louisa's complaints.

"Goodness, George, do you have to pull that paper out during breakfast?"

Clara had heard Louisa ask that question hundreds of times. From behind the paper, Clara's father only grunted an affirmation.

Louisa persisted. "Is that the same paper John Rolley reads in the mornings?" She sounded absolutely disgusted as she pointed her finger at it. "Because I have seen him take that paper to the privy. Not that I keep such a close watch on the servants, but really, once that paper has visited the privy, I cannot abide sharing a breakfast table with it!"

Clara could hear her father's muffled laugh.

"George!"

"I don't know about John, but it is the same paper I take to the privy with me."

"Shocking!"

This time Clara laughed too. She could imagine her father and Louisa teasing each other as children. They got on well most of the time, but Clara's father always enjoyed getting a reaction out of his sister.

Louisa had come to live with them right after Clara's mother died of influenza. Clara was only eight years old and had contracted influenza as well. For a time, the doctor had worried they might also lose Clara. Not one to give up, however, Louisa nursed Clara to recovery and helped her and her father get through those first difficult weeks and months. Louisa had been with them ever since. Though Clara was grateful for her aunt, she sometimes wondered why Louisa had never married. Was it possible the midnight conversation had something to do with Louisa's past? Clara would ask about that too.

She cleared her throat when she saw her father put down his paper. The words were rising on her tongue when, right at that moment, Mr. Rolley walked in humming to himself and said good morning to everyone. He placed a stack of newly arrived letters in front of Clara's father, who became just as absorbed in sifting through them as he had been with his paper.

Clara cleared her throat even louder, and the letters stopped shuffling. Finally, she had his attention. But the puzzled expression he gave her made her pause. Was it possible he already knew she had been listening at the door? She was so focused on how to word her admission to such behavior that she didn't at first notice the letter he was holding out to her.

Realizing it was for her, she slowly took it, aware that her aunt was watching too. Clara usually didn't receive letters, but she remembered a certain someone who said he would write.

"Thank you, Father." Her face grew hot as she tucked the letter into her robe.

"Clara, dear, don't you think—" her aunt started to say but was cut off by her father.

"Clara, you are excused if you wish to read your letter in private." Louisa rolled her eyes.

"Thank you, Father," Clara said. *Thank you.*

She made a point of taking three more bites of ham and sipping twice from her cup of chocolate before excusing herself, lest she seem overly eager to read her letter. She even counted her steps when she left the table to keep them even. One. Two. Three. Otherwise, she would have skipped like a child with fresh sweets.

Alone in her room, she took care to quietly shut the door. At the sound of the click, her grin broke free, along with the seal, before falling to her bed to read.

Dear Miss Everton,

I have stared at this paper for days, wondering how to begin. If only there were a way to make feelings and intentions condense straight into ink and words! After all my wondering, I am forced to conclude that staring at paper will do nothing to help me gain your favor. So, I have attempted to articulate my thoughts to you here.

The simple explanation of why I am writing is that you have made an impression on me, and I wanted you to know. It happened during the Stratford ball, less than a fortnight earlier, when your uncle introduced us. I looked for an opportunity to dance with you, but each time I built up the courage to ask, I was beaten to it by another fellow. Though you and I only exchanged a few words that night, I was drawn in by the way you laughed, the way you smiled, and something in your countenance that felt familiar, even though we had just met. I hardly knew the effect you were having on me until I learned from your uncle that you were to be leaving for home soon. I had missed my chance. Your uncle, who has been a friend to me for many years, observed my distress and encouraged me not to forget you. He continues to praise your kindness, intelligence, and beauty whenever I see him, and he tells me I should wait and seek you out next season.

Your uncle has convinced me that you and I would suit each other well, and he nearly convinced me that he has seen our fates written in the stars, but he has not convinced me that I should wait. Why not find a way to seek you now? Waiting leaves too much to fate, and all things considered, my experience informs me that I should not wait again, no matter what the ton would think of this letter.

Now I face the daunting task of sufficiently endearing myself to you. Would it help if I said I am unusually charming and hard-working? Have I mentioned that I am enjoyably clever? Or handsome? Or— never mind. I won't mention it because I am really quite humble! I could go on about myself, but more than anything, I wish I could know your thoughts at this point. Though I did not want to wait to make my regard known to you, I am more than willing to wait for any reply you might offer.

Most humbly,
James Thayne

Clara felt like she had just sat through a rushing gust of wind. James Thayne? Not Mr. Shaw? And such a letter! Such a shocking, delightful letter! She laughed out loud in disbelief that she had done anything to inspire such a man to compose it for her.

She stood up and looked in the glass, smiling to herself. *Well, well. It would seem my first season was more successful than I thought!*

She kept smiling as she folded the letter and tucked it into her bedside table before dressing for the day. *James Thayne?* She was baffled. *Who was he?* The name did sound familiar. She had a vague memory of being introduced and perhaps even dancing with someone who might have been Mr. Thayne, but his letter stated that they had not danced together. Perhaps her memory could not be trusted.

She was tempted to write him back just to tell him how much his letter had cheered her up. *Written in the stars! Humble, indeed!* It really was a pity that a gentleman who could write such an entertaining letter would be disappointed. It almost made her regret her preference for Mr. Shaw. Almost. Despite her relatives' warnings, she wasn't ready to give him up yet. She only hoped that whatever letter he wrote was as interesting as Mr. Thayne's.

Chapter 4

Owen Shaw woke with a headache and realized he had slept half the day away. No matter. He slept late most days. As the clock downstairs chimed noon, he sat up and rubbed his eyes, grateful, at least, that his pompous brother, Philip had returned to their country estate in Lanford and was no longer there to glare at or lecture him for such habits.

While their parents remained in the country, Philip had come to London for the season at their behest to exert a steadying influence over Shaw, but that was nonsense. Shaw wouldn't be steadied, least of all by Philip, no matter how much their parents praised his manners. At least now they had lost their main informant and could only speculate over Shaw's less scrupulous activities. As long as they remained in the country, Shaw remained in town.

He sat on the edge of his bed trying to remember whether he had plans for the day. Was it Saturday or Sunday? If it were Saturday, his family's long-standing housekeeper, Mrs. Hamilton, would be bustling through all the rooms, taking inventory of the linens, ordering the maids about, and generally making a lot of noise. Excepting Saturdays, Shaw kept her busy in the servants' quarters and kitchen as much as possible to keep her less informed about his private parties and lost wagers. Word got back to his parents less frequently that way.

Her alto voice echoing in the hall told him it was indeed Saturday, and his head throbbed anew. He would have to miss cards at Brooke's that afternoon, but perhaps it was for the best.

In the past few weeks, Shaw had begun to see that his habits were ruining him. His luck had never been so bad. His old chum, Brenton Harris, had begun to feel the same way, so after losing more pounds than they cared to admit, they took off their hats to each other and swore they would be respectable. *What a night that had been!* Though the memory was hazy, Shaw recalled flinging his hat over the Thames as a symbolic gesture of his commitment to reform. Part of Shaw had meant it, but mostly he and Harris were just kicking up a lark that night. *Good old Harris!* Shaw chuckled as he dressed and wandered to the breakfast room.

Mrs. Hamilton was there inspecting all the candlesticks.

"Good morning, Mrs. Hamilton!" he said with a bow and a flourish.

She, however, cast a sour glare. "Well, this morning certainly was a lovely one, and it's unfortunate you missed it. It's now the afternoon."

Shaw ignored her as he took a seat at the table and ordered his breakfast to be brought in. After one of the maids obliged him with a plate of bread, butter, and potatoes, Mrs. Hamilton unceremoniously dropped a small stack of papers next to his arm.

"There's a letter in there from your mum."

Shaw stopped chewing. His mother wrote him every month telling him how much she wished he would mend his ways and settle down, how it broke her heart to see him living the raucous life of a bachelor, how she missed him and wished he would spend more time at home, and so on and so on. He didn't need to read her letter to know its contents, but he did know that Mrs. Hamilton would stand watch until he had. What with all her children grown and married, as she would often comment, she knew how his mum felt.

"Well?" she asked sternly, though it really wasn't a question.

Shaw reluctantly dropped his fork to open the letter and found there the same pleas he had read in nearly every letter his mother had sent that year. Until the end, where his eyes paused. He had to reread the last few lines several times to take in their meaning.

Owen, your father will be arriving in town soon, probably around the time you receive this letter. He has some news for you.

*Please understand. I couldn't change his mind. I hope you know
he certainly wants what is best.*

> *Always,*
> *Your loving mother*

Shaw groaned. What could this news be? The last thing he wanted
was a visit from his father.

With his head pain increasing by the minute, Shaw heard the
front door open.

"You're writing me out of your will?!" Shaw stood gaping.

His father, tall, big boned and heavily muscled, grunted and
leaned against the fireplace mantle as if in thought. The smothering
flames on the logs dried the air and overheated the room, but the elder
Mr. Shaw did not seem bothered.

"I just saw the solicitor about it this morning while you were sleeping off last night's revelries."

Shaw didn't have a response to that. His father had an uncanny
ability to read his face. It took Shaw a moment to recover, but he shook
off the guilt. "I can't believe you would do that to me, your son!"

"I am at my wit's end with you, Owen. Your behavior this year
has been positively shameful! Do you realize how your mother frets
over you?"

Mrs. Hamilton walked in at that moment carrying a tray of
tea and biscuits and gave the younger Mr. Shaw a narrow look. She
proceeded to dust, humming low to herself, but Shaw saw her steal
glances of him and his father as they talked.

"What do you have to say for yourself, Owen?"

"Well, I—"

"I don't want to hear it!"

"Father, I—"

"Here is the situation as it stands, son. Your recklessness is eating
away at your inheritance, and it's marring our family's reputation.
Not to mention, your actions are hurting your brother's chances of a
respectable match just as much as they are hurting your own."

"You're worried about Philip?"

Shaw clenched his jaw. He hated being compared to Philip. As children, they had played well together. Shaw taught him things like how to climb trees, how to plant facers, and how to recognize a good wager, but as they grew older, Philip grew distant. To use their father's words, he became *studious* and *responsible.* To Shaw, that was just another way of saying Philip had gotten boring. Yet, Philip got all the praise and Shaw all the reprimands. "Why do you have to cause so much trouble, Owen? Philip spends his days studying!" "When are you going to grow up, Owen? Judging by how little you tend to your responsibilities, I would think Philip was the older one!" Father was *so* proud of Philip. As Shaw thought about it, he was sorely tempted to break the gleaming vase that Mrs. Hamilton was fastidiously polishing.

His father's voice rose. "We are all worried for you, and I am worried for all of us! You have to understand that as the head of this family, I have to do what is best for everyone."

"But don't you think this is extreme?" Shaw had never seen his father make these kinds of threats before.

"Your behavior has been extreme!"

"I'm not half as bad as some of the other fellows out there."

"Huh!" His father did not seem impressed. "You think I don't hear everything they are saying?" He gestured toward the door. "The gambling, the debts, the leading on innocent girls!"

"Father, I realize it is time for me to . . . uh . . ." He struggled to articulate his thoughts, ". . . take matters more seriously . . ."

"I agree," his father said, "which is why I am writing you out of my will." There was a heavy pause. "Unless . . ." He seemed reluctant to continue.

"Unless what, exactly?" Shaw asked.

"Unless you quit the gambling and settle your debts, of course, and . . ."

"And what?"

"And marry a respectable girl by the end of the year." His father strode right up to Shaw and cast one last disapproving glare over him. "I leave in the morning," he said fiercely. "So, mark my words, Owen.

I'm through with your nonsense." He turned his back and marched out of the room.

The fire crackled loudly, and Shaw stood gaping. As his father's footsteps sounded on the stairs, Mrs. Hamilton's humming turned to a *tsk tsk*, and in an impulsive need to exert his will, Shaw snatched the dust rag from her hands and tossed it into the fireplace. He waited for her reaction, eager to see someone get as angry as he felt, but she just shook her head and walked out.

Alone in the drawing room, Shaw's grasp on the world was dissolving. Of all the conditions his father could have placed on him! With some discipline, he could probably limit his visits to the gaming halls and clubs, which was where most of his gambling occurred anyway. But marriage? Who would he marry? There wasn't any girl he fancied enough to settle down with, but that was exactly what his father was telling him to do. Settle. It sounded bad enough, but giving up his inheritance? Letting it fall to Philip? That would be dreadful. Marriage it must be.

Then a worse thought crossed his mind. What if he couldn't find a girl in time who wanted to marry him?

Chapter 5

Clara watched patterns of sunlight and shade flash on the ground as the phaeton passed under the trees. Looking up, she closed her eyes and let the shadows play over her lids. Louisa held the reins, which gave Clara the freedom to rest or enjoy the surroundings as she pleased.

They were on their way to join Mrs. Peters, the vicar's wife, and a handful of ladies for tea. Mrs. Peters often organized these gatherings to discuss the needs of the parish and how each lady could help. Clara usually found some way to contribute either through time or donations. Having a father and aunt who had once been quite poor, she understood that the comfort and modest luxuries she enjoyed were merely the result of good fortune. Giving to those in need was Clara's way of recognizing her kinship with them.

Developing friendships with the wealthier ladies, however, was much less straightforward. Clara always had difficulty, for example, with the way Mrs. Wright and her daughter, Frances, rambled through the town gossip until some poor listener fainted with shock. Of course, there was Catherine Blakely and Eliza Warren, both lovely, accomplished young ladies whom Clara was accustomed to having for tea on occasion, but Catherine and Eliza shared so many more interests with each other than they did with Clara. Try as she might to find common ground with them, they continued to cling to each other rather than admit Clara into their confidences.

When Clara had learned that they would all be in London for the season, she had hoped it would be a chance to become better friends with them, but their circles of acquaintance in town hadn't overlapped with Clara's, resulting in very little time together.

"Are you looking forward to seeing Catherine and Eliza today?" Louisa asked, startling Clara with her perceptive question.

Clara gazed at the path and trees ahead. "I am."

"You don't sound very enthusiastic."

Answering slowly, Clara said, "I admit, I'm nervous to talk about London with them. I didn't see them as often as I would have liked."

"I see," was all Louisa said, leaving Clara to her thoughts.

The horses cantered along as they came to the bend in the road that would lead them to the vicar's house. When they arrived, Clara and Louisa were shown into a quaint sitting room where most of the ladies were already gathered. Clara had barely stepped through the threshold when Mrs. Wright took her by the arm.

"Clara! How good to see you! You look absolutely lovely, dear, though perhaps a bit paler for all that time in town. How did you like London? I heard it did not quite agree with you." Mrs. Wright kept a firm hold on Clara as several snickers escaped from mouths hidden behind teacups. Mrs. Wright never even paused for an answer. "And Clara? I simply must say, I was so relieved to hear you had returned home safely. After the misfortunes you survived with such a dreadful rake! It's so good of you to show yourself here in any event. I commend you for holding your head high. Such experiences do have a way of lowering spirits, I'm told."

Clara looked around at a room full of curious faces, including Catherine and Eliza's. What had Mrs. Wright been telling everyone?

"I beg your pardon?" Clara managed calmly but feared her face revealed too much.

"No need to look so guilty, dear!" Mrs. Wright answered with a chuckle. "No one here doubts your intentions were good, however misplaced your trust." She smiled knowingly at the other ladies.

Louisa stepped between them, freeing Clara from Mrs. Wright's grasp. "I'm afraid, Mrs. Wright, that you are seriously misinformed. My niece has had no such misfortune. Clara is the perfect picture of proper!" Flecks of spittle flew from Louisa's mouth, and Clara smiled at her loyalty.

Mrs. Wright raised her eyebrows. "I am never misinformed."

"Then kindly sit down," Louisa enunciated, "and tell us what you've heard so we can set you to rights."

Mrs. Wright brought her hand to her chest. "Goodness, Louisa! I meant no harm. Frances told me she saw Clara spending time with Mr. Shaw who, I'm sure you know, has been earning himself quite a reputation. So naturally, I have been interested in seeing that our dear Clara is all right."

Clara saw Frances Wright on a nearby settee observing the scene. When Clara's eye met hers, Frances quickly looked down at the teacup she held. Clara didn't remember seeing Frances at the ball that night, but then again, she hadn't bothered to look for Frances. They had never spent much time together apart from Mrs. Peter's gatherings, and their paths had hardly crossed in town. It never occurred to Clara that Frances might have seen her dance with Mr. Shaw, but even if she had, Clara couldn't fathom how Mrs. Wright could derive such gossip from two innocent dances. It was almost enough to make Clara lose her composure.

Keeping her voice steady, however, Clara explained, "Mrs. Wright, it is true that Mr. Shaw and I spoke and danced together during the Stratford ball, but that was the extent of it. I am not ignorant of his reputation, and," she took her aunt's arm, "I was fortunate to have Louisa as well as my other aunt and uncle there as chaperones. They certainly will vouch for my good character."

Mrs. Wright gave her daughter a sideways glance and stumbled, "Why, I only thought . . ."

"Well, you can stop thinking it," said Louisa with a tight smile. "Now please excuse us while we thank Mrs. Peters for inviting us to tea."

They walked off and left Mrs. Wright standing alone by the door with several sets of eyes on her.

To Clara's relief, Catherine and Eliza eagerly waved her over and each gave her a kiss on the cheek. Once everyone was seated, Mrs. Peters called for their attention and proceeded to outline the needs of the less fortunate in the village. Most ladies volunteered to mend clothes or donate money, but Mrs. Peters emphasized that many new mothers, widows, and young families simply needed a good meal. Clara and Louisa volunteered to deliver baskets of food to these families, as did Mrs. Wright and Frances. Mrs. Peters thanked the ladies and continued to make assignments until all the needs of the parish were covered.

Catherine, sitting just to Clara's left, whispered, "Do you think Mrs. Peters will mention one of her ailments? She always does you know."

Clara gave Catherine a sideways glance and tried to focus on what Mrs. Peters was saying.

"Thank you," Mrs. Peters concluded. "Everyone will be so grateful. I just hope this strange sore on my elbow heals in time . . ."

Except for a small giggle that Catherine didn't fully suppress, the ladies nodded politely, and with their efforts thus organized, they relaxed around a selection of dainty cakes and biscuits. Just as Clara turned toward Catherine to talk, Catherine turned toward Eliza, and the two began chatting away.

Clara picked up her fork and pretended to be content with her small square of cake while Mrs. Wright's raspy whisper on the other side of the room grew louder.

"I really shouldn't wonder at it, even if it was just a few dances. The poor girl didn't attract a single suitor, so it came as no surprise when I saw her flirting with the only man who would pay her any attention. A rogue like Mr. Shaw is never particular, you see . . ."

Clara clenched her jaw. *What a bothersome gossip!* Clara had done nothing wrong, absolutely nothing, but Mrs. Wright would have her share of amusement. *Of all the silly nonsense!* Clara considered asking for her thoughts on whether it were a greater evil to dance with a rogue or spread rumors about an innocent girl.

Looking over her shoulder, she saw Louisa and Mrs. Peters conversing by the window. Louisa's mouth was twitching slightly as Mrs. Peters described the various colors her elbow sore had recently turned.

Clara, suddenly wary of her cake, pushed it away and quietly listened to Catherine and Eliza. It was difficult, what with Catherine's back to her, but she did catch a few things, descriptions of new gowns, sparkly evenings at Almack's, and the men who tried to woo them. Wearing collusive smiles, Catherine and Eliza finally turned toward Clara.

"Clara," said Catherine, "tell us who the best kisser was of all the men that courted you."

"Why are you asking her?" asked Eliza, looking very entertained. "No one courted her. She doesn't have any experience."

"But of course she does!" Catherine countered. "You forget Mr. Shaw!"

Clara stared in disbelief as they simultaneously erupted with giggles.

Eliza was the first to compose herself. "Catherine, don't embarrass Clara like that. Can't you see? Just the name of Shaw turns her face red." Eliza shook her head with a pitying smirk. "Poor thing answers without meaning to."

"She can't even speak!"

"Then the rumors must be true!"

A new round of giggles broke out. Clara bit her tongue to hold back the rebuffs that threatened to spring loose. Was this the change in their friendship she had been fearing? Or had it been this way all along? When Clara saw their eager faces, she decided against responding to their bait.

Frances Wright walked over and gave the girls a measuring glance. Clara shut her eyes. If Frances was anything like her mother, Clara would need to bite her tongue harder.

"You're one to talk, Eliza. What did Mr. Shaw whisper to you that turned your ears so red?" asked Frances.

Clara's eyes sprung open in time to see Eliza's ears turning red.

"And you, Catherine," Frances continued. "I'm surprised you would be so quick to believe silly rumors, especially considering the ones I've heard about you and Mr. Matthews. Just imagine if such rumors reached your mother's ears! I don't suppose there's any truth to them?" Catherine's eyes followed Frances's across the room to where Mrs. Blakely sat. Catherine's expression immediately subdued. "I thought so," said Frances coolly as she sat next to Clara.

Clara sat very still. Of all the young ladies present, Frances was the last she would have expected to become her ally.

Frances smiled and tilted her head. "Did you enjoy London?"

Clara examined Frances's face. Did she really want to talk? Her sunny yellow dress, pale blue eyes, and bouncing strawberry-blonde curls were in perfect alignment with the mischievous grin she wore.

"Yes, it was quite pleasant." Clara hoped her simple answer would satisfy Frances, but Frances kept looking at her. Clara finally asked, "You?"

"Oh, yes!" Frances jumped at the chance to talk. "I've never met so many charming men in my life. I'm pining for next season already." Frances looked up at the ceiling and sighed.

Clara couldn't relate to Frances's sentiments, but she did her best. "I wouldn't mind a chance to attend the theater again."

On the other side of the room, Mrs. Wright could still be heard leading the gossip. An occasional gasp or "no!" from one of the ladies accented the whispers.

Frances cleared her throat, and Clara realized her attention had lapsed.

"Did you hear that Mr. Frandsen made me an offer?"

No, Clara hadn't.

Frances put her hand on Clara's arm. "Imagine that! I would have been Mrs. Frances Frandsen!"

Clara did think that sounded silly. She gave a small chuckle while Frances laughed out loud. "The poor man! I should have done more to discourage him early on, but he never was good at catching hints." Frances smiled again, and this time, though Clara couldn't explain why, she believed it was sincere. Clara relaxed, and Frances leaned closer. "I didn't mean to give my mother the idea that your reputation had been . . . smudged. Please forgive me."

"Of course," Clara said, and she meant it. She had always assumed Frances didn't like her, but perhaps she had been wrong. Clara ventured a question she thought Frances would enjoy discussing. "Was there a particular man in London, besides Mr. Frandsen, who caught your eye?"

"Oh, one or two," she said lightly. "Did you get the chance to meet Mr. Garrett or Mr. Thayne?"

Mr. Thayne? What did Frances know about *him*? "I believe I met them both, though I don't remember either particularly well."

With feeling, Frances said, "Oh, you would remember Mr. Thayne!"

Clara searched her mind for something she could say in response. "Well, I . . ."

Clara realized Catherine and Eliza had not completely withdrawn from the conversation.

Eliza perked up first. "Did you say Mr. Thayne? Don't get your hopes up, either of you. He was always eager to dance with me. He followed me around like a lost puppy half the time." Eliza whipped out her fan and waved it over her smug face.

Catherine glared at Eliza. "He only followed you around because you told him you knew where they were serving cake."

"You're just jealous he didn't ask you to dance!" Eliza jabbed.

Clara held back a smile as she listened to their bickering and thought of a certain letter tucked away in her drawer.

Frances shook her head and whispered to Clara, "Don't believe a word they say. I doubt Mr. Thayne noticed either of them."

Clara looked at Frances and tried to sound casual. "Tell me what you thought of Mr. Thayne."

Clara quickly learned that talking about men came naturally to Frances.

"Mr. Thayne is the kind of man who really stands out. He was one of my favorites to dance with! He never stepped on my feet, which is more than I can say for some of my partners. You danced with Mr. Thayne at the Stratford ball, didn't you?"

Had Frances been watching her the whole time?

"I'm not sure. I might have." Clara could feel the heat rise to her cheeks, and she was certain Catherine noticed.

Frances, however, raised her eyebrows and gaped. "You *might have*? Goodness, Clara! Is there no one who meets your standards? If you're entirely uninterested in someone who is cheerful, wealthy, and handsome, I can understand why you took no notice."

"Well, how much can one really tell after a single dance?" Clara didn't appreciate Frances's sarcasm or the implication that she was being proud. She tried to think of something to say, something she had noticed about Mr. Thayne, but she couldn't think of anything. If he hadn't written her a letter, she wouldn't have given him a second thought.

Frances was still going on about him, and for some reason that Clara couldn't explain, the more Frances praised him, the more Clara wanted her to stop. "Who else did you say caught your attention in town? Did you say something about Mr. Garrett? Tell me what you liked about him."

Thankfully, Frances didn't need to be asked twice. Mr. Garrett was rumored to be wealthier than Mr. Thayne but was not as skilled a dance partner and so on. Clara forgot most of what Frances said after that.

Sometime later, Clara joined Louisa and thanked Mrs. Peters as they took their leave. Back in the phaeton heading toward home, Clara looked down at her lap and frowned. "I shouldn't be surprised by Mrs. Wright's behavior. We all know she can't resist spreading rumors, true or not, but I can hardly believe that Catherine and Eliza would treat me that way."

"You seemed to be getting on well with Frances," Louisa noted.

"Yes, that's true . . ." Clara admitted, her gaze drifting up as she thought about their conversation.

For a time, Louisa was uncharacteristically quiet, which Clara didn't mind until Louisa let the phaeton ride past its usual turn. That could only mean one thing. Stallings.

"Louisa, please tell me we're simply taking the scenic way home."

Louisa stared straight ahead. "Mr. Platt was very disappointed not to see you the other day. I promised I would bring you with me next time."

"Why didn't you consult me? I'm not prepared to meet him!"

"Because I only just thought of it. We're already out, and I don't see why we shouldn't make a short call."

"I can think of several reasons why we shouldn't." Clara was suddenly sick with the swaying of the phaeton on the uneven road.

"Clara," Louisa pleaded, "I wish I could tell you all the reasons I worry about you so much."

Clara sat straighter. Was Louisa about to tell her what she and her father had been whispering about the other night?

"What reasons?" Clara asked.

Louisa shook her head. "Your father . . . he's so stubborn. It's because, well . . ." Louisa's face shifted through expressions of frustration and resolve. "It's mostly because I care about you."

Oh. Clara knew that already.

"The truth is, Clara, as I was leaving Stallings the other day, Mr. Platt hinted to me that he would very much like a private audience with you soon."

Clara clenched her stomach and gasped. "No!" A private audience could only mean one thing.

Louisa held up her hand. "I'm not going to try to convince you to accept his offer, but I do want you to hear it, and I do want you to consider it. All I'm asking is that you don't say no right away."

"Why would I do that? I'll say no eventually. It would be pointless, not to mention unkind, to mislead him like that."

Louisa tilted her head toward Clara and added, "I just want to see you taken care of. I want to see you happily settled, and I don't want to see you missing an opportunity simply because you said no too quickly."

Clara's mind was racing. Sweat made little hairs stick to the back of her neck, sending shivers all through her, despite the outside warmth. This all felt wrong. Mr. Platt felt wrong, and she was panicking. Clara was not going to face Mr. Platt today, and she would not allow him to think that she would even consider an offer of marriage from him.

But the phaeton rambled on, and Clara fumed. Mrs. Wright was spreading rumors about her. Catherine and Eliza mocked her. And now she was being forced to receive the attentions of a man whom she suspected was much less of a gentleman than her aunt realized. What kind of talk would that lead to? If she let herself be persuaded to hear his proposal, what else might she be pressed to do?

No. She wouldn't allow it. Something inside Clara snapped, and with one fluid motion, she snatched the reins right out of Louisa's hands.

"Clara!" Louisa exclaimed as the horses stomped in confusion. "Hand those over at once."

"Not a chance, dear aunt," Clara answered amiably. She already felt better as she gained control and maneuvered the phaeton to a clearing where she had room to turn around.

"Clara, this is very unladylike." Louisa grumbled.

Clara preferred to be unladylike than endure a proposal from Mr. Platt.

She was watching the dirt road ahead, ever inviting with its open space, when she realized that Louisa had also dispensed with being ladylike. As soon as Clara had turned the phaeton toward home, Louisa was grappling for the reins.

"I will have those back!"

"No, you won't," Clara said between gritted teeth as she fought to keep the reins.

The horses started to dance and shake their heads as Clara and Louisa sent confusing messages down the reins. One horse let out a startling squeal, demanding that both ladies take notice. Louisa was forced to give up as Clara pulled on the reins, urging the horses back to submission.

When all was calm, Louisa quietly renewed her pleadings. "Clara, I implore you, please turn back around. I promise, if there were any other man—"

"What about Mr. Sh—"

"Don't say it! Anyone but him. If there were any other man besides Mr. Shaw, I would leave you alone."

Clara paused. Any other man? With the promise of being left alone? Clara could not let such an opportunity pass, and inspiration struck. There was a charming letter still lying in her chest of drawers, proof that there was, indeed another man in her life. She had day-dreamed about writing a reply to Mr. Thayne but never thought she should. Until now.

"Aunt, there is someone else. Besides Mr. Shaw." Clara spoke calmly, keeping her eyes on the road.

Louisa put a hand on her heart and gaped at Clara as if she had just sprouted wings. "There is?" she gasped.

Clara nodded.

With narrowed eyes and a pinched smile, Louisa patiently added, "I need not remind you that my spirits once thoroughly raised could not withstand the blow of disappointment if such news were untrue."

Clara adjusted the reins and shifted in her seat. "I need no such reminders."

"Well, who is it? I need to know who! How did it escape my notice?" Louisa's voice grew louder.

This time, Clara shook her head. If Louisa and her father kept secrets, she could keep hers.

"Oh, Clara! This is torture! You won't tell me?"

Clara shook her head emphatically.

"You must tell me! I order you to tell me!"

Clara bit back a smile. Louisa only tried to order Clara to do things when she knew she had already lost.

Louisa persisted. "Please, Clara! You promise you're telling the truth? There really is another man?"

Clara handed Louisa the reins and spoke with surety. "Definitely."

In the dim candlelight of her room that night, Clara dipped her pen in ink and let it hover over a blank sheet of paper.

A letter is an innocent thing, she thought, *nothing but lines of ink spread across parchment, a few friendly words exchanged between acquaintances. Such a small thing.*

So why was it giving her such trouble? Hadn't she already been inclined to write to Mr. Shaw whenever his letter arrived? This was hardly different, but her conscience struggled. It was unheard of for a respectable lady to write to a man she was not engaged to, much less one she did not know.

Several dots of ink speckled the top left corner of her paper, evidence that she had attempted to start, but every time her pen made contact, her hand instinctively rose up, too uncertain of her plan. She knew that as soon as the words *Dear Mr. Thayne* graced the top of her paper, she would no longer be the proper young lady her aunt thought she was. But she had to write this letter. She had promised Louisa only hours earlier that there was another man in her life, and this was the only way she could think of to make that true.

Still, she hesitated. Clara could easily imagine the slandering tales Mrs. Wright would spread if ever she found out. Oh, the scandal she would raise! The thought was chilling enough to make Clara leave her desk and fetch her shawl.

A letter is a misunderstood thing, she argued, *a carefully crafted creation, like a poem or drawing.* It didn't have to be improper.

What was the point in fearing Mrs. Wright? That woman would find scandal wherever she set her foot. Did that mean Clara had to give Mrs. Wright weight in her decisions?

Absolutely not.

When Clara had snatched the reins from Louisa earlier that day, she had also snatched them from Mrs. Wright, Catherine, Eliza, and even her own doubts. She couldn't let their voices live in her thoughts anymore. This time, Clara would keep the reins.

She tossed the shawl on her bed and returned to the desk with renewed resolve. She reread Mr. Thayne's letter and considered again how to respond. Even if she was about to go against all sense of propriety, she could at least take comfort in knowing that he had gone against it first. Maybe he hadn't stood out to her at the ball, but his letter stood out to her now. If she wrote him a reply, he might possibly send another letter. They would share thoughts and ideas and become better acquainted. As scandalous as some might call that, Clara realized that sounded delightful. The desire to hear from him again finally outweighed her doubts. She wouldn't make the mistake of dismissing him, or anyone else for that matter, too easily again.

Clara ran her hands over the smooth paper with renewed excitement. Her father once told her that life hinged on the most unexpected of moments. She swiveled her pen and thought, *What if now is one of those moments?*

Chapter 6

James Thayne dipped his hands in the wash basin and splashed his face, curing his eyes of lingering sleepiness. Though he still sometimes felt the urge to sleep late, his father had taught him the value of the morning hours. He could almost hear his father's voice, *The master of an estate should be an early riser, always alert and clear of mind.* Thayne nodded to himself and acknowledged how much sharper his mind felt in the mornings.

He continued to dress, strapping on his boots and dark blue coat and enjoyed the freedom of completing the task without the help of a valet. He had servants who were willing to assist, but tending to his own appearance was central to his need for independence. Thayne looked in the glass and pondered another of his father's maxims. *A true gentleman's appearance should reflect dignity and inspire trust.* Thayne turned his head from side to side and considered his face. *Better get rid of this stubble,* he thought. He picked up his razor and slowly edged it around his jaw, the scraping sound reminding him of pen etching paper.

Satisfied with his appearance, he exited his bedchamber and headed for his study. He always had breakfast in his study so he could answer letters while eating. This morning he needed to write to the bank regarding interest on some investments. Such work had become his responsibility a year ago when his father died, a responsibility he was still learning to manage. Thayne had no particular reason for hurrying to his business, but working through breakfast was preferable to eating at a large, formal table that only served to remind him that he was alone. At least his cook's savory concoctions provided a temporary distraction from his predicament.

However, it was not true to say he was entirely alone. He still had Mr. and Mrs. Andrews, his reliable steward and housekeeper who oversaw the modest band of servants that kept Felton Park running efficiently. They had been there longer than Thayne could remember and were practically family, but even with them for company, the house still felt too large.

He had once cherished the hope of bringing a bride to Felton Park to fill the emptiness, but all his hoping had come to naught.

Three years ago, Thayne had courted a lovely girl named Lucy Conway who had come to stay with her aunt in a neighboring estate. Thayne was easily smitten with Lucy, and she seemed to reciprocate, but Thayne was cautious and slow to show his admiration. Then one day, she became less talkative, less animated when he called, and shortly after, her engagement was announced. To his friend, Gilbert Farnsworth. He had stolen Lucy right out from under Thayne's nose, and worst of all, Thayne hadn't done a thing about it. Mired in frustration, he bore his pain in silence and watched them marry and move out of his life.

That was a time full of regrets. Thayne spent long nights reviewing conversations, smiles and gestures, wondering how he never knew until it was too late. His father had tried to reassure him that he had behaved properly throughout the affair, but Thayne believed that was the problem. He had been too proper, too strict about being a perfect gentleman to remember what really mattered. He hadn't fought for what he wanted. Maybe Lucy never knew how much he cared.

So, Thayne made some decisions. He would not repeat the same mistakes. He would not live with regrets. If ever he found someone who attracted him the way Lucy had, he would put forth every effort.

Making such plans, he discovered, was the easy part. The difficult part was actually finding someone. Eligible girls were scarce around Felton Park, and Thayne did nothing to put himself in their society, not since losing Lucy. After several solitary months and persistent hinting from Mrs. Andrews that he would have a better chance of finding a bride in town, he went to London.

He went with a cautious hope, but he never expected to find anyone like Clara. Beautiful, charming Clara! It was all thanks to William Martin, friend to both Thayne and his late father.

Martin had first introduced Thayne to several pleasant girls, but Thayne was having trouble keeping track of them all. He was so much better at remembering faces than names, and unfortunately, the ladies did not like it when he accidentally addressed them by the wrong name. He was feeling rather discouraged until the Stratford ball. There he found a young lady who just seemed to shine. Clara! Thayne hadn't expected to feel shy around her. It wasn't his way, but this time he did. What a stroke of luck that Martin was not only acquainted with her but related to her! When Thayne failed to secure a dance with her, he inadvertently despaired aloud, voicing his interest in becoming better acquainted with her. Martin and his wife showed such enthusiasm for the idea that Thayne was emboldened to take action.

But the ball had come to an end, and Clara was due to return home. What options did he have? If he risked waiting for another opportunity, as Martin suggested, some other coxcomb would, no doubt, try to woo her, just as Farnsworth had furtively courted Lucy. If Thayne did not act quickly, his moment would pass. So, he made up his mind and wrote Miss Clara Everton a letter.

He knew it went against social expectation for him to write to her, but he had decided that he would not allow society to limit him when his conscience was clear. Was it asking too much to hope she might feel the same?

With these thoughts brewing, Thayne entered his study and sighed when he saw the small breakfast tray laid out on his desk. He slowly sat, sipped from his hot mug, and began sorting through the morning post. His hand was moving routinely when suddenly, he paused. There was a letter among the usual mix that clearly stood out. It could only mean one thing. Clara had written a reply. He hadn't expected her to, but in some corner of his mind, he had hoped it all the same.

He looked at his name written on the front and hesitated. What if her reply merely contained a request that he never write to her again? What if he had insulted her with his letter? What if she were angry with him for sending it? He rose from his chair and lightly tapped her reply in his hand. Soon, he would know whether she had any inclination to ever receive his attentions.

Don't be stupid, he told himself. *It's just a letter.* He could handle its contents, which, he reminded himself, could be positive. Either way, he had to read it. He unfolded the paper and absorbed its words.

Dear Mr. Thayne,

> *Are you certain we did not dance? I will not argue if you say we did not because I hardly remember the details of our meeting. I cannot claim you made the same impression on me at the ball, but you have made an impression through your letter. Your boldness is refreshing. What young lady does not like to be told she is kind, intelligent, and beautiful? I am rather inclined to admit you into my good graces. How you knew I would enjoy a letter more than a dance, I have no idea.*
>
> *But I am too hasty. Though you seem charming enough on paper, I am still making up my mind about you. All I know thus far is that you have a healthy disregard for the ton and a sound taste in female beauty. And you are acquainted with my uncle, which means you are likely to know more about me than you are letting on. I think it only fair that I ask you to tell me more about yourself, that we may stand on equal footing. What will you tell me, I wonder?*
>
> *Kind regards,*
> *Clara Everton*

After reading the letter a third time, Thayne held it up to the light from the window and laughed at the trepidation he had felt before opening it. He reclined in his chair and, for the briefest moment, forgot all about his responsibilities. His risk had paid off. Clara now knew of his interest and was willing to receive his letters. Unstopping his ink, he prepared his pen and paper. What would he write to Clara next?

A knock on the door followed by Mrs. Andrews, however, reminded him that his responsibilities had not forgotten him.

"Sir, one of your tenants is here to see you."

"The same man who came last week?"

"I believe so," she answered with a nod.

Thayne leaned forward on his desk and rubbed his brow. He knew why the man had come. There were improvements needed in the southeast part of the estate where he resided, such as structural repairs, drainage routes for areas that tended to flood, and the clearing of land for planting more crops. Various plans had been proposed and discussed when Thayne's father was still alive, but nothing had ever been decided. The burden now fell to Thayne, and the tenants were awaiting his decisions.

He closed his eyes and thought, *How can I do this without you, Father?*

Mrs. Andrews waited patiently for his response. Looking up, Thayne's eyes landed on Clara's letter splayed open on his desk like a spring blossom. She was still making up her mind about him. Would she be impressed that he was still struggling to fill his father's shoes?

Thayne sat straighter and told Mrs. Andrews to show the man in.

Chapter 7

*C*lara was glad the post came early that morning. It meant she could intercept a certain letter before anyone else saw it. Since exchanging their first letters, she and Mr. Thayne had written a handful of notes sharing the kind of lighthearted details they might have discussed in person to become better acquainted, mostly things about their homes and daily lives, but they always ended with a jest as to whether or not they had actually danced together. Mr. Thayne had also insisted that, though her aunt and uncle had spoken highly of her, their descriptions lacked the substance he hoped to gain through corresponding with her.

So far, such brief letters had been entertaining and flattering, but Clara was hoping to learn something more personal about Mr. Thayne and had hinted as much to him in her last letter. It hadn't taken him long to reply, and she was more eager than usual to read what he had written this time.

Unfortunately, time was short. She had a full day ahead helping Mrs. Peters deliver baskets of food to the needy in the village, and Louisa was waiting for her downstairs. So Clara hid her letter under her pillow to save for a quiet moment.

As she opened her bedchamber door to leave, she could hear Louisa and Olivia talking below. They didn't sound like they were in a hurry. With one last eager look at her pillow, Clara decided they could wait just few minutes more. Leaping onto her bed, she freed her smile and pulled out the letter.

Dear Miss Everton,

I know how we shall finally settle the question of whether or not we danced together at the Stratford ball. We shall simply call a truce and promise each other a dance the next time we are both in town. What do you think? Because whether or not we danced, I simply wanted more time with you.

Now to tell you more about myself. I could go on about things I enjoy, such as roast venison and apple tarts, which is my favorite dessert, but perhaps you would like me to share something riskier. I will indulge your request without delay and tell you a secret.

I am good with a needle and thread. My dear grandmother taught me when I was a child. It began with her showing me how to mend my own socks. One thing led to another and before I knew it, my grandmother and I had the start of a blanket. When my father saw me sewing, he immediately took me out to chop wood and ride horses. My father taught me much, and I love being out of doors and riding horses because of him, but I have never forgotten my grandmother's lessons. She and I finished that blanket together, and I still keep it to remind me of her.

She always told me how smart I was, what a fine lad I was. You must be saying to yourself, "There he goes being humble again," but I assure you I only say this to paint in your mind a picture of how much I loved her for believing in me. Not many know about my talent with a needle, but I have enjoyed sharing my secret with you. What secret would you share with me?

Eagerly waiting,
James Thayne

Clara held Mr. Thayne's letter and smiled, blissfully unaware of Louisa's calls until Olivia knocked on her door with the warning that Louisa was growing impatient.

"Please tell her I will be down shortly," Clara called back.

She could imagine Olivia on the other side of the door walking away with her head shaking, but Clara only wanted a moment. She didn't have time to compose a reply, but she did have time to savor her letter another way. She went to her desk, pulled out a blank sheet of paper, and let her hand fly. At first, she sketched an apple tart. Mr. Thayne should know it was her favorite too. Then she added speckles and shading and could taste the memory of cinnamon on her tongue.

Flipping to a new page, she outlined a boy sitting with his grandmother and a blanket shared between them, each holding a needle and thread. Clara usually preferred to draw such scenes from live models, but the image came so clearly to her mind that she sped across the paper, making lines everywhere, some faint, some bold. Now that Clara had committed it to paper, she could fill in the details later.

When Clara finally came down, Louisa commented on the extra spring in her step, hinting that she suspected it had to do with this secret gentleman in Clara's life.

"Is he handsome? Is he wealthy? Does he live in London? Does he have a large family?"

Clara was surprised at how much she didn't mind these questions. Apparently, having an actual gentleman in her life made them more tolerable, and—dare she admit it?—enjoyable. A smile was the only answer she ever gave Louisa because, even if Clara hadn't been too embarrassed to talk about Mr. Thayne, the truth was, she simply didn't know the answers. But that didn't matter. Clara was happy and Louisa seemed equally satisfied.

Since the weather was fair, they walked to the village that morning, passing through wooded lanes and fields, and met Mrs. Peters, Mrs. Wright, and Frances to deliver baskets of food to the designated families in the area.

When the ladies stopped to deliver a basket to a young widow living near the market, Clara saw Mr. Platt walk by. In broad daylight, with his reddened nose and oiled hair, he looked like he might have been twice her age. She did her best to focus on Mrs. Peters and the other ladies, but Clara was certain he slowed his pace to stare at her, causing the hairs on the back of her neck to prickle. Only once he was out of sight could she breathe freely.

When Mrs. Peters suggested they split into smaller groups to cover more ground, Clara and Frances went to the south corner of the village with some baskets while the older ladies headed north. As they went about their task, Clara noted how Frances knew all the families and always knew what to say and what to ask. Frances smiled and listened, and the time passed quickly in her company.

When all the baskets were delivered, the ladies met once again on the high street. Louisa, worn out from all the walking, rode back with Mrs. Wright in her curricle, while Clara and Frances decided to remain in the village to see the shops and enjoy the fine weather. It was the kind of comfortable day Clara had always wanted to spend with a friend but could never before think of who that friend might be. Now, as she watched Frances swinging a handful of newly purchased yellow ribbons, it occurred to her that good friends might not be as scarce as she once thought.

When Frances accidentally sent the ribbons flying, Clara turned back with her to pick them up. Dusting off the ribbon and looking up, Clara saw a man leaning against the stone wall of the milliner's shop they had just passed. He was directly facing them, but his hat was pulled forward so as to cast a shadow on his face, and his shirt collars were high enough to obscure his cheeks. His attire was that of a gentleman's, nothing that should have caused the hairs on Clara's arms to stand up as they did. She stared at him as discreetly as she could, straining to see any feature that might reveal his identity, but the only one she saw clearly was his chin.

Looking at the road ahead, about three miles to Milton Manor, Clara felt a twinge of worry. She clenched the ribbon in a fist and told herself that she had safely walked that road hundreds of times.

The girls continued on, but Clara did not laugh as easily anymore. She kept looking behind her, trying to be inconspicuous, and each time, there was the same man, keeping his distance but definitely following them. Clara still couldn't see much of his face, but there was something familiar about his build. She searched for any memory that might help her identify him, but it was like trying to recognize a shadow. *Who was he?* Had she seen him before? Why would anyone she knew be trying to hide?

Her thoughts were interrupted by the sounds of rickety wheels hitting rocks on the road. A familiar phaeton pulled up next to Clara. Sitting atop was her family's servant John Rolley. *Thank goodness,* thought Clara. She didn't dare look back yet again, but she could feel the stranger's eyes on her.

John Rolley dispensed with the usual formalities and spoke quickly. "Miss Everton! Your father is ill, very ill, I'm afraid. This afternoon he has taken a turn for the worse."

"A turn for the worse?" When had her father become so ill? Clara had noticed him coughing, but nothing more. "Take me to him at once, please!" Clara approached the phaeton to climb in, but Mr. Rolley motioned for her to stop.

"No, no, miss," he hurried. "Begging your pardon, but I am on my way to fetch the doctor, and I've been instructed to make haste. I'm sorry, miss. I only stopped to let you know."

He tilted his hat and rode on, sending a small cloud of dust rolling at the girls' feet.

Clara knew there would not be enough room for her, Frances, and the doctor in the small phaeton, but perhaps Mr. Rolley could send the doctor riding ahead and accompany them back on foot.

"Mr. Rolley, wait!" Clara called after him, but the clacking wheels drowned her out. Her hopes of evading the strange man pulled away with the phaeton.

Clara stood there unsure of her next step until Frances tugged her arm, urging her toward the road. "Clara, we should get you home."

The girls kept a brisk pace as the sky grew dusky. Clara jumped at each bird trill and scurrying squirrel as the setting sun cast strange lights and long shadows before them. The minutes passed uneventfully, and before long, they saw Mr. Rolley drive past again, this time with the doctor. Sometime later, when Clara estimated they were halfway, she checked the road behind and saw no one, but near the road ahead, there was movement in the bushes.

"Probably a deer," Clara whispered.

Frances nodded, and they quickened their steps.

When a twig snapped, Clara jumped and snatched Frances's arm so suddenly that Frances let out a yell. Clara looked back again, and this time, there was a dark figure, nothing more than a tiny silhouette against the setting sun. Though quite a ways behind them, the silhouette walked purposefully, making Clara's legs grow shaky.

"Frances," she whispered, trying to keep her voice steady. "Don't look back, but I think someone is following us."

"Clara!" Frances tightened her grip on Clara's arm and timidly pointed ahead.

Two men stepped out of the trees and staggered onto the road, laughing when they saw the girls. One of them was Mr. Platt.

"Good . . . evening . . . Clara," Mr. Platt slurred between hiccups. Clara cringed to hear him speak her name with such familiarity. "We . . . wanted . . ." He didn't finish his sentence, and now he and his companion were blocking the girls' path and stepping close enough for Clara to smell their sweat.

The other man, who looked both older and dirtier than Mr. Platt, grabbed Frances's free arm and yanked her out of Clara's grasp. In a gravelly voice, he said, "I'll take this one! Aren't you a pretty thing! Why don't you take a walk with me?"

He pulled on Frances, but she gritted her teeth and pulled back. Clara took hold again of Frances's other arm. Looking over her shoulder as she tugged, she saw that the silhouette was closer, now recognizable as the stranger from before, still hiding his face with his hat and high collars. Clara realized that pulling Frances back would only be stepping closer to him. What if the strange man was in league with Mr. Platt and his comrade? Clara looked at the bushes, gauging their height and thickness, and wondered how quickly she and Frances could move through them.

Mr. Platt locked his hand around Clara's arm and yanked her close, making her lose her grip on Frances again. His hot breath spread across her face as he leered over her. "You'll make me a fine wifey." He belched and hiccupped again. "But I don't"—belch—"like the way you strut around"—hiccup—"like a proud cat . . . thinking you're better than me!" Mr. Platt leaned in with a look both angry and hungry.

Clara reacted as best she could. She kneed him with all the force she could muster, sending him to his knees, groaning. She had to run a few paces to catch up to Frances, who was digging her heels in the dirt to keep her assailant from pulling her away.

Clara tried to take hold of Frances by the arm and then the waist, but just when she got a firm enough grip, Clara felt two heavy hands land on her shoulders and pull her away. A scream escaped her throat as she was then pushed to the side, discarded. The strange man who had been following them had finally caught up and was joining the fray.

With her eyes on his back, Clara crept closer and angled her elbow for just the right jab until she realized the stranger was prying the filthy man's hands off Frances. With his lowered hat and high collars, the stranger threw his arm back as if pulling a sling and let it fly in a well-aimed hit to the assailant's jaw, sending him spinning to the ground. Next, this stranger-turned-rescuer took two long strides toward Mr. Platt, who had barely risen to his feet, and delivered an off-kiltering blow to his face. Blood dripped from Mr. Platt's nose as he writhed on the ground.

Every inch of Clara trembled. She still couldn't get a good look at her rescuer's face, and she still didn't trust him. He had stepped in front of her to fling his fists, but he stood between her and Frances.

Clara braced for another struggle, but nothing could have prepared her for what happened next. Frances, also trembling, looked at this stranger with uncontained emotion, threw her arms tightly around his neck, and pressed her lips to his. Clara crimsoned as she heard their kiss.

His rough whisper followed. "Take your friend and get home, Frances. I'll ensure these knaves don't follow. I'll be all right. Now, go!"

Clara stood confounded by what she had just witnessed, but her questions would have to wait. Her desire for home overruled everything else. With the yellow ribbon forgotten, Clara took Frances by the hand and pulled her into a run.

After a few strides, Clara turned back for another look at the man who had helped them, but the sun still cast shadows over the men's forms, melting away the details of the scene. All she could discern was that the strange rescuer was snarling threats at Mr. Platt and his accomplice.

Not waiting to see the outcome, Clara and Frances lifted their skirts and ran the remaining mile back to Milton Manor. They tripped a few times in their haste, but eventually, they stumbled through the house's threshold completely out of breath and collapsed into the nearest chairs.

Olivia came in unaware of the danger Clara and Frances had just fled from, but apprehension burdened her every feature. "Oh, miss! I'm glad you're back. Your father is very ill."

Clara caught her breath and gathered her thoughts. "Is the doctor here? What can I do?" She quickly stood, willing her weary legs to bear her up for any task that lay ahead.

She listened as Olivia explained that the doctor was currently upstairs examining her father. "Your aunt is already doing everything she can to make your father comfortable. I'm afraid the doctor has ordered that you be kept from your father's room to prevent exposure to the illness. The doctor was quite firm about it, as were your father and aunt."

As Olivia left to fetch some tea, Clara sank back into the cushions of her chair and closed her eyes. She understood the reasoning behind the order. Ever since her mother had died of influenza, her father and Louisa had always been overly cautious to protect Clara from getting sick, despite her healthy constitution. To ease their worrying, she usually submitted to their precautions, knowing it was their way of caring for her, but it was never easy. With each measured breath, she hoped for her father's recovery.

Moments later, the rattle of a tea tray roused Clara from her thoughts. Olivia placed the tray on the table in front of Clara and left. That's when Clara realized Frances was still there watching her.

With a concern that contrasted her usually bright features, Frances reached out her hand and said, "I hope your father is all right."

"Thank you," Clara breathed out, grateful to have a friend with her. "I hope so too."

They sipped their tea for a while, not saying anything else. Then, despite Clara's exhaustion, there was one question she had to ask. "Frances . . . the man who came to our rescue . . . who was he?"

Frances took a deep breath. "He is my . . . betrothed."

Guilt folded Frances's stomach. Was it foolish of her to think this question might not arise? "You didn't recognize him, did you?" she asked timidly.

Clara shook her head. "Should I have recognized him? I never got a clear look at his face."

Frances was grateful for that. She wasn't ready to share everything yet, but she owed Clara an explanation. "Well . . ." Frances twisted a loose piece of string on her sleeve and sighed. "I'm not sure it's the best time to tell you. Your father is ill, and you and I haven't always been close . . ."

"It's all right," Clara reassured her. "You can trust me, but you don't have to explain if you don't want to."

Frances hesitated to confide in Clara so quickly, but keeping it all inside was taking its toll. "Mr. Frandsen wasn't the only man who made me an offer."

"Oh?"

"It's not official yet, but the man you saw tonight, the one who helped us . . . it's been nearly a year since he asked me. I'm worried he will tire of waiting." Frances took another deep breath and was quiet.

Clara looked skeptical. "Come now, Frances, what was all that talk last week about the different men you liked in town? You even said you were pining for next season."

Frances waved the thought aside. "I was only talking like that to make you smile. We were at a ladies' social. I wanted to find out who you liked. Besides, hardly anyone knows he proposed. Or that I accepted."

Clara paused. "What do you plan to do?"

Frances looked around, then whispered, "Clara, what would you do if you were in love with a man your family did not approve of?"

Clara shrugged. "Honestly, I don't know."

"Neither do I," Frances admitted, her shoulders sinking. "I know why my family disapproves, but they misunderstand him. I told him to give me more time. I've been trying to convince my parents to accept us."

"What did he think of that?" Clara asked.

"Oh, he is such a gentleman." Frances went from sad to smitten. "But I can't keep him waiting forever, and personally," she sat up and straightened her shoulders, "I don't think I can keep myself waiting either."

Clara gave her a narrow look. "What does that mean?"

Frances debated how much to tell. She and her betrothed had made some rather spur of the moment plans, but she didn't want to explain the details and hear all the arguments and warnings from Clara that she had already heard from her mother. Frances already knew about the uncertainties surrounding her betrothed's inheritance, or lack thereof, and she already knew about the rumors connected with his name. None of it mattered to Frances.

When she didn't answer, Clara made a suggestion that caught her off guard.

"Frances, why don't you stay here at Milton Manor for a few days? You can send for your things tomorrow and arrange it with your family. It will give us time together to consider your dilemma."

All doubts about trusting Clara fled. "You would do that for me?"

"Of course."

Frances reached for Clara's hand but stopped midway. "Well, there is one problem."

"What is it, Frances?"

Frances bit her lip, torn between a smile and an apology.

"I might be eloping tonight."

Clara knew her mouth hung open as she stared at Frances. She wanted to protest or at least ask questions, but before her mind could form them, Olivia came in to give Clara news regarding her father.

Fortunately, it was good news. Her father was doing better under the doctor's administrations. The violent coughing had subsided, and the fever seemed to be going down, but caution was still needed. Her father's improvements were too tenuous to trust yet. He slept fitfully, and it would be a long night.

"Please inform me of any change," Clara instructed Olivia. "I want to know the minute I can see him."

After Olivia answered the rest of Clara's questions, she handed a note to Frances. "This just come for you, miss."

With wide eyes, Frances accepted the note. She said nothing and neither did Clara. When Olivia was gone, Frances stood up and pressed the note to her heart before tearing it open and reading its contents. Clara watched Frances's breathing grow faster as her face flushed.

"Oh, my!" Frances whispered. "Clara, I . . . I'm so sorry. I have to go!"

Before Clara could say a word, Frances was gone.

Clara sat by the fire, staring at the doors Frances had just walked through. True, Frances had said she might be eloping, but Clara had no idea it would happen so soon. She felt as though her blanket had been stripped away in the cold of the night, making Mr. Platt and his accomplice feel too close and her father's health more uncertain. Frances had left, quite easily, to run toward a possibly ruinous fate, and there was nothing Clara could do. What if Frances's betrothed was dishonorable? What if he couldn't be trusted? He had defended them, but what if his motives were selfish?

Clara's eyes swelled. She didn't know what to do. The wind blew outside and floorboards creaked above as she sat in the large, empty sitting room. From somewhere deep and raw, she sighed for comfort and connection, for a listening ear. But there was no one.

She wandered over to the table on the opposite side of the room and pulled out some paper with the intent to alleviate her solitude with drawing, but instead of images coming to mind, she envisioned the page being filled with words. There was one person she could still reach out to.

Dipping a pen in ink, she sat and wrote line after line without worrying about what she was saying or how she was saying it. Nothing she wrote felt very important, but the simple act of writing a letter was comforting. She just needed to reach out in some way to someone, and tonight, Mr. Thayne was that someone. With her eyes watering and her heart somewhat relieved, she folded the letter and tucked it into her dress.

When Clara heard footsteps approaching behind her, she assumed it was Olivia with more news about her father.

"Are you all right?"

Clara stood and spun around. Frances stood before her with drooped shoulders and glistening eyes. A glance at the clock revealed that it had only been half an hour since she had left. And now she was back?

"Frances? What happened? I thought you'd left." Clara rose from her chair at the desk and gestured for Frances to sit with her by the fire.

Frances sat down and slowly shook her head. "I'm so sorry. My intended. He wanted me to run away with him. Tonight. Just now. But I said no."

Clara blinked. "You what?"

"I had every intention to run off with him tonight, but then I thought of you sitting here alone worrying about your father. And I just couldn't do it. I told my intended I couldn't leave you right now, that it was the worst possible moment."

"Oh, Frances!"

"The man I marry needs to have compassion and understanding for things like that."

"Well, what did he say?" Clara was eager to know what this all meant for Frances.

"At first, he just looked at me in stunned silence. Oh, Clara, the seconds that followed after I told him I couldn't go were the worst moments of my life! I doubted I knew him as well as I thought."

"And then?"

"He was disappointed, but I think he understood. In fact, he agreed I should stay. Clara, it was such a relief to hear him say that! We'll probably have to elope no matter what, but I don't want to be selfish about it. We'll find another time." Frances looked down and smiled. "He told me that having me as a wife was something worth waiting for." A dimple appeared in her cheek as she spoke.

"And when will that be, Frances?"

Her shoulders slumped and the dimple disappeared. "I don't know. He leaves tonight."

Clara nodded, and for a while, the only sound was the light snapping of the fire on the logs.

Frances let out a big yawn, and Clara felt her eyelids droop. The excitement of the day had finally caught up to them. Arrangements were soon made for Frances to spend the night, and after a brief dinner, Clara and Olivia helped Frances settle in.

As Clara walked to her own room that night, she imagined herself in Frances's position. She didn't think she could ever defy her father by running off and eloping, but then she thought of the letters she had exchanged with Mr. Thayne. Did that pleasant little secret mean she was already defying her father? She hoped not. Her father would understand, wouldn't he? Even if she had wanted to talk to him about the letters, she didn't want to burden him when he was ill. It would have to remain her secret. After all, her father was keeping secrets too. That secret, the one between him and Louisa, felt unfair while Clara's felt so innocent. It was just a few letters—letters from a man who was kind and clever and interesting and . . .

And then she remembered Mr. Shaw. Where had that thought come from? Some far-off part of her mind whispered his name just to test her reaction. What did she think of him? Truthfully, she had hardly given him much thought since writing to Mr. Thayne. She tried to think of Mr. Shaw and their last dance together, but it seemed insignificant now. He had said he would write to her, but he never did.

Chapter 8

Shaw sat down and made a list of the most attractive girls he knew, and by attractive, he meant good looking and rich. Several of the girls on his list were those he had flirted with merely for his own amusement. With time being short, he needed to focus on those who seemed most promising.

After a few scratches, four girls remained on his list. He read through the names and crossed off one more because he didn't like her high-pitched laugh. Then he crossed off another because, although she was rich and pretty, he didn't like that she was taller than him.

Two names remained, Elizabeth Watson and Clara Everton. They weren't as rich as he would have liked, but both were attractive and interesting in their own way. He had danced with both at the Stratford ball a few months ago and recalled something about having promised at least one of them that he would write to her. *That would be a good start*, he thought.

He got out a sheet of paper and looked around for inspiration. Mrs. Hamilton had put a vase of fresh flowers on the table. He laughed to himself as he began to compose.

Dearest —

> *I saw a rose today and thought of you. Its beautiful bloom reminded me of your crimson lips and youthful glow. Though it has been only a few months, it feels like years since I have seen your graceful figure on the dance floor. Would that I could ask*

you to dance this moment so I might have the pleasure of holding your hand and hearing your lovely laughter!

That's perfect. Shaw was quite proud of himself when he read it over again, but he couldn't think of anything else to say. He got up and paced around the room. Did he really need to say much more? He snapped his fingers and sat down to finish.

> *I will keep this letter brief so I may send it all the more quickly. I don't know when our next meeting will be, but I earnestly hope to have the opportunity to see you soon. In the meantime, please consider me your humble, yet devoted admirer. Please reply soon so I may have the satisfaction of knowing you understand my sentiments.*
>
> *Passionately yours,*
> *Owen Shaw*

That will do, he thought as he made a second copy. It contained just the sort of thing a girl who wanted to be in love would want to read. With both copies in hand, he addressed one to Miss Watson and the other to Miss Everton and wondered which girl would be the first to answer.

As he sealed the letters, hot wax dripped on his finger, stinging his skin and flaring his bitterness. Why did his father ruin everything? Sending love letters to pretty girls should have been entertaining. Instead, Shaw felt like a fool, but what choice did he have? His inheritance was at stake. With a sneer, he added the letters to the outgoing post and decided to see what Harris was up to.

Chapter 9

$\mathcal{J}$ ames Thayne ran the brush over his horse's short, black hair and praised him for being such a fine animal. Knight was his favorite horse for many reasons. Not only was he strong and obedient, but he was the last gift given to Thayne by his father before he died, a reminder of all the times they had ridden together.

The horse's muscles eased under the brush, and, like water flowing down a stream, a tension Thayne hadn't realized he was carrying slowly left him. He had just returned from a visit with the tenants who lived in the southeast corner of his estate. Thayne had gone around with them to various sites and listened to their complaints. The need for repairs was greater than he had realized, but already a plan was forming in his mind which he could implement the following week.

Leaving the stables, he ran his fingers through his dark, wavy hair that had become thick with sweat and admired the sand-colored stone exterior of his home. He still felt too small for such a grand house and all the responsibilities attached to it, but lately, the renewed hope of bringing home a bride filled the empty space.

He entered the door and checked with Mrs. Andrews to see whether there were any letters. Since writing to Clara Everton, the post's arrival had become the most anticipated event of the day. Mrs. Andrews handed him a small stack, and he began sifting. Business, business, business. Then his hand paused with the letter he had been waiting for. He recognized Clara's handwriting, her small, even loops slanting gracefully across the paper. He turned the letter backward and forward and took a satisfied breath. Dropping into the nearest chair, he broke the seal and read.

Dear Mr. Thayne,

What a strange day it has been. As I write, I feel as though I am trying to hold the ground still while the world relentlessly spins. Change comes like a whirlwind, and it's difficult to catch my breath. Just now, my father is ill and my friend is gone, and all I want is someone to talk to about ordinary, predictable things. So, as I write, I will imagine you are here listening.

I'll begin by saying that I am in favor of the truce you propose. What better way to settle our dispute than with a dance! I can only think of one improvement to this plan. We must also share an apple tart when next we meet. They are my favorite as well.

I enjoyed learning your secret and reading about your grandmother. She sounds lovely. Unfortunately, my skills with a needle and thread do not extend beyond my girlhood samplers. Instead, I spend my time drawing. Did my uncle tell you I draw? Ever since I was little, I have loved the feel of a finely crafted pencil trailing across paper as it leaves its mark. Each time I finish a drawing, whether it's of an apple tart or a boy and his grandmother, I feel as though I have gained a new truth or made a new friend.

Thayne paused to pull out two other sheets of paper and laughed when he realized she had drawn things he mentioned in his previous letter. The drawing of an apple tart looked as appetizing as any he had ever eaten, but it was the other drawing that displayed Clara's real talent. Somehow, through the expressions on their faces, she had managed to capture the feeling of love between the grandmother and child. After admiring the drawings a few minutes more, he returned to the letter.

I enjoy riding as well but only if I am on the right horse, and there is only one horse I trust. She is a light brown mare with long ears. My father gave me this dear horse for my twelfth birthday. It struck me then that her face, with her ears sticking up and her nose twitching, looked more like a rabbit, so I have called her Rabbit ever since.

And now, Mr. Thayne, I have a sensitive question for you. Do you ever eavesdrop? Before your first letter arrived, I happened to overhear my father and aunt whispering about me in the middle of the night. I was not sure of the context, but I am certain they are keeping secrets from me. Neither has ever said a word to me about it. I try not to worry, but I overheard them having a similar conversation again just the other night. My father has been taking ill more often lately, and my aunt tends to him so frequently that she has forgotten to pry into my affairs. Everything seems to hang in such a delicate balance these days. Your letters bring a welcome cheeriness, which grounds me. The only problem is now you know I eavesdrop.

> *Most sincerely,*
> *Clara Everton*

Mr. Thayne was struck with Clara's letter. With other ladies, he never could get past their outer layer. Yet, he already knew several things about Clara that resonated with him, and for the first time in his life, he realized that the woman he married should first be his friend.

One phrase from Clara's letter lingered in his mind, *when next we meet* . . . In his opinion, it would happen sooner or later, so why couldn't it be sooner?

He made the decision right then. He would not wait until next season to spend time with Clara.

Chapter 10

Clara ran for the pure enjoyment of it. She wanted to be outside where the only thing between her and heaven were the clouds. Tall grass whipped her skirts while breezes sent tiny hairs racing over her face. She was running to her favorite place under the oak tree by the pond to read her newest letter from Mr. Thayne. Reaching the tree, she looked up at the wide, green leaves and determined to relish the last warm days before autumn chills settled in and sent leaves falling. Holding his letter tight, she read,

Dear Clara,

I hope you have found time to catch your breath since your last letter. Change can be merciless indeed, especially when it is not of our own choosing. Unfortunately, I have resisted change of any sort at Felton Park for far too long, and I begin to feel the consequences of it. I am now compelled to make several decisions regarding repairs and improvements which will require a great deal of labor and resources. If only I had made the repairs long ago. But I should not complain. I know such changes will be for the better, even if the process is difficult.

I must thank you for the excellent drawings. Your uncle did mention that you draw, but I enjoy seeing the evidence of your skill firsthand. Though you have never seen my grandmother and can only guess what I looked like as a boy, you expertly captured the love within the memory. I hope the small gift I have included here, along with a flower that grows abundantly around Felton Park, will convey my thanks as well as my enthusiasm for your talent.

Clara unfolded a separate sheet of paper that contained two finely crafted graphite pencils, the sort that would be the envy of any artist, entwined with dried clusters of forget-me-nots. She loosened the pencils from the flowers and ran her finger along their thin frames. Mr. Thayne must have gone to some trouble to find them. After carefully wrapping them back up, Clara finished her letter.

I am delighted you will reserve a dance for me. I will not forget your promise. When next we meet, we should not only share an apple tart, but we should also go riding together, you on Rabbit, and I on my horse, Knight, named such because I always feel like a knight when I ride him. Now that I have the notion to ride with you as well as dance, I grow ever more impatient to see you again.

To answer your question frankly, yes, I have been known to eavesdrop, but I blame it on the fact that I am unable to stop and start my ears at will. Eavesdropping can lead to fascinating discoveries, but it is a responsibility that comes with a burden. I have learned that I can choose to stay and listen, but I cannot choose to forget what I hear. I do not always like what I hear, and I would venture to guess you did not like what you overheard. Your consolation might come in knowing that your father and aunt care about you. If you are disinclined to approach them about their secrets, perhaps trust is the only logical option.

Knowing that you eavesdrop, I shall mention, is no problem at all. I believe people become true friends when they share their imperfections with each other. How else are they to know if they are loved and accepted for who they are? My parents were great examples of loving each other despite their imperfections and sometimes because of them. Though they have both since passed, and not a day goes by when I don't miss them, their examples shine clear in my memory.

Dear Clara, is it safe to say we are friends now? Am I allowed to say I have been thinking about you? Each letter you send gives me a charming glimpse into your character, and I am eager to learn more.

Your constant admirer,
James Thayne

Chapter 11

Frances sat across from Clara, sipping tea and thinking about her betrothed. It had been a little over a fortnight since Clara's father had taken ill, and Frances had turned down her betrothed's offer to run away with him. She didn't regret her choice. It was the right thing to do, but she couldn't help but wonder when another opportunity would arise.

After that night, Frances had tried to convince her mother to allow her to stay at Milton Manor for a week or two, but her mother, always suspicious that Frances might run off in the night to elope, had said no.

Her mother didn't seem to mind what she did during the day, however, so Frances frequently found herself wandering to Milton Manor for the afternoon. Sometimes, she and Clara walked around the estate. Other times, they rode horses together, and sometimes Clara gave her a drawing lesson. It didn't really matter what they did. Clara was excellent company, and being at Milton Manor gave Frances a much needed reprieve from the tense discussions she had lately been having with her parents over what constituted a prudent match.

Despite the difficulties, Frances continued to correspond with her intended whenever she could, usually through disguising her letters and choosing discreet messengers. He knew she was often at Milton Manor, and though a specific time to run away had never been decided, she would be ready to leave at a moment's notice.

When tea was finished, Clara suggested they take their sketchbooks to the pond to draw. Frances loved the idea, mostly because the pond was a convenient place to listen for approaching carriages, should her intended arrive, but when Clara suggested they go out in the rowboat, she loved the idea a little less. Still, she agreed to go.

Frances didn't know what to think when Clara declined the help of the servants, but Clara was surprisingly adept at maneuvering the boat out onto the water. Stepping in without help had been awkward, but Frances had managed. Once Clara stepped in, getting her feet and skirts wet in the process, she used an oar to push off and began to row effortlessly. Frances assumed it was because of the calmness of the water, but when she took a turn, she realized how difficult it was. Her hands were quickly chafed by the constant motion of the oars rubbing her skin, so she didn't mind pausing when Clara pulled out a sheet of paper. At first, Frances thought Clara was going to begin their drawing lesson, but then she saw the guilty look on Clara's face and the lines scribbled across the paper.

"I received a letter today," Clara said, "from Mr. Shaw."

Frances almost let one of the oars drop in the water. Surely, she hadn't heard Clara correctly. "From Mr. Shaw?" Frances asked, trying to sound only mildly interested.

"Yes," Clara confirmed, looking off to the side.

Apparently, Frances would need to help Clara speak more openly. "What do you think of his letter?"

Clara took a deep breath. "I don't know. It's . . . it's a love letter of sorts. At least, that is what I think he meant by it."

Frances gasped. She couldn't help it. She leaned forward. "Are you actually interested in Mr. Shaw?!" She sounded more eager to know than she had meant to.

"No . . ." Clara looked down as her cheeks reddened.

Oh, no. Frances didn't want Clara to feel judged. She tried to row casually, despite the effort it required, and asked, "Well then, what troubles you?"

"Frances, I can trust you, can't I?" Clara looked up expectantly.

"Of course you can!"

"The truth is, that night at the ball, I really did begin to like Mr. Shaw, but my uncle and aunts discouraged it."

"Oh, dear." Frances knew how it felt to be thwarted in love.

Clara shook her head. "Oh, no! You misunderstand me! Mr. Shaw's letter is ridiculous! His words are so . . . empty. I'm almost convinced he is laughing at me."

Of course his words would feel empty, Frances thought. She knew Mr. Shaw would not mean whatever he wrote to Clara. "Well, have done with it, and throw the scoundrel's letter in the water!"

Clara gave a short laugh. "You don't think he deserves a response?"

Frances looked to the side as she rowed and said matter-of-factly, "Clara, I am too lady-like to tell you exactly what I think that man deserves."

Clara tilted her head back and laughed. "You're right!" She tore the letter in half and tossed it in the pond. A moment later, her expression turned pensive. "There is more."

"More letters?" Frances's interest was piqued.

"Yes— no! Well, not from Mr. Shaw. You see, I have been writing to another gentleman."

Frances eyes widened. "Are you secretly engaged?"

"No . . ."

"But you are writing to someone?"

"Yes."

Frances didn't know what to say. It was not the kind of thing a respectable girl like Clara did. Then again, Frances considered herself a respectable girl, and there she was intently trying to find a way to elope.

"Are you in love with this man?" Frances asked. "Do you expect to be engaged soon?"

"Frances, you must promise not to laugh or be shocked."

Frances promised, then tightened her grip on the oars as she waited. Maybe it was her mother's influence, but she still enjoyed a good secret.

Clara sighed. "I hardly know him. I've only met him once."

Frances didn't understand. "Then why do you risk sending letters? If my mother knew, she would spread the news like wildfire. Imagine the harm that would do to your reputation."

"Well, what about you?" Clara asked defensively. "Does your mother know that you and your betrothed exchange messages, trying to arrange your elopement?"

Frances handed the oars back to Clara and folded her arms. "She suspects."

"Do you ever worry she would say something to damage your reputation?"

Frances shook her head. "I'm her daughter. If my reputation were hurt, it would reflect poorly on her. I live with constant reminders of what society expects from me, which equals what she expects from me. Sometimes I think she spreads rumors so quickly because it's her way of protecting our family. If she spreads stories about other people that are sufficiently shocking, no one will notice what I am up to."

Clara pressed her brows together. "How have you lived like that? I hear my share of society's expectations from my aunt, but my father always tempers her and allows me a great deal of freedom. Don't you tire of hearing your mother go on like that?"

"It's incredibly exhausting!" Frances breathed out, but when a look of pity swept Clara's face, Frances cleared her throat and shifted on the wooden plank that acted as her seat. "But we were talking about you."

"Oh." Clara pulled in the oars and let the boat glide on its own. She picked up her notebook and ran her fingers along the edge. "I care about my reputation, but . . . I was very flattered by the first letter Mr.—" Clara stopped and brushed a curl out of her face. ". . . this gentleman sent me. I hadn't planned on writing a reply, but I wrote one eventually because I wanted Louisa to think there was a man in my life. I wanted her to stop bothering me about Mr. Platt."

"Mr. Platt? Are you serious? That beef-wit? That jug-bitten, no good—" Frances felt her temper flare at the idea, after what he did to them!

"Exactly," Clara confirmed.

"Well, then I can't blame you if that was your reason."

"That was how it started," Clara explained, "but now I would write to him regardless of Mr. Platt. We've become real friends. I feel I can trust him. Oh, Frances, I know it sounds a bit . . ."

"Imprudent? Naïve?" Frances suggested. She could hardly believe what she was hearing.

"I was going to say . . . daring . . . or romantic." Clara smiled, then sighed. "I know it breaks with tradition. I was hoping you would understand and perhaps help me know what to do."

Frances could see Clara's guard coming down and didn't want to do anything that might disrupt it. Frances held still and listened.

"I have thought about it a great deal, Frances. This is one decision I can't let society make for me. I haven't done anything wrong. In fact, I feel good about writing to Mr. . . . to this gentleman. Why should I assume society would be a better judge than I am of the best path to my happiness?"

Frances looked out over the water, considering Clara's words. "Perhaps I have been listening to my mother too much, Clara, but aren't society's rules meant to protect us? I'm sure they exist for a reason."

Clara looked surprised. "You're one to talk! Where do society's rules fit in with your plans to run away?"

Frances shook her head. "Oh, no. We are still talking about you. I already know I live with contradictions."

Clara gave Frances a half-grin. "I just think society's rules are unreliable in too many ways. When I was in London, I met girls who wanted nothing more than an advantageous marriage. It was all to strengthen estates and preserve legacies. It was hardly ever about the girl. Society is fickle. The rules protect against some dangers but leave us vulnerable to others. What kind of anchor is that?"

Frances nodded. When had Clara become this thoughtful? Had she always been this way? Frances thought of her own marriage predicament. She didn't want to break her mother's heart, no matter how ridiculous her mother could be sometimes, but Frances realized she agreed with Clara. She had to do what she thought was best.

The tiny boat drifted on the water as the girls sat silent. Then, as their eyes met, each girl reached in the water and gave the other a splash. It would have been a pleasant end to a pleasant afternoon but for one thing. Frances's betrothed did not come.

Chapter 12

M r. Thayne had a particularly strange mix of letters that morning, but a letter from Clara made him forget the rest. In his favorite chair, he leaned back and read,

Dear Mr. Thayne,

Thank you for your gift. Wherever did you find such perfect pencils for drawing? By artist standards, they are very fine. I promise I will put them to good use.

To answer your question, yes, we are friends now. I have been thinking about you as well. Your letter came at just the right time. I will try to follow your advice and not worry about what I have overheard because, for the time being, I can't control what my father and aunt do not tell me. I wish you and I could talk about it in person, but for now, I must be content with letters.

I am sorry to hear that your parents have passed. My mother died when I was eight. Like me, she liked to draw, and my father says my temperament is very much like hers. I often imagine what life would be like right now if she were still alive. I can remember being very young and sitting in her lap as she placed my hand on an empty sheet of paper and traced its outline for me. What magic it seemed at the time! It has been years, but I still recall the feeling of my little hand in hers. The sadness of her loss never entirely leaves me, as I'm sure you understand, but my memories of her are happy.

My memories of you, I will mention, are still quite hazy, and I do not understand it. Why did we connect through letters but not in person at the ball? If I am honest with myself, I think it is my fault. I was not myself that night, and I was too dismissive. All I can say is I regret it. If I had been more open, perhaps you and I would have more than letters to build off of right now. Regretting only takes me so far, though, so I have decided upon two remedies. First, I must make the most of our letters. I want to learn everything I can about you, and second, I am determined to look for the good in everyone. My father always says that most people are likable once you get to know them. It has certainly been true with you.

Always,
Clara

Chapter 13

Shaw walked briskly down the street with resentment in his step and anger on his breath. He was determined to do something more aggressive to preserve his fortune. He hadn't yet heard from Clara Everton or Elizabeth Watson. He didn't have time to keep writing stupid love letters, and there were no girls in town he fancied at the moment. It was time for more drastic measures.

When he arrived at the solicitor's office, he pounded on the door until it creaked open. He was shown into a musty office lined with old books on one end and certificates neatly framed on the other.

"Good afternoon, Mr. Shaw. How are you?" asked Mr. Barnes, the solicitor, from behind his desk, not bothering to take his eyes off his papers even when he stood to shake hands. His small silver spectacles barely hung on his nose, and his salt and pepper hair grew to his shoulders.

"I would like to talk with you about my inheritance," Shaw declared with an edge to his voice. He saw no point in wasting time with pleasantries.

Mr. Barnes grunted, "Yes, your father told me you would stop by."

Shaw cursed under his breath. Was he so predictable?

Mr. Barnes finally looked up and smiled sharply. "There is no way out of this, boy. A fine bed you've made for yourself!" He gave an impolite chuckle. "Don't be too hard on yourself. After all, your father has made provisions for you to rescue the situation. I couldn't help but think you might even fancy my own daughter. Been trying to get her off my hands, you see. She has a few years on you and would be a little particular about what kind of jacket you wear sometimes, but when you pause to consider . . ."

Barnes's words fell on deaf ears. Shaw wasn't that desperate yet. Without any concern for civility, he turned to leave. As Shaw swung the door open, ready to march out, he was hit in the shoulder by another man trying to enter at the same time. Shaw took one look at the man and felt his sweat steam.

"Philip!" he exclaimed. "What are you doing here?"

Philip Shaw stood close to his brother in the doorway. Philip was an inch or two taller, had slightly darker hair, and a larger smile. Otherwise, the two brothers looked very much alike. Philip remained unruffled by his brother's short temper and gave him a friendly pat on the back.

"Owen? What a surprise. It's good to see you."

Shaw shoved Philip away from him. "I know why you're here. Come to gloat, are you? Come to check on your inheritance?"

Shaw could hear Barnes groan from his desk.

Philip shook his head, looking confused. "Have you talked to mother lately? I didn't know if you knew. I came to talk to Mr. Barnes about—"

"I know all about it. It's not yours yet, you know. This isn't over!"

Shaw stormed out, ignoring whatever Philip was yelling to him down the hall. He marched past the clerk and pushed his way through the main doors. What was Philip doing back in town? He was supposed to be in Lanford with their parents. How dare he come talk with Barnes! He should be grateful Shaw didn't pummel him right there in the office.

But Shaw was apt to pummel something soon if he didn't find a release. He strode along the pavement with impressive speed, heading straight for Harris's.

The walk helped take the edge off his temper, but he remained in a foul mood.

Harris was stepping out his front door when Shaw reached the gate. "Harris!" he hollered. "You can't be going somewhere right now! I need your help."

"Shaw!" Harris walked over and gave him a friendly slap on the shoulder. "Why don't you walk with me, eh? I'm just on my way out."

He carried a rolled newspaper under his arm and stuck his hands in his pockets.

"On your way where?" Shaw asked skeptically. "A bit early for gaming isn't it?"

Harris frowned. "I'm not on my way to gamble."

"Out with your secret, then, Harris! I want in on the fun!" Shaw elbowed him in the ribs.

"Haven't you heard?" Harris grunted. "Miss Dalton is expecting me to make her an offer today."

"And what kind of offer are you making her?" Shaw jeered. "Are you buying one of her horses? Or do you want her to come take care of yours?"

Harris whacked Shaw over the head with his paper. "That's my future wife you're talking about!"

This was too much. Harris was always good for laughs, but marriage? Not likely. It had to be one of his jokes. Shaw was about to make some other jab, but he hesitated when he took in Harris's appearance. Harris was wearing one of his nicest jackets and a serious expression, and his brown hair looked neater than usual. Was it really possible?

"Well," Shaw ventured, "when did this happen?"

"While you've been sobering up the past few days, I reckon."

Shaw still could hardly believe it and would have remained unconvinced had Harris not looked so offended. "Harris, old fellow, I apologize. I truly thought you were having a go at me. By all means, tell me about it. And . . ." He paused again, cocking his head in consideration. "Come to think of it, you might be in a better position to help me than I thought, seeing as how you have more experience in these matters than I realized."

Walking along, Harris explained how it had all been arranged by his mother, on whom he still relied for his living. She insisted it was time for him to wed and that this was a good match. She also insisted that if he didn't follow her recommendations, he would be the most ungrateful child ever to be born, and she would henceforth reduce his living to such an amount as to make him obliged to seek out Miss Dalton's hand for her wealth if not for his mother's approbation.

"What do I care?" Harris continued unaffectedly. "So long as Miss Dalton obliges me during the hunting season, I've no reason to prefer any other lady to her. So long as a comfortable living is secured, I've no reason to complain, eh?"

Shaw was speechless. Since when did Harris care a lick about what his mother thought? And since when was Harris interested in getting married at all? Shaw had often heard him talk of living out his days as a comfortable old bachelor.

Shaw stumbled over a rock in the path and remembered what he needed to talk to Harris about. He explained his own situation which, he remarked, was surprisingly similar to Harris's new one. Harris listened and nodded, much less surprised than Shaw expected.

"Well, what am I to do?" Harris asked carelessly. "See if Miss Dalton has a cousin?"

"Harris, you're useless!" Shaw swatted at the air and turned to leave.

"Now, wait a minute, Shaw!" Harris grabbed him by the arm. "Don't leave in a huff. I'm about to propose for goodness sake! If you leave me disgruntled, I'm certain I'll botch things up with Miss Dalton. Now let's sit here a moment and think this through."

Shaw's shoulders relaxed. Even though Harris tried to give the impression of being cold and unconcerned, Shaw always found him to be helpful in a pinch.

"Now look, Shaw," Harris began. "The way I see it, there are plenty of ways to go about this, but there's no use in complicating the matter. Just find some pathetic girl and make her an offer."

"I could never tolerate just any girl," Shaw said as he looked at a crack in the pavement.

"Well, there's the real problem." Harris jabbed him in the ribs with his finger. "You're too particular. I'm about to be happily married myself soon, but that might not be if I fretted over every detail."

"You really fancy that you'll be happy with Miss Dalton? Especially when it's a match your mother is pushing for?"

"I've no reason to think otherwise."

"Do you love the girl?"

"I've no reason to think I won't love her by the end of it all."

"Harris, you're insane." This time Shaw gave Harris a push to the head.

"Now look here, Shaw." Harris grew serious. "I want to help. I'm not a romantic by any means, so if you're looking for love, you'd best be looking elsewhere for advice. But if you want my opinion, you just need to choose a girl and have done with it. Find out how to persuade her." Leaning close, he added in a low voice, "Make it impossible for her to say no."

Shaw pondered this advice. "And how in the world are you going to persuade Miss Dalton?"

"That is between me and Miss Dalton." Harris gave a mischievous grin, and with a tip of his hat, he walked off.

Shaw stood on the pavement musing over Harris's words. *Make it impossible for her to say no.* The letters Shaw had been writing were simply not enough. He scratched his cheek, considering what lengths he might go to this time. Capturing a bride would require more effort than he had initially planned, but he could be very persuasive when he wanted to be.

When Shaw arrived home, Mrs. Hamilton walked over and handed him a letter. She bustled all over the house now, at his father's request, whenever she pleased, probably to spy on him. Shaw didn't try to hide his scowl as he yanked the letter out of her hand and watched her walk away.

The address was written across the paper in a hand he didn't recognize. Was it possible one of his love letters had finally gleaned a reply? Without bothering to get his hopes up, he broke the seal and read.

Dear Mr. Shaw,

I was not expecting your letter, but the sentiments you share come as no surprise. I felt your gaze on me more than once when last we met, and it is a shame we did not have more time to get acquainted.

However, I must tell you that my mother does not approve of my corresponding with you. I send this letter to you in secret only to inform you that, while I may share a portion of the eagerness you express to meet again, my family forbids me to write to you. I assume that if your sentiments are in earnest, you will find another way for us to meet before next season. I am the kind of person who is very strong in my affections, but if kept waiting long, I see no point in delaying my search for another object of my affection. It should be no secret that I have more than one admirer at the moment. Please understand that I send this letter to give you the upper hand.

Sincerely,
Elizabeth Watson

Well, well, thought Shaw. This was good luck! Miss Watson was foolish enough to feel flattered and wrote him back out of her own vanity. She seemed like the type of person who would want something more because it was forbidden. This gave Shaw something to work with.

If he was quick to make the arrangements, he could travel to Miss Watson's home the very next day. He would need to employ his most charming tactics, but if his luck held, he could be engaged by the end of the week.

He read the letter a second time and considered her eagerness. Was Miss Watson really so enamored with him that she would give such obvious encouragement after a few mere flirtations and one short letter? And what of her threats to find another suitor if Shaw did not hurry? Was it possible she wanted to rush him along for her own purposes?

Shaw tapped the letter in his hand. *What do I care?* he thought. So long as her motivations did not conflict with his, he would marry her. He walked upstairs, ready to plan his visit, but questions started buzzing through his thoughts like houseflies. What if Miss Watson wanted to marry Shaw to escape sudden poverty? Perhaps she merely wanted to spend his fortune. Or convince him to use his wealth to pull her family out of debt. Had there been any recent scandal? Was there a reason why no one else would want her?

Shaw's pace slowed. He had no problem rushing into marriage as long as he knew exactly what her reasons were. He might risk his domestic happiness, but he would not risk the unknown, not when his inheritance was at stake. No, it was absolutely necessary that he be the one in control of his marriage choices.

Hopefully his worries would come to naught, but if Miss Watson were involved in any sort of intrigue, he would find out.

Shaw was dreading the visit he was about to make. It shouldn't have come to this. If the situation weren't dire, he never would have sought out his cousin. At least this time, there was a need.

His cousin, Mrs. Emily Trent, lived within walking distance of his own townhouse, but he avoided her as much as possible. Besides being the most well-informed gossip he knew, she was married to the most boring fellow he had ever met, besides Philip, so Shaw was reluctant to bask in their society. Visiting his cousin was always tedious, and he expected this time to be no exception.

He knocked heavily on the door and was shown in by the housekeeper. He only waited a minute before his cousin burst into the room.

"Oh, it *is* really you, Owen!" Mrs. Trent, in a dress covered in ruffles, bustled over to shake hands with Shaw and invited him to sit down. She spoke quickly and punctuated each sentence with a wave of her hand. "I told Nancy, that couldn't be Owen Shaw! He never comes to visit this time of year! But here you are! Such a surprise! Mr. Trent is upstairs in his study and won't be disturbed, but I'm happy to receive my cousin. To what do I owe the pleasure?"

Shaw shifted in his seat. Mrs. Trent was a year younger than he, but she was far more outgoing and outspoken. She always appeared eager to put Shaw at ease, but Shaw ended up uncomfortable regardless. He usually spent his time trying to gauge whether he had stayed long enough to politely excuse himself. This time, he would try to act more amiable and allow her to prattle on. At least that part wouldn't require much effort.

Shaw made the first civil comment he could think of. "Well, I have only seen you and Mr. Trent a few times since your wedding last year, and I thought I would come see how you are getting on."

Mrs. Trent clapped her hands together and told him how much she enjoyed purchasing new china and running her own home. Choosing colors, directing servants, spending money, and so on and so on. Shaw had never suspected it possible to have so much to say on the subject, but he listened patiently and waited for the break.

When Mrs. Trent finally paused for air, he asked, "What's the latest news?"

She jumped at the bait. "Owen, it really is simply amazing that you have come here today of all days. Why, only last week, a solicitor called on my husband and me to see if we could help him find the nearest relative of Mr. George Everton."

Shaw listened but was waiting for the right moment to inquire about Miss Watson without betraying his interests, which would be no simple feat. His cousin was skilled at divulging gossip because she had a talent for detecting it. She would be quick to make assumptions, regardless of what he said.

"You see," she continued, "Mr. Everton's estate is entailed, and he only has one daughter."

Shaw braced himself to hear the whole history of the Everton family, their rises and falls in wealth, their scandals and so on. Somehow, he would need to steer the subject toward Miss Watson.

Mrs. Trent smiled the whole time she talked. "Mr. Everton has hardly any relatives, and his health has been failing him, poor soul! His solicitor is going about the unpleasant task of tracking down who is to inherit once Mr. Everton is gone. It would appear that Mr. Everton does not spend much time in society and is unaware of who his closest kin might be. All he has is a sister who never married, and a cousin rumored to be lost in India."

Shaw fidgeted with a string that had come loose on his jacket. Mrs. Trent was rambling on, and he began to doubt whether there had been any point in coming at all.

"And here is where it gets interesting, cousin." She leaned in. "Mr. Barnes believes that your mother is actually a relation of Mr. Everton's, the closest he has! Which means . . ." She trailed off and raised her eyebrows.

He paused and rubbed his chin a few times. "Are you saying you think I am in line to inherit his estate?"

"Indeed!" She clapped her hands together and beamed at him.

"Did you say . . . Mr. Barnes told you this? Mr. Barnes the solicitor?"

"Right again, cousin."

Shaw sat back. This was news! With another inheritance to rely on, Shaw could forget the whole marriage deal and his father's approval. At least, he could if he was willing to let Philip be appointed heir of the Lanford estate, which he absolutely wasn't. It would be too humiliating. If only there were some way to use the situation to further his chances of marriage so that he could have both estates. Then a realization struck.

"Did you say this was about a Mr. Everton? Who has a daughter?"

"We are sharp this morning," Mrs. Trent teased.

"Did Mr. Barnes give you the name of his daughter?"

"Oh yes," she cleared her throat. "Miss Caroline. Mr. Barnes told me that he had mentioned the eligibility of his daughter to you during a recent visit you paid to his office. Miss Caroline Barnes sounds like she might be interested in receiving a visit from you . . ."

"No, no, no!" Shaw interrupted. "Not Barnes's daughter! Mr. Everton's!"

"How silly of me!" Mrs. Trent laughed and waved her hand as though she were fanning herself. Shaw was growing impatient. "Yes, he did mention her name . . . What was it? . . . Give me a moment to recall." She tapped her face with her finger and smiled.

Shaw knew she was doing this on purpose. Mrs. Trent didn't need a minute to recall. She was waiting for his reaction so she could detect whether Mr. Everton's daughter meant anything to him. He tried his best not to betray the suspense she was keeping him in.

"Clara! Yes, that's it! Miss Clara Everton. You don't happen to know her do you?"

Shaw rolled his eyes at her pretenses. He had heard all he needed to. If he was actually to inherit the Everton's estate, and possibly soon if Mr. Everton's health was that poor, then Shaw had good reason to believe it would be a simple matter to secure Clara as his bride. With her inheritance combined with his own, he would be guaranteed every indulgence he could want. And there would be nothing left for his perfect brother.

Splendid.

Chapter 14

Dear Clara,

Though you say you were dismissive at the Stratford ball, I never saw it, nor do I regret how things have transpired thus far. If you had opened yourself up more to others that night, perhaps I would be competing with another gentleman for your attention. I was fortunate to see something unique about you that night, and my only regret is that I was not more bold with you.

Being overly cautious has plagued me most of my life until recently. Perhaps you will not believe me, given my letters, but I will explain. You see, I once fancied myself in love, but a friend stole her affections from me. Looking back, I can see that I was so worried about doing something wrong that I hardly did anything at all. It was a great blow at the time, which led to many hours of solitary reflection. I promised myself I would base my choices on living with no regrets. It has been a few years since then, but seeing you at the ball awakened me to that promise. Writing to you has been my first opportunity to test my resolve. I now see I was not really in love those years ago, and somehow the regrets of the past are put to rest by the joys of the present. I would never change how things have transpired.

Clara, I am eager to learn more about you. I won't ask any questions this time because I can't decide what to ask. There are too many things I should like to know all at once. It is good we have letters right now because they pace me. They pace my

*feelings, and I would rather discover you just as you would choose
to unfold yourself to me. Though letters are all we have right now,
I am hopeful that one day we will have more.*

Truest regards,
James Thayne

Clara loved how letters between her and Mr. Thayne were gaining
momentum, swinging from him to her like a pendulum. She loved
everything she learned about him. His words and ideas were becoming so impressed on her mind that she would often imagine what he
might remark about a book she was reading or a drawing she was
working on.

Every now and then, however, Clara itched with the worry that
there was still much she didn't know about him. But, wasn't the purpose of letters to become better acquainted? She already sensed he was
a rare sort of gentlemen, the kind of man who was worth knowing.
And he liked her. So, she would keep writing.

Chapter 15

Dear Mr. Thayne,

Your letter disarms me! What can I do but reveal myself to you exactly as I am? If you were any other gentleman, you would only see the outer layer, the one that shows I am an innocent, quiet girl who tries, on occasion, to be proper. But for you? Such flat impressions will not do. You must be given a deeper view and see what a tangled process it is to truly know me. I certainly want you to see my best qualities, but I also want you to see me as I am. I will be honest. I can be good but scheming, kind but lazy, motivated but frustrated, elegant but messy. I live each day knowing I am capable of more. I reach out to those in need, and I love my family, but is it enough?

My father tells me all the time that I am enough, and I believe him, but I do not think he means that I need no further improvement. There is still a divide between who I am and who I want to be. I struggle sometimes to close that distance, but since writing to you, I have found it easier to see the good in everyone and everything. There is a lesson in every experience, and though I still feel like an unpolished stone, I try to listen more honestly and smile more genuinely. I must be successful some of the time because I am certain that Louisa and I argue less frequently than before.

What I am trying to say is that each letter you send stirs something inside me that urges me to be better while still making

me feel accepted for who I am right now. I am not even sure how
you do it, but the sun shines brighter. Because of your letters.

> *Yours,*
> *Clara*

Thayne stood pacing in front of his desk. On the one hand, he was smitten with Clara's most recent letter. He was glad his letters were having the desired effect. Oh, how he was falling for her! In fact, he was certain he knew and loved more about Clara than he ever did with Lucy. That pain had finally found its place in the past.

But on the other hand, Thayne was bothered by three other notes he had spread across his desk. He knew they were ridiculous. They were absolutely absurd, but he was still puzzled by them. The first note simply said, "Stay away." The second note said, "Not clever enough to take a hint, are you?" The most recent one, however, carried more edge. It said, "Come near Clara again, and I will end you myself." Thayne hadn't thought much about the first two notes, but this last one definitely caught his attention.

All three letters appeared to be written by the same hand. They came through the post with no signature and no distinguishable seal. He couldn't think of anyone who knew about his correspondence with Clara, so perhaps they were written by someone she knew. Was it possible her father was an excessively protective parent who wrote threats to his daughter's suitors? Thayne had heard of such things happening, but it felt entirely different to have it happen to him. Did Clara have any other relatives who might feel threatened by his letters? Was someone calling him out? Was this what happened when someone breached society's rules?

Thayne was pacing back and forth when he heard a knock on the door.

Mrs. Andrews came in and announced, "Mr. William Martin here to see you, sir."

"Thank you, Mrs. Andrews."

William Martin walked into the room wearing an easy smile. Thayne met him halfway and exchanged a hearty handshake and slap on the back.

"Good to see you, Thayne!" cried Martin.

"You too, old friend," Thayne replied.

"What do you mean old? I have a few grey hairs, but I've got enough spirit to keep up with you." He chuckled and sat in the seat Thayne gestured toward.

Thayne sat across from Martin as he amended his statement. "I meant longtime friend. Thank you for coming all this way to see me, Martin."

Martin shrugged and folded his hands comfortably in his lap. "What's a few hours' drive from London? Sometimes it's nice to escape town."

Thayne asked how Mrs. Martin was, how she was settling in after their journey and so on. Martin asked how things were at Felton Park and how Thayne was handling the responsibility of running the estate. Eventually they started reminiscing about Thayne's father and memories they shared of him, and even though Martin was the guest, he was making Thayne feel at home.

Thayne had invited Martin and his wife to spend a few days at Felton Park for various reasons. One, he invited them every year, and two, they happened to be Clara's aunt and uncle. Thayne was hoping to find a subtle way to learn more about Clara and the unfriendly notes he had received.

"What's got you so distracted, Thayne?" Martin asked.

Thayne sat a little taller. He had been caught. "Oh, well, I—" Then he laughed. "You know me too well, Martin."

"I should. I've known you nearly your whole life."

"Well, there is something I want to talk with you about."

Thayne showed Martin the mysterious notes, even the last one that specifically mentioned Clara.

"Can you think of anyone who might have sent these?" Thayne asked. "A jealous would-be suitor? An overly protective father?"

"George would never write a note like that, no matter what he thought of you."

Thayne sighed in relief.

Martin scratched his cheek and added, "I can't think of anyone who would send such crude notes. Certainly none of my acquaintances."

Thayne rubbed the back of his neck. "I'm not sure who else knows about my regard for your niece. What do you think I should do?"

Martin tapped his chin. "Is it really a question? Ignore the notes."

"But I don't want to cause Miss Everton any trouble."

Martin nodded. "Anyone who would send notes like these is a coward. Don't be intimidated, Thayne. Just do your research and be on guard."

Thayne acknowledged Martin's point and considered what to do to be ready if a confrontation arose.

Martin sat back, rubbed his hand across his eyes, and grumbled. "Actually, I can think of someone crude enough to send these notes. And he was there the night I introduced you to my niece."

Chapter 16

Clara gazed out at the sky as Frances mounted her horse. Clara didn't know how long they would be able to ride that afternoon. The clouds in the distance looked heavy with rain, but the air was crisp and calm.

Clara brushed a leaf off the sleeve of her riding habit as she waited for the stable hand to assist her. The leaf slowly spun to the ground, and, looking down, she noticed another stuck to her skirt. Reddish gold, nearly the same color as her dress, the dried leaf was one of many that would soon scatter across Milton's grounds. Instead of casting off the leaf this time, Clara plucked it up and held it between her fingers, noting how its thin, papery quality was similar to the blank sheets that sat on her desk waiting to be filled with words that would spread into lines like the veins of the leaf.

Her thoughts soon shifted from leaves and letters to apple tarts and eavesdropping, and by the time the stable hand had helped her mount Rabbit, her mind had already ridden off alongside a strong, ebony horse that carried a tall, handsome gentleman.

Frances cleared her throat and sang, "I can tell you're thinking about him."

"What?" Clara felt like a child caught sneaking a spoonful of sugar.

"Your face tells me everything," Frances smiled warmly.

Clara couldn't hide her smile. "I was just thinking about where we might ride."

"Is that *all* you were thinking about?"

Clara lowered her lashes and smiled wider. "I might have been thinking about my friend." Clara and Frances had an unspoken agreement that they did not mention the names of their secret gentlemen.

"Friend, indeed," said Frances meaningfully. "I hope you will not think it rude of me to inquire . . . but have you considered the fact that this friend of yours might look better on paper than in person?"

Clara tilted her head. "I suppose I have, but in all fairness, he has the right to wonder the same thing about me, and he continues to send letters."

The girls leisurely rode toward a rippling stream that ran just beyond the boundaries of the Everton's estate.

"Clara, is it accurate to say you have feelings for a man you know only through letters?"

Clara reddened but answered coolly, "His letters are very endearing."

"Well, that may be," Frances nodded, "but you should find a way to meet him in person soon rather than carrying on an indefinite correspondence. Find out what he is really like. And Clara?" Frances paused as the girls led their horses over the stream and through a cluster of trees. "Do not be so hasty in any of your letters as to make him any promises."

Clara arched her eyebrow. "And is an elopement not a hasty promise?"

Frances lifted a shoulder and grinned. "Not for me."

"I see," Clara laughed.

"But you and I are both aware that anyone who catches you writing to this gentleman will think you are engaged. So, what is he to think?"

"I doubt he has any specific expectations. We are just becoming acquainted with each other. I don't think he views our relationship any differently than I do."

"Can you be so sure? He would never write to you if he were not interested in more. You are my friend, Clara." Frances looked earnest as she added, "I don't want to see you get hurt by this man, especially if he turns out to be different from what you expect. Don't let your feelings get in the way of your judgment. Promise me you won't give him grounds to take advantage of your goodness later on."

Clara sat silent. There was sense to what Frances was saying. After the many ways she had lately proven herself to be a loyal friend, Clara felt she should listen.

"I promise to be careful," Clara reassured her. She had to admit she was developing an attachment to Mr. Thayne, and Frances was right that she needed to determine the true nature of his character. She needed to meet him under proper circumstances to learn what their relationship meant to him, but until she knew how or when, writing letters still seemed like the best way.

Clara was lost in these thoughts when she heard the approach of another horse's hooves and a voice that made her shrink.

"Well, well, well," said Mr. Platt, sounding oily and satisfied as he cantered up alongside Clara's horse. "If it isn't my bride-to-be."

Clara stiffened in her seat and tightened her grip on the reins. Even Rabbit shifted uncomfortably beneath her. "I don't recall ever coming to such an understanding, Mr. Platt." She tried to sound confident and firm, but her hands were shaking. Frances was close but quiet.

"We don't need to be so formal, Clara. I thought everyone knew we were intended for each other."

"You take too much liberty, sir." Without pausing to deliberate, she turned Rabbit around and started leading her back toward the manor, assuming Frances would follow.

"Oh, don't worry," he sneered. "I'm not here to court you today."

"Is that what you call this?" she countered.

Ignoring her comment, he said, "I only came to deliver a message."

"Then deliver it so we may finish our ride."

Mr. Platt cleared his throat and rode very close to her. "My grandmother tells me that, according to your aunt, you have some mysterious new suitor. Well, that won't do at all, now will it? I've been made a fool of too many times before, but not this time. I won't see you looking down your nose at me. I'm not taking orders from anyone anymore. This time, I'm taking what I want." Mr. Platt breathed through his nostrils. "You tell this man of yours that if he comes anywhere near you, he'll regret it." He then pulled out a pistol, breathed on the barrel, and polished it on his sleeve.

Clara caught a sickly sweet smell on his breath that made her recoil. She didn't realize that, in her anxiousness, she had pulled on the reins hard enough to make Rabbit stop. Clara looked straight on, unable to move and unable to look at Mr. Platt or Frances. For a moment, her courage faltered, but she looked up at the sky and breathed deeply. She wasn't alone. Frances was with her, and they were both on horses. Clara did not want to be afraid of a man who relied on intimidation and threats.

"Mr. Platt," Clara managed, though she still trembled, "you have stumbled on perhaps the only thing we have in common. I'm not taking orders either. Any suitor who comes near me will only do so with my permission." She forced herself to meet Mr. Platt's eyes. "You can put that pistol away now."

Mr. Platt threw back his head and laughed, but a tiny click brought it to an abrupt stop.

Frances had produced a silvery grey pistol. "Tell me, Mr. Platt, is your pistol as accurate as mine?" She held it awkwardly, like she was examining it for the first time. Then, in an instant, she held the pistol firmly in front of her and aimed it at a rusty bucket that sat next to a feeding trough about a hundred yards away and only slightly to the right of Mr. Platt and his horse. The pistol sounded and the sting of metal hitting metal cracked the air.

The horses all shuffled, but Clara and Frances quickly calmed theirs. Mr. Platt, however, struggled with his, and for a moment, Clara thought he would ride off.

When he didn't, Frances pretended clumsiness with her pistol again and casually pointed it toward him. "Mr. Platt, you had best be off. Our suitors don't take kindly to men who threaten us." Emphasizing her words, she added, "And neither do we."

With nostrils flared, Mr. Platt stared in disbelief. After several uncomfortable seconds, he spat on the ground and kicked his horse to a gallop in the opposite direction.

When he was out of earshot, Clara put her hand on her heart and released a big breath.

"Bravo, Clara!" Frances had her hand on her heart as well.

"You deserve the praise, Frances. I was a complete mess!"

"Not at all! You stood your ground. That was very brave! And it gave me the courage to show him this." Frances held up her pistol again before securing it somewhere in her sleeve. "I've been carrying it ever since the night he and that dolt threatened us. My betrothed gave it to me, but my father taught me how to use a pistol years ago."

"Well, let's hope it was enough to scare off Mr. Platt!" Clara exhaled.

Chapter 17

Dearest Clara,

I am humbled to know my letters inspire you to be better. That is one of the most generous compliments I have ever received, and I must tell you, your letters have had the same effect on me. I used to feel, for example, that being the master of Felton Park was a burden I was not fit to carry. I never wanted to assume my father's responsibilities because they only served to remind me he was gone. It is why I procrastinated the repairs I needed to make. Yet, writing to you has refreshed my spirits and turned my mind toward more hopeful thoughts. I feel greater peace when I remember my father. I no longer go about my responsibilities out of reluctant duty, but I approach them with concern for the people I love.

Such is your influence on me, dear Clara, but I believe it has the potential to become much more. Within our letters, I see a friendship worth pursuing and a foundation on which we might build something lasting.

Lovely Clara, I must not let another letter pass between us without telling you that you have grown very dear to me. Though we have spoken few words to each other in person, you are more real to me than any other lady I have ever met. With you, there are no pretenses, no formalities, nothing but the real you on every page you send.

I do not know how to go on, but there is much I should like to say to you in person. Next season in London still sounds too far away. Might there be some way for us to see each other sooner? Or am I too hasty? What are your wishes?

Humbly yours,
James

Clara's hand trembled as she held his letter. It was too good, too beautiful to be true! James Thayne cared for her!

She went to her desk and pulled out a fresh sheet of paper, filled with a desire to immediately convey to him the depth of her affections. She sat down but could hardly steady herself as her heart pulsed down to her fingertips. She was sure she would have to rewrite her letter to make it legible. No matter. She would allow her words to flow as true as she could.

Why was this so difficult? Clara crumpled what must have been the ninth or tenth draft she had attempted over the past several days. Writing a love letter sounded simple enough, but nothing she penned seemed good enough for Mr. Thayne. Each time she attempted to answer him, her mind tied itself in knots trying to work it out.

If Mr. Thayne came to Milton, he would have to meet her father and Louisa. Of course, Clara would have to explain the letters. Louisa would secretly plan a wedding. And Clara's father? She had no idea how he would react. Would he be welcoming or excessively protective? She wished there was a way to meet Mr. Thayne without explaining things to her family, but that would mean waiting for next season.

Clara stood and paced around the room, tapping the feathered end of her pen against her cheek. Regardless of the obstacles, she wanted to reassure Mr. Thayne that she felt the same way he did. Yet, somehow, her words always fell short. Any expression of care and affection lost its impact when she attempted to explain the awkwardness of meeting in Milton.

Oh, but she needed to return his letter before he doubted her feelings! She pulled out Mr. Thayne's most recent letter and gawked at the date. Had it taken her this long to respond? *Oh, bother*! That was one more thing she needed to say in her reply; *sorry for taking so long*. This was bound to be the worst love letter ever!

When Clara was honest with herself, she knew there were other reasons for her delays, other fears and hopes that battled in her heart, and she didn't know how to write them all in a letter without hurting Mr. Thayne or their chances of being together.

She pulled out a fresh sheet of paper for another attempt, but as she laid it on her desk, her finger grazed the edge, and she flinched from the sting of a cut.

A letter is a dangerous thing, she thought, *alive with words, yet deceptively still . . .*

She took a steadying breath. *Calm down*, she told herself. *It's just a letter.*

Not just a letter. A love letter.

This letter would be different from the others she had exchanged with Mr. Thayne. This time, Clara would commit her heart to paper, raw and vulnerable, and wait for him to receive it. Her heart ached to think of all that could go wrong, and the paper in her hand no longer felt safe. Her words held power and would take on a new life once he read them.

A letter is an uncertainty, a risk.

What would happen after she sent it? Would Mr. Thayne be as wonderful as she thought? Would his feelings persist? Didn't she have reason to hope? Hadn't Mr. Thayne just declared how dear she was to him? *Yes! A letter could also be a promise, a hope for a happy future.* She would give their love a chance.

Clara held to that idea and knew she could not risk letting Mr. Thayne think she didn't care. She rolled back her shoulders and sat at her desk with renewed determination. She reviewed all the letters he had written her. How she admired him! How she wanted to see him! An idea sparked in her head, and her words poured from the place in her heart reserved just for James Thayne. He might get her letter later than usual, but it would soon be on its way.

With the next dip of her pen, her hand shook with unsteadied nerves, aware that her message was too unrestrained for a lady, and a stray drop of ink fell and seeped into the corner of the letter. She flinched and imagined her own blood had dripped there. Was her heart already so fragile, pricked by a mere thought?

Perhaps, but she would give it to him regardless. If only she knew how he would receive it.

Chapter 18

Thayne ate his breakfast but hardly enjoyed it. The bread was dry. His tea had grown cold, and there was nothing special about the post that morning.

Deciding to dispense with table manners, since no one was there to care either way, he dropped his fork and knife with a clank and stood abruptly. He scowled at the empty seats as if his mood were their fault. Why he had opted for the breakfast room over his study that morning, he couldn't say, but it had done nothing to alleviate his dismay over his lack of letters.

Clara hadn't written him for a month. A whole month! Why hadn't he heard from her? He strode out of the room and down the hall to sort through the post again. He flipped through the letters three times to be certain. All letters of business.

He paced a few times and headed outside with no destination in mind. As he forced the door to make way, the crisp air stung his eyes, but he didn't mind the cold. He needed to be outside moving in order to think. Why was this bothering him so much?

The last time he had written to Clara, he had expressed his feelings for her and suggested they meet in person. He wasn't sure of the best way to arrange it since they lived so far apart, but he felt confident they could overcome the obstacles.

Only, now he feared he had misjudged her feelings. Perhaps their relationship was too tenuous, too undefined to raise the idea of meeting. Would it make him her suitor? Part of him hoped so, but he dreaded the thought that Clara might not feel the same way. Her previous letters suggested she might, but what if she only viewed their relationship as amiable? Now that Thayne had expressed deeper feelings for her, she was silent.

Thayne kicked rocks down the path as he stewed. He was wandering to the stables where Mr. Andrews was likely to be tending the horses and overseeing the stable hands. As Thayne got closer, he saw Andrews stepping out with a large saddle balanced in his grasp.

"Hello, Andrews!" Thayne called out.

Andrews shifted his hold on the saddle and waved. "Hello there, Master James!"

Despite his mood, Thayne smiled at the familiarity with which Andrews addressed him. "How are you doing?" Thayne said, patting Andrews's shoulder and helping him place the saddle on its stand inside.

Andrews wiped sweat from his forehead and regarded Thayne. "I'm well enough to be sure, but you look like you come with bad news." Andrews could always tell when Thayne was troubled.

"No, no bad news," Thayne nervously laughed. "It's more a matter of not receiving any news."

Andrews nodded like he understood and pointed a finger at Thayne. "Does this have anything to do with that young lady you have been writing to?" Andrews's voice was worn but mirthful.

"How did you know about that?" Thayne couldn't hide his surprise. He hadn't told anyone about his correspondence with Clara. He knew what kind of gossip it could stir up, and he especially didn't want to cause mischief for Clara.

Mr. Andrews just laughed and patted Thayne's shoulder. His eyes gleamed as wisps of grey hair flew out from under his hat. "James, I may be old, but I see what goes on around here. She hasn't written for a while, has she?"

Thayne noticed Knight in his stall swiveling his ears toward the conversation as if waiting for Thayne's response.

"You have hit the mark, Andrews. She has not written for longer than usual. I . . . I'm not sure what to think or what to do. I told her how much I've grown to care . . . and I suggested we find a way to meet, but . . ."

"But she hasn't replied to your letter yet?"

"That's it." Thayne slouched. "Now, I'm unsure whether I should write to her again or take it as a hint that she no longer wishes to hear from me."

"Don't give up so easily, James!" Andrews patted Thayne on the back. "I can tell just by looking at you that she means something to you."

It was true. What had started as infatuation had grown into an abiding care and admiration for a woman who represented his hope for a life full of laughter and affection. The more Thayne learned about Clara, the deeper his feelings ran.

"She means a great deal to me, but all we have are letters!" Saying it out loud sounded so insubstantial.

Andrews's eyes wrinkled as he smiled. "James, I've kept my eye on you as you've been writing to this girl. I see the way you grow animated when you receive a letter from her. I've seen you go about your business and manage this estate with more ambition than I knew was in you. Why, the expert way you handled the repairs for the tenants in the southeast end of the estate was most admirable. I cannot quite put my finger on it, but you seem happier with everyone and with yourself. Whatever happens between you and this Miss Everton—"

"How did you know her—"

"Think, boy! I handle the post!"

Thayne felt ridiculous for not thinking of that.

Andrews nodded and chuckled as he gave Thayne a friendly elbow jab. "She certainly has you distracted, hasn't she?" Then Andrews put a hand on Thayne's shoulder. "Whatever happens between you and Miss Everton, she lit something inside of you that needed kindling. I'm glad to see it. You have more direction in your life. Too many of these fancy young dandies have nothing to do but play cards and lose money. There is too much idleness. But you are paying attention to the part of you that craves work and companionship! I may be making too many assumptions by saying that Miss Everton is the cause of it, but if that is all Miss Everton ever gives you, I'm glad for it!" He paused to wipe his head again with a handkerchief before going on. "You and your family have been so good to me these many years. I want to see you happy, James. Don't let her get away."

Thayne walked back to the house grateful for the advice. He was only beginning to realize what Clara meant to him, and he could feel the embers glowing inside. He would not lose her for lack of trying. As a hazy plan took shape in his thoughts, his feelings settled. He knew what to do. It was time to plan a trip to Milton.

Chapter 19

Frances rushed upstairs with her letter, barely containing her laughter on the way. Once in her room, she closed the door, and released her excitement in one breathy gasp. Until this letter, she hadn't heard from her betrothed in weeks, and she was starting to doubt whether she would ever have her chance at happiness. Now, she had evidence that despite his silence, he had been waiting and watching for the right opportunity to communicate with her.

For the past three days, Frances had been staying at Milton Manor as a guest and could still hardly believe that her mother had finally consented to the visit. Frances had certainly pestered her mother long enough, but her mother only agreed once she became entirely preoccupied with planning a trip to London. When Frances's week at Milton was over, she and her mother were to travel to town to help plan her cousin's wedding. Once all the plans and preparations were settled, they would then travel to Teniford for Christmas and the actual wedding.

Such a long trip with multiple destinations meant that Frances would be constantly engaged with the social obligations a wedding required. She would hardly have a moment to spare. Communicating with her betrothed, not to mention running off with him unnoticed, would be more difficult than ever, a fact her mother surely took into consideration.

Frances's hope had been dwindling, but now that she held a letter from her betrothed, she was more determined than ever to find a way to be with him. Unfolding the page, she saw the handwriting she knew as well as her own.

My darling Frances,

I hope I have heard correctly that you are at Milton Manor and that this letter finds you well. My affection for you remains as strong and as constant as ever. However, I grow uneasy being separated from you for so long. I am searching out new ways to come to you. I hear that you and your mother will be in London soon. Be ready, my darling. I shall be nearby. Till then, you are always in my thoughts.

Faithfully,
Yours

Excitement rippled through Frances like a bubbling stream. She could almost feel the wedding ring on her finger! On an impulse, she grabbed the lacy bottom of the nearest curtain, draped it over her head like a veil, and danced around, swaying from side to side.

A sudden knock on her door startled her, making her spin herself into the curtains until she lost balance and bumped into the writing desk. In her efforts to unravel herself, she sent a chair toppling.

Louisa poked her head inside just as Frances was shaking off the curtain and smoothing her skirt.

"Miss Everton," Frances said, her voice higher pitched than normal. "Do come in."

Her eyes darted to the place on the bed where she had dropped her letter, as obvious and awkward as if it had been her chemise on display. Frances searched for a way to hide it before Louisa's penetrating glare landed on it, but nothing came to mind.

"Are you all right, dear? I heard a crash." Louisa's eyes roamed the room, pausing on the upturned chair.

Frances brushed a few loose curls out of her face and clumsily righted the chair. "I'm quite well. Yes, I apologize. I bumped into the desk and then knocked over the chair. But I'm fine. Certainly fine. And you? How are you, Miss Everton?" Was the room growing warmer?

"I'm as well as can be, dear. Do you have a moment?" Louisa surveyed the room a second time.

"Yes, of course." Frances stood still, willing herself not to look at the letter on her bed.

"I hope you understand, dear, that while you are in this house, I consider it my responsibility to look after you as your own mother would, just as I look after Clara."

Why was Louisa saying this? Frances didn't want anyone extra looking after her, at least, not like her mother would, but Louisa sounded so genuine that it was endearing. Frances might have hugged her if it weren't for the guilt that sunk inside her chest.

Louisa added, "I could never face your mother if anything happened to you while staying with our family." This time she looked at the bed, and Frances was certain she saw the letter. "As it happens," Louisa continued, "your mother has sent a message asking that you be ready to leave early tomorrow morning. She instructs you to pack your belongings as you will be heading straight to London with her. I don't know the details, only that she apologized for the haste but saw no reason to delay the journey. I'm sure she'll explain it all to you tomorrow."

Frances flushed at the prospect of heading to meet her betrothed so quickly. What impeccable timing he had! What a remarkable man! If only she could convince her mother of it.

Louisa made some statement about what a pleasure it had been for the family to host Frances. A few more polite words were exchanged, and she exited with a small curtsey.

Alone once again, Frances burst into a squinty-eyed grin and began packing immediately. She wondered why her mother hadn't written to her directly, but as Frances considered it, she assumed her mother must have warned Louisa that she might try to run off to elope. Oh, but it didn't matter! Frances's mother probably thought this trip would be the perfect way to separate Frances from her betrothed. Little did she know it would bring them together.

Chapter 20

Mischief was definitely afoot. Louisa could tell by the way Frances had trembled and blushed when she looked at that letter on the bed. Louisa didn't like to insert herself in others' affairs, but she had meant what she said about looking after Frances. Perhaps Mrs. Wright was right to worry that her daughter might try something stupid like running off with a fellow she hardly knew. Mrs. Wright would never forgive Louisa if Frances snuck out under her watch. So, Louisa dutifully spied on the girls at night, a task she always dreaded, but at least it was only for one more night.

Louisa had to admit she was also concerned about Clara. She trusted Clara more than Frances to act prudently, but Louisa couldn't rid herself of the feeling that Clara was up to something just as clandestine. Clara was most likely falling in love with the mysterious gentleman who kept sending letters, but who was he? It must have been someone she had met in London. That was Louisa's best guess, but no matter what Clara claimed, Louisa could only think of one man who had caught Clara's interest at all. Heaven forbid she should end up with that conniving Mr. Shaw!

No. Louisa wouldn't insult Clara by thinking it possible. Clara had far too much sense to fall in love with Mr. Shaw. After all, Clara had been the first to see what a twit Mr. Platt was. Louisa felt guilty for ever suggesting Mr. Platt to Clara, but there was no point dwelling on it now.

Who else could have caught Clara's attention? Clara wasn't one to gush about her feelings, and Louisa could very well imagine Clara feeling too shy to talk about fancying someone. Was it possible she was simply corresponding with a friend?

Would a letter from a friend make her blush so deeply?

Louisa hated to admit it, but her instincts told her that Clara was secretly engaged. What news that would be! It could solve all the worries and disagreements she was having with Clara's father. Louisa walked down the hallway twisting a handkerchief in her hand. If Clara was engaged, shouldn't she share her secret with her family? What good would it do to keep such news hidden unless she were engaged to a scoundrel like Mr. Shaw . . . please, not Shaw! Louisa needed to know who this letter-writing gentleman was and why Clara wasn't talking about him. Not knowing was driving Louisa mad.

Louisa considered how to get Clara to open up about it. George would be no help. He was always so stubborn about letting his little girl have her own way. It was a miracle Clara wasn't more spoiled. Louisa took credit for that. She had guided Clara with a caring but firm hand, just as she would have for a daughter had she ever married and had children. *Ah*, Louisa sighed. *If only*. George, on the other hand, was too indulgent and definitely too trusting. Louisa decided that if he wouldn't push Clara in the right direction, she would.

She would just confront Clara about those letters. That's all there was to it. She had to be careful, however, not to offend her sweet niece by implying that she doubted her judgment or thought her capable of deceit. Louisa knew Clara loved her, but she feared pushing her away or, worse, pushing her toward someone like Mr. Shaw.

Louisa walked slowly toward Clara's room, inwardly composing a speech that would be so patient and convincing that Clara would want to confide in her and receive her guidance. If Clara was engaged to a respectable man, Louisa wanted to see it brought to a respectable marriage.

Oh, if only that girl knew the predicament she would be in if she didn't marry soon! Louisa shuddered at the thought. Not telling Clara was George's choice. He didn't want her to rush off and marry the first man she met because she was afraid of losing her home. Louisa couldn't stand it when her brother was unreasonable, but Clara should know that the property would not pass to her. Louisa wished she hadn't promised not to say anything about it to Clara. Where would she and Clara go once George died and the closest male heir took over? No doubt, he would be a man of questionable honor who would turn them out of the house at the earliest opportunity.

Clara's father had often insisted that a male heir had never been found and probably never would be. Louisa thought it was foolish to rely on such chance, so she had written to the solicitor about it. George may have prohibited her from informing Clara about the entailment, but he hadn't said anything to prevent Louisa from learning for herself whether a male heir existed. She only hoped that Mr. Barnes wouldn't find one after all.

Louisa paced the halls for several minutes. Perhaps there was a subtler way to help Clara. If Clara could somehow spend time with her intended and see that her family approved, she and her secret gentlemen could solidify their plans and announce their engagement.

Then Louisa gasped, struck with an idea. It was perfect! She would send Clara to London with Frances. Clara could stay with Rose and William and make it known she was in town. When her suitor came to court her, Rose would properly steer Clara toward marriage while William kept the scoundrels away. They wouldn't even have to know about the letters! Then Clara and her gentleman could make wedding arrangements. Louisa felt quite proud of herself once she had worked it all out. Her plan would spare her and Clara an awkward conversation and perhaps solve their most pressing worries.

Instead of turning toward Clara's room, she headed for her own to compose a letter to Rose and a note to Mrs. Wright. She could tell Clara all about it at supper. Clara would be in good hands, and Louisa would be free to remain at Milton to look after her brother who was trying to deny the fact that his health was going swiftly downhill.

$\mathcal{Chapter}$ 21

$\mathcal{T}$hayne ran his fingers through his hair and paused to savor the reality of his surroundings. Forested land stretched before him, green and rolling, as lovely as Clara had described them. Had Thayne really gathered the courage to journey to Milton? It had been easy in the comfort of his home to talk of travel, but it was only after an abundance of encouragement from Andrews that he actually did it. Now on the road with hardly a mile to go, his courage wavered and he relied on pure momentum to carry him, one foot in front of the other. A carriage from the inn would have been faster, but walking sharpened his focus and the outdoors gave him space to think.

He looked at the sky as he took a steadying breath and wondered what he would first say to Clara. How should he present himself? Should he be formal or familiar? They knew each other well enough on paper but had hardly spent any time together in person. What if Clara was upset with him for coming uninvited? Thayne's pace slowed as he deliberated. With luck, she would be impressed, but if not, he would persist. He would charm her, fight for her, whatever it took. If her family disapproved, he would work to gain their favor.

What if she wasn't upset? What if her family did approve and Clara expected a proposal? Thayne's stomach flipped at the thought. It felt too soon for that, but not making an offer after all those letters might give the wrong impression. He didn't want Clara to question his intentions. He just wanted her to know he cared. Hopefully, he would know what to do when he saw her. Whatever happened, he determined to give it his best effort. No regrets.

When the road bent by an abandoned well, just past a cluster of trees, Thayne had a clear view of Milton Manor. There, across a large field with the sun's rays splayed around it and autumn trees standing guard, was Clara's home. And somewhere nearby was Clara.

After all those letters, he was so close! Propelled by a new surge of excitement, Thayne left the meandering road for the more direct route through the field, disturbing overgrown grass and the occasional sheep. As his determination increased, his strides lengthened, and his view of Milton Manor sharpened. He took in the brick and ivy, the chimneys and windows and the path to the right which led to the pond. Clara's descriptions of the place made the house feel familiar, and he was more certain than ever that she would be happy, if surprised, to see him.

Leaving the field behind, Thayne shook off his doubts and brushed off the grass that stuck to his trousers. He walked up the gravel path that led to the large, wooden door and knocked without hesitation. He explained who he was to the maid who answered and was shown into a cheerful, pale yellow sitting room where he was asked to wait.

So, he waited.

And waited.

Despite the chill outside, Thayne had worked up a sweat that he only just noticed, so he stood up to walk around and fan the lapels of his jacket. After several minutes, he sat back down, wondering whether the maid forgot to announce his presence. Just as he stood back up to check the hall for the maid or some other servant, an older man and woman entered the room.

Their manners were civil as they invited Thayne to sit in the armchair across from them. Thayne could see the old gentleman moving stiffly, so he reached out to help him sit, but the man waved Thayne off and managed it himself. Meanwhile, the woman regarded Thayne with knitted brows and a pinched frown.

At first, no one spoke, but Thayne had planned for such a moment, having already decided that he should start the conversation.

Smiling as pleasantly as possible, he began. "My name is James Thayne. You must be wondering why I am here."

"Yes, young man," the older man, who Thayne guessed was Clara's father, replied with an upward tilt of his lip. "Although I am certain I could make a few good guesses, there is more entertainment in hearing what you have to say first."

Thayne liked the way Clara's father jested. Perhaps he was better informed of the letters than Thayne had realized. The older woman, who must be the aunt Clara had described, looked at Clara's father and rolled her eyes. She sat quietly, but Thayne suspected she was restraining herself.

Thayne cleared his throat. "I know this is very untoward, but I would like to see Miss Clara Everton."

"I knew it!" said the aunt, squeezing her eyes shut and shaking her head. "I knew that girl was hiding something."

Thayne couldn't tell whether she was upset or satisfied with herself.

She looked Thayne square in the eye and asked, "Are you engaged to my niece?"

Thayne blinked. "No, madam, but I can certainly understand at your wondering so."

Clara's father nodded and gestured with his hand as he spoke. "Well, Mr. Thayne, I am George Everton, and this is my sister Miss Louisa Everton. We welcome you to Milton and invite you to share with us your story."

"Right," Thayne cleared his throat and his mind went blank. While walking, he had practiced exactly what he would say, but he forgot it all the moment Mr. Everton invited him to speak. Thayne would have to improvise. "Well, your daughter and I were briefly introduced at a ball at the end of last season. I had little time with her, but there was something about her, something that made me want to know more about her. Again, I know it is untoward, but I made a few inquiries. I know her uncle, William Martin, you see, and I sent her a letter. She has written back to me . . ." This was the awkward part. No easy way to say he had shamelessly gone against proper decorum by writing to her, but he hadn't thought about how awkward it would be to tell her family that she had done so too. At least he didn't have to tell them how many letters they had exchanged. "The simple explanation is that I have come because I was eager to become better acquainted with Miss Clara Everton in person. I am eager to demonstrate that my intentions are honorable, and I would like to see her, with your permission, if she is home."

"Well, I'm afraid that—" the elder Miss Everton began but Mr. Everton cleared his throat and held up his hand.

"Before we get too hasty," he said calmly, "I would like the chance to become better acquainted with you first. Do you fish, sir?"

"Oh. Well, yes . . ." Thayne was surprised by the question. It made sense that Clara's father would want to know more about him, but he hadn't counted on being delayed from seeing Clara.

"Then I should like you to accompany me to our pond for a chat." Mr. Everton slowly rose from his chair and, with the use of his cane, shuffled toward the hall. Thayne stood to follow. What could he do now but go fishing?

When all was prepared, Thayne followed Mr. Everton, carrying poles, bait, nets, and buckets. Mr. Everton refused all other offers of assistance, and Thayne politely ignored his light wheeze. Though Mr. Everton hobbled along with his cane, his short steps quickened when they neared the pond.

Thayne occasionally glanced back at the manor's windows, wondering which one Clara might be sitting behind. If all went well today, perhaps he would have the chance to take her out for a row tomorrow.

When they reached the boat, Thayne deposited the supplies in the middle and held out his arm for Mr. Everton, but Mr. Everton was set on climbing in on his own. As Thayne observed how Mr. Everton stubbornly did things his own way, Thayne understood why Clara had felt free to write him back. She took after her father in that regard.

Thayne settled in his seat and took the oars, pushing off from the shore as Mr. Everton began to prepare the lines with bait. With everything in place and a moment to catch his breath, Mr. Everton wiped his forehead with his handkerchief and sighed.

The calm ripples and cool breeze urged Thayne to be at ease, but just when he was getting comfortable, Mr. Everton cleared his throat and asked Thayne about his family, then his estate, his opinions on politics and business, his favorite books, whether he had chicken pox as a child and so on. Somewhere in the middle of it all, Mr. Everton added his own comments, and their talk became less of an interview and more of a conversation. Thayne enjoyed Mr. Everton's sense of humor, and Mr. Everton nodded appreciatively at Thayne's insights, noting that these were the kinds of topics Louisa never had much patience for.

After nearly two hours of talking and fishing, the conversation dwindled, and Thayne couldn't think of anything else to say.

Finally, Mr. Everton raised the inevitable topic. "Tell me what you know about Clara."

Thayne had been waiting for this. He tried not to think too hard about his answer. He would say whatever came to him, whatever felt right and true. "I know she is very kind. Her goodness shines on every page she writes. She is smart, and talented, and . . ." Thayne was thinking how to put his feelings into words. "She makes me want to be a better person."

Mr. Everton looked at Thayne as if he were mildly amused. "Do you think you deserve her?"

Thayne paused. He had never asked himself this question before. "I'm not sure how any man can truly deserve her, but I hope to come the closest."

"Hmmm." Mr. Everton nodded and grew quiet.

Thayne's wooden seat was suddenly very uncomfortable. What did Mr. Everton think of Thayne's correspondence with Clara? Should Thayne ask for approval to court her? Did she even know he was there? He looked up again at the manor windows. What would she think when she found out he was there but had gone fishing before saying hello?

Mr. Everton finally asked, "Does that mean you want to marry my Clara, Mr. Thayne?"

Thayne sat straighter and rubbed the back of his neck. There was so much he didn't know, but he had to answer truthfully.

"I . . . I think I might." Should he say more? Should he say that they hadn't spent much time together in person and that he needed to gauge Clara's feelings before making plans? That all they had were letters, but he really hoped their relationship would develop into something lasting? "When the time is right, I would like your permission to marry your daughter, if she will have me."

Thayne thought he had been nervous earlier, but that was nothing compared to the cold tension that strained his body as he waited for a response.

"Well, I will have to think about it."

Thayne leaned forward. "Is it because of the letters?"

Mr. Everton chuckled. "No, no. I don't worry about something as harmless as letters, whatever society says. London's high and mighty do not rule me. I care more about your reasons for writing the letters. I believe in letting our conscience guide our choices. Clara and I are much alike in that regard, as I imagine you are." Mr. Everton looked out across the water. "I just want to make sure you understand how special she is." He leaned back slightly and regarded Thayne. "I can see why she likes you. Just give this old man some time."

Chapter 22

*B*lood rushed to Thayne's head from standing up too quickly. "You mean she's not even here?"

Unbelievable! He didn't even try to hide the disbelief from his voice. He had come all this way! He had just spent the entire afternoon with Clara's father, nervous the whole time about whether he was making the right impression, wondering whether Clara knew he had come, and she was not even there. He felt like an idiot.

"You are correct, sir," Miss Louisa Everton replied, folding her hands together with her head held high.

Thayne stared at her, dumbfounded, then shook his head, trying to comprehend the disappointment that sat in his stomach like a rock.

At first, Miss Everton stood still, unable to look Thayne in the eye for more than a second, and she began to clasp and unclasp her hands, examining her fingernails. Finally, she shook her head and sighed. "I must apologize for my brother. I intended to tell you when you first arrived, but he seemed set on talking with you. And now he has retired to his room." Her eyes wandered up as if to send Mr. Everton a disapproving glare through the ceiling.

Despite his disappointment, Thayne could sympathize with the awkwardness she must have felt, but he also understood why Mr. Everton had retired early. Their afternoon excursion had obviously exhausted him. Thayne had done his best to accommodate him, but Mr. Everton chose exhaustion over dependence. When they had arrived back at the house, Mr. Everton wiped his head with his handkerchief and excused himself, leaving the elder Miss Everton alone with Thayne.

She shook her head and added, "My niece has gone to London."

"To London?" Thayne was feeling increasingly foolish for coming unannounced to see Clara. She had gone to London and hadn't bothered to tell him. It probably meant she had lost interest in him. He slumped down on the sofa and leaned forward with his head in his hands.

Miss Everton scratched her arm, frowned, and looked at the floor. Thayne stood up to excuse himself, but she held up her hand to stop him. "I will admit I am completely surprised by your visit. I knew Clara had been writing to a gentleman she met in town last season, but I had no idea who, and I feared it was someone untrustworthy. You seem a respectable gentleman, but you will forgive me if I still have my misgivings."

"Madam, I understand you. You have every right to have your concerns, especially after the way I imposed on your kindness today. I . . . I will leave you now." Thayne bowed and turned to leave.

"One moment." She stood there considering him. "You seem truly distressed at not finding Clara here."

Thayne nodded. "I was hoping to spend time with her."

"Well, I am sincerely sorry for the way my brother led you on today without any explanation." She pinched the top of her nose and closed her eyes. "He must have his reasons." She lowered her hand and looked back at Thayne. "I will talk with him. If you have made a sufficiently good impression on him, then, with his approval, I will tell you where Clara is staying in London."

Thayne beamed at Miss Everton who, with those few words, became his ally. He could easily guess that Clara was staying with her aunt and uncle, but it would feel better to go after her this time with her family's approval. Miss Everton was giving him another chance. He had already promised himself that he would not give up on pursuing Clara, so he accepted Miss Everton's conditions. She told him to come back tomorrow, and she would let him know what the verdict was.

Chapter 23

$\mathcal{F}$rances looked out the carriage window and listened to her mother's aimless conversation. Frances had expected her mother to barrage her with questions about her stay at Milton Manor, whether she had received any letters or heard any interesting news, but instead, Mrs. Wright directed all her questions at Clara. Having Clara along for the journey to London was an unexpected treat, one Frances was most grateful for, but she guessed Clara did not feel as fortunate, especially when Mrs. Wright once again pressed her for thoughts on Mr. Shaw.

"Do you think Mr. Shaw is in London, Clara?" Mrs. Wright asked. "As I recall, you once had a certain interest in that man."

Frances gave Clara an apologetic look as their carriage rambled along. Eager for the last stretch of road to end, Frances looked out the window and happily noted that the houses and buildings were growing denser, a sign they were getting close. Hopefully, Clara could endure her mother's questions a little longer.

Clara glanced out the window as she answered. "I hardly know him."

"Oh, don't worry, dear," Mrs. Wright continued with dramatic sympathy. "I know things between you two never developed into anything worth mentioning, nothing like his previous escapades. I don't know why I even thought of it. Most likely, it is because we will be staying so nearby his home in town, and I wonder how often we will be in his company. His parents do not often come to London, but Mr. Shaw prefers being in town almost year-round, you see. More opportunities for games and wagers."

Frances inwardly pled for her mother to stop talking.

Clara leaned forward in her seat and spoke without pretense. "Forgive me, Mrs. Wright, but don't you think people are apt to believe you take a special interest in Mr. Shaw if you continue to discuss him so frequently?"

Mrs. Wright sat silent and blinked. Frances had to suppress a giggle. If only Clara knew how true her arrow had struck!

Mrs. Wright looked out her window and mumbled, "I hope we stop soon. These roads are always so bumpy, and I could use some air."

The carriage wheels squeaked as they bounced along the cobblestone streets now lined with townhomes. The volume of people in town compared to the country could be stifling, but Frances felt comforted knowing that her betrothed was among them. He would be close, watching for her. Somehow, they would find a way to be together.

Chapter 24

Thayne walked back to the inn with much more to think about than when he had left for Milton Manor that morning. True, he had not seen Clara, but he had spent time in her house and with her family, and most importantly, he had received approval from her father to address her in London. He still wondered why she never returned his last letter, but now he also puzzled over why she never mentioned anything about going to London. Was it possible she didn't want him to know she was there? He decided it didn't matter. He had to see her and make his sentiments known, whatever the reasons for her silence.

He shuffled along the road with his hands in his pockets, imagining how he should inform Clara of his presence once he arrived in London. He hadn't been walking long when he heard someone approaching from behind.

"Well, well. You must be Clara's mysterious suitor. I was beginning to think she made you up."

As Thayne tuned into the man's oily voice, he instinctively knew who it was. He stayed calm and simply greeted the man with a, "Good day to you, sir," and kept walking, keeping his eyes on the road.

As the man caught up, Thayne could feel his heavy stare on him.

"Come here to do some courting, have you? Well, it ain't common knowledge yet, but I feel it my duty to tell you that Clara and I are engaged."

Thayne stiffened and gave this man a narrow look from the corner of his eye. He knew the man lied, but he didn't like hearing it. "Is that so, Mr.—?"

"Platt." It sounded like he spat.

Thayne mechanically responded, "Pleased to make your acquaintance. I'm Mr.—"

"I know who you are, Thayne!" Mr. Platt belched and put a hand on Thayne's shoulder, making him stiffen further. "You obviously don't know Clara like I do. I, however, know all about you and her conquests. Mind you, I don't complain if she has her share of amusement before the wedding. Gives her character, if you ask me, but she needs a man like me who can handle her, so as a gentleman, I thought I should warn you not to keep dangling after her."

Thayne flexed his hands. He knew how to control his anger, but he would not tolerate anyone dishonoring Clara. For now, he kept silent.

Unfortunately, Mr. Platt did not. He made a wheezy sound that might have been a laugh or a cough and added, "It's all such rubbish!"

"Sir, I warn you—" Thayne tried to cut him off, but Mr. Platt was not done.

"I mean, there's no way a man of your caliber could be so easily taken in by the sentimental rot she actually wrote to you!"

This declaration was fuel to the fire. "How would you know what she wrote to me?"

Mr. Platt snickered. "It's amazing what you can learn for a few guineas."

"Miss Everton wrote me back, didn't she? You intercepted the letter!"

Again, Mr. Platt laughed. "Figured it was my right if I'm to marry her."

Both of Thayne's fists were now clenched. "And you wrote me those ridiculous notes, didn't you?"

"Only for your own good. Didn't want to see an innocent fellow like you getting mixed up with a light-skirt like Clara. Then again, I don't know but that you might just be looking for a little amusement as well." He ended in coughs and chortles.

Thayne felt a shift inside him. Like a storm cloud releasing lightning, his fist swung and cracked down on Mr. Platt's face with startling speed. He grabbed Mr. Platt by the collar and pulled him up to look him in the eye.

"Do not ever speak such lies about Miss Everton again."

A bruise was already forming around Mr. Platt's eye as he hung trapped in Thayne's grip. Both men breathed hard.

Mr. Platt inhaled sharply and spoke through his teeth. "Or what? You won't always be around."

Thayne tightened his grip on Mr. Platt's collar and carefully calculated his words. "I won't let you near Clara when I am around, but if I'm not, I happen to know plenty of men who will come take care of you for me, particularly Mr. Rothmeyer."

Mr. Platt's face blanched, further highlighting the bluish-purple ring forming above his cheekbone. Thayne knew his words had hit their mark.

With the help of Martin, he had done some research before coming to Milton. Because of the strange, threatening notes that kept arriving, Thayne made it his business to find out which gentlemen resided in the area who might take an interest in Clara. Mr. Platt was an obvious choice, so Thayne made some inquiries. He discovered that Mr. Platt had several outstanding debts and was hiding from a particularly aggressive moneylender named Rothmeyer. Rumor had it that Mr. Platt was hoping to garner money from his wealthy grandmother, but she hadn't given him anything. Once Thayne made it clear that he would not hesitate to contact this famed moneylender if the need arose, Mr. Platt was profusely promising never to bother Clara again.

Chapter 25

Clara sat by the fire in the small drawing room of her aunt and uncle's London townhome. Having just been outside with Rose, Clara stretched her feet by the hearth to warm up. The frost and heavy clouds were reason enough to cut short their morning walk, but Clara didn't like strolling around London nearly as much as she enjoyed the open country, even when the weather in town was fair. Instead of nature's peaceful lulls, she heard squeaky carriage wheels disturbing rocks in the road, horses' hooves clopping on stone, and other unidentified clanks and calls.

With pencil and sketchbook in hand, Clara drew a large carriage wheel rolling over a cobblestone road as she listened to the thrum. She hadn't planned on being in London again so soon. The past few days had gone by in a whirl. Why had Louisa felt so urgent about sending her to London with Frances, nearly demanding that she go? Did it have anything to do with the secrets Louisa and her father were keeping, which Clara still suspected involved her father's health? She hated to leave him when he was only recently recovered from another bout of sudden sickness, but he seemed to agree with Louisa this time. He wanted Clara to spend time with her friends and relatives. Frances was so thrilled with the idea of Clara accompanying her that by the end of all the fuss, Clara felt obligated to go.

Seeing Aunt Rose and Uncle William again was pleasant, but London held no other draw for Clara. She would have to adjust to the noise and social shuffle if she was to enjoy herself. It was sure to be an uneventful visit, but as Clara sat by the hearth adding shadows to her drawing, the maid came in with a message for her that altered her every expectation.

James Thayne was in town. Apparently, he had left a note while Clara was out with Rose. He also left a card, proving he had been physically present. Clara turned the letter over and over in her hands. How had he so quickly discovered she was in town? She slowly unfolded the paper and read:

How are you, dear Clara?

I am thrilled to discover we are both in London. I wished to see you in person right away, but I am once again thwarted in my efforts. Your maid informs me you are out with your aunt. I write these words from the sitting room in hopes that you may soon walk through the door. I am in no hurry to leave, but the maid continues to hint that I am in her way. I've thought about calling on you tomorrow, but the truth is I am in suspense as to what your desires are. I would like to see you soon, so if the idea pleases you, I propose we meet tomorrow night at the ball Mrs. Chelsea is throwing for her niece. I have enclosed a small gift that I hope you will wear to the ball. I will watch for you, ask you to dance, and then, if you are inclined to say yes, I shall hope to visit you for as long as you are in town.

Sincerely yours,
James Thayne

Clara hadn't realized until she finished reading that her heart was pounding. Mr. Thayne was in town! He wanted to see her! He wanted to dance with her! She unfolded a second paper that had been wrapped within the letter to reveal a cluster of tiny silk forget-me-nots. To say she felt flattered was an understatement. Clara laughed and grew light-headed just thinking about James Thayne being so close by.

She looked out the window and scanned the streets to see if she might be able to spot him. He had walked those very streets only an hour earlier! To think she had almost seen him! No doubt, had she been there to receive him, she would have burned bright red and stumbled through the whole visit! At least this way, she had time to prepare.

With her hands to her cheeks, Clara left the window and paced the room. Was this really happening? She had spent so much time writing to Mr. Thayne, and even more time thinking about him that the idea of finally standing face to face with him made her pulse quicken. Would she be able to speak with him as easily as she had been able to write to him? What if she couldn't think of anything to say? What if she tripped while dancing with him? Or worst of all, what if she came across as uninterested? She could not let that happen, not after the personal letter she had just sent him. She looked at the small forget-me-nots he had given her. Holding them tight against her chest, Clara promised that James Thayne would know she meant every word she had ever written him.

Clara winced as Aunt Rose pulled a curl too tight. Rose insisted on helping the maid arrange Clara's hair, wanting everything to look perfect. Clara appreciated her aunt's help, but the extra attention was making her nervous. Clara reminded herself that it would be like any other ball. Except this time, there was a gentleman attending whom she wanted to see, and she wanted to look stunning. Aunt Rose finished adjusting the curls, fastening them with pins studded with white pearls. When she was finished, she loosened a few curls to hang around Clara's face. The end result was very flattering. Clara sat for a moment in front of the glass admiring Rose's handiwork and the effect it had on her overall look.

"I daresay," began Rose, "Mr. Thayne will find you even lovelier than he remembers." She placed her hands on Clara's shoulders and gave her a quick hug.

Clara spun around to face her aunt. "Mr. Thayne?" she stated, surprised that her aunt had read her thoughts.

"Oh, Clara! Of course, Mr. Thayne!" Rose said nonchalantly. "Your uncle and I know how much he has been looking forward to seeing you again. I hope you will be willing to give him a chance tonight."

Clara blushed. Of course, she would give him a chance! She was relieved Rose didn't seem to know about the letters.

Clara took a sip of the peppermint tea that had been brought up to calm her nerves and warm her up. The mint was just as soothing as refreshing. As Clara felt the warmth spread, she had another comforting thought. Frances would be attending the ball that night. Clara had learned from Aunt Rose that Mrs. Chelsea's niece, whose upcoming marriage the ball was meant to celebrate, was Frances's cousin, the very same whose wedding arrangements Mrs. Wright was helping with. Clara couldn't remember ever looking forward to a ball so much.

As the time to leave drew near, she thought about what to say to Mr. Thayne when she first saw him. Would he be as attractive in person as he had come across on paper? She had tried to keep her expectations and feelings in check over the past few months, but since reading his most recent letter, she had given her heart free rein to believe that James Thayne was the most perfect man she would ever find.

As a final touch, Clara took the small forget-me-nots and pinned them at her shoulder. She was ready.

Chapter 26

Thayne was one of the first to arrive that night. After greeting and thanking his hosts, he only had one desire. Find Clara. Every muscle wound up for that moment, so much so that he began to jump at every pretty face and turn toward the call of any name sounding remotely similar to Thayne. Unfortunately, there seemed an inordinate number of girls named Jane in attendance.

At least he was certain Clara was coming. He confirmed as much with Martin yesterday. Otherwise, he couldn't have born the suspense. He couldn't sit still or stand in one place for too long either, so he strode from one room to the next, constantly scanning the crowd.

There were times, in the soft candlelight, when he thought he had spotted her only to be disappointed. His senses strained against the sights and sounds, and it didn't help that several ladies and gentlemen had overdone it with perfumes and scented oils, leaving Thayne coughing in their wake. All he wanted was to see his beautiful Clara. He decided to return to the main hall to check for her again.

Then he stopped.

Finally!

After months of writing to each other, sharing thoughts and secrets, there she was on the other side of the room talking with two other ladies. She was just as beautiful as he remembered, even more so now that he felt so familiar with the strength and beauty of her character. Golden hair, amber eyes, a glowing complexion. He had pictured her face many times as he read her letters.

Now that he stood only a few strides away from her, he cursed his nerves, which gripped hard and held him to the spot. *Miss Everton, we meet at last,* he rehearsed to himself . . . *No, sounds like I'm greeting an enemy.* Or perhaps, *Are you having a pleasant evening? . . . No, no. Too boring.* He wanted to make an impression. He would be bold.

Thayne saw his chance. The other women who had been standing with her walked away, leaving her alone for the moment. She stood with her back toward him, so she didn't see him shake out his arms and roll back his shoulders. Five steps later, he was right behind her.

He cleared his throat. "I was wondering whether you received my last letter." He smiled but inwardly grimaced at his lack of *savoir faire.*

She turned around frowning. "I beg your pardon?" Her eyes were cold and suspicious.

She will be happy to learn who I am, he thought. "I'm James Thayne." He tried to give her his most pleasant smile. Perhaps she was nervous too?

"Oh." Apparently, she had a talent for conveying the utmost disinterest. "Well, I personally prefer a more formal introduction, so if you will excuse me, I really should be getting back to my—"

"Forgive me. I thought you were here because you wanted to meet in person, Miss Everton." Thayne saw her confusion and wanted to clear it up as soon as possible.

"Miss Everton?" she said with disdain. "I'm afraid you are mistaken. If you must know, I am Elizabeth Watson." She gave him a reproachful glance and walked away.

Mind blank. Completely blank.

Thayne didn't know how long he stood there petrified until someone bumped into him from behind with a, "Begging your pardon."

Thayne blinked.

Elizabeth Watson?

His stomach twisted and writhed. He was certain she was the girl he saw last season at the Stratford ball, the one he sheepishly followed around hoping to dance with, looking for an opportunity that never came. He was certain it was her, this lady who called herself Elizabeth Watson. This was definitely the girl he had pointed out to William Martin, who claimed her as his niece. Oh, what a mistake to have made!

What have I done? he thought, almost doubling over with disappointment. If the woman he had been so smitten with was Miss Watson, then who was Clara Everton?

Thayne felt the ground shift beneath him as he looked around completely unsure of himself. He saw Elizabeth Watson talking with the same two women from before only now they were eyeing him and whispering things behind their hands. Leaving all other considerations aside, he knew he had to get out of that room.

He no longer trusted his legs, but he willed them to move regardless. Each step felt unnatural and slightly off balance as he left the main room and followed the hallway. He needed fresh air immediately. Colorful gowns swished and circled round him like animals closing in on their prey, but he persevered with the hope that he was heading toward a balcony or window. After a few more steps, he saw the main doors. Even better. He would just go home.

Then, at the other end of the hallway, he saw Martin walking with two ladies. The first Thayne knew to be Mrs. Martin, and the second was a girl that looked only vaguely familiar. She had chocolaty brown curls that twisted round her face and glistened bronze in the light. She was quite lovely, but what struck Thayne the most was the cluster of blue forget-me-nots pinned at her shoulder. This was Clara, the one he had actually been corresponding with. He stared hard, searching for some intuitive recognition, but nothing came to him. He didn't know her at all.

He wasn't prepared for this! How could he face her? What would he say? *Oh, what an idiot I am!* They hadn't seen him yet, but they would all soon be face to face in the hall if he did not do something quickly. Panicking, he looked around and grabbed a large vase of flowers from a nearby table and hoped it would hide his face. It was heavier than he thought, and he grunted at its weight.

He heard Martin chuckling. "I say, Thayne, you certainly have a flair for style!" He continued to laugh as he pointed to the vase. "Those are lovely flowers, but they look like they would be awkward to dance with! Ha ha!"

Thayne's face grew hot. He gave a modest laugh and slowly placed the vase back on the table. He looked back and forth between Mr.

and Mrs. Martin. He could not bring himself to look Clara in the eye. *What a disaster*, he kept repeating to himself. *Stupid, stupid, stupid!*

Martin cleared his throat. "You know my wife." She gave a small bow. "And here is my niece, Miss Clara Everton, who I introduced you to at the Stratford ball last season, as you may very well recall."

Thayne repressed a groan. Did Martin have to wink?

Clara gave a small bow and smiled wide.

Thayne forced a smile in return but knew it came out wrong. "Yes, well, it's good to see you again."

"Mr. Thayne," she said with a satisfied breath. "We meet at last."

That was supposed to be my greeting! He took a large gulp of air and didn't know what else to say. He watched helplessly as Clara's face slowly changed from eager smiles to blank realization. Her lips parted ever so slightly and her eyes pled with him before dropping under heavy lashes and turning away.

"I beg your pardon," he managed to get out, "but if you will excuse me, I need to step outside." He swallowed hard and walked right past them and out the door.

He advanced quickly toward the carriages, but before he could find his own, he heard his name being called.

"I say, come now, Thayne!" Martin sounded winded from hurrying after Thayne. "What was that back there? I know you sometimes have difficulty starting a conversation, but that was downright disastrous!"

Thayne stopped and let his head droop down. "You have no idea," he sighed. He had hoped to postpone this discussion with Martin, but there was no point in avoiding it. He explained as best he could what had happened. Martin stood there gaping as Thayne finished.

"But I even introduced you to Clara! I thought you were just having trouble remembering her name!" Martin waved his hands all about as he talked.

Thayne tried to remember what had happened that night at the Stratford ball. He could remember her face, the one who he now knew to be Miss Watson. The rest seemed hazy. "Perhaps they were standing next to each other when I pointed her out. I . . . I don't know!"

Martin groaned as he rubbed his face. "Good gracious, boy! What an uproar this will cause among the ladies!" He started pacing. "And

I'm the one to blame! I thought my niece was the one you pointed out. Oh, what a predicament!" He mumbled and continued to rub his forehead.

As Thayne watched Martin panic, he regained a little of his own composure. "I don't blame you, old friend. The fault is mine."

"What do we do now, Thayne? I've got two ladies in there who will be growing more uneasy the longer I'm out here. What is to be done? We've raised Clara's hopes! Oh, what a predicament! What a mess! This is all my fault!"

"As I said, Martin, the blame is mine. I convinced myself that I had good reason to overlook the imprudence of writing letters to a lady I hardly knew."

"You . . . you what?" cried Martin. "You have been writing letters to my niece? Thayne, this is worse than I thought!"

"I know!" Thayne hollered in dismay. He tried to explain to Martin how compelled he had felt to write, how he saw no point in waiting and leaving so much to chance. "So, I wrote her a letter," he explained. "I hardly expected a reply, but well . . . as I said before, I have been writing to a lady I hardly knew." Thayne let out a nervous laugh. "Turns out I knew her even less than I thought."

Martin's eyebrows rose. "That's not entirely true," he remarked. "You know her quite well, I should say, if you have exchanged that many letters."

"All those letters! To the wrong girl." Thayne bent over with his hands on his legs for support. He took one great breath and said, "I'm sorry. You have no idea how unnerved I feel right now. I must go!"

Chapter 27

When Clara saw her uncle rush out after Mr. Thayne, she ignored Rose's protests and quietly followed. She knew it wasn't a good idea. It was probably very improper of her, but she had to know what was happening. She got as close as she could and watched the men from behind a tree. Clara could only make out some of the words, but one thing was clear. She was the wrong girl.

Her mind spun, and her stomach heaved.

She was the wrong girl. Mr. Thayne had never intended to write to her.

She wrapped her arms across her chest and tried to breathe, unsure how she could walk back to the ball and face everyone. She leaned against the trunk of the tree, smelling the damp earth and listening to the men's footsteps fade, wishing she were anywhere but there.

"Clara?"

Clara quickly stood and looked around. There was Frances waving to her from the path on the left, looking like she had just arrived.

Thank goodness it was only Frances! Clara ran over and threw her arms around Frances's neck like a child. Clara didn't cry, but she could hardly speak.

"Oh, Clara!" Frances gave her a quick embrace, then pulled her back by the shoulders. Speaking in hushed tones, she said, "Whatever is going on, I want to help, but you must compose yourself. Quickly!" Frances gestured with her head toward the people behind her.

Clara glanced back. Among the various people on the path, she could see Mrs. Wright intently conversing with another matronly woman. They hadn't yet noticed Clara.

"You do not want to be discussed in every sitting room within twenty miles of our house. Do you understand?"

She certainly did. She hastily pulled out a handkerchief and wiped her eyes, even though they were dry. She took a few deep breaths and, with Frances there for support, she managed to walk back to the house.

Clara had hardly stepped inside before Rose took her hand and, in an urgent whisper, asked, "What on earth is going on?" Noticing Frances, Rose smiled weakly. "Oh. Good evening. Forgive my outburst. I . . ."

"It's all right, Aunt," Clara said, barely keeping her voice from shaking. "Frances is the reason I'm not still outside making a fool of myself."

Rose leaned closer to whisper. "Can you tell me what happened? What is the matter?"

What was the matter? What could Clara say? She was the wrong girl. She didn't want to explain any of it. "Not now, Aunt. Not here. I'll be all right. Allow me a moment to speak with Frances."

Clara linked arms with Frances, grateful for her friend's support, and together, they searched for a quiet place amidst the crowded rooms where they could sit and talk freely. When they came to a small window seat with long velvety curtains hanging on each side, Clara let herself drop to the cushions. It was as private a place as they would find that evening.

"Tell me what has happened," Frances urged.

Clara opened her mouth, but she knew if she tried to explain, her composure would crumble. What had just happened with Mr. Thayne only minutes ago . . . it was too fresh, too painful. All those expectations, all those hopes built on the thrill of having found someone she cared about—gone in an instant! All she could do was ask Frances to excuse her from explaining just yet.

Frances's eyes were heavy with concern, but she said she understood.

Clara attempted a change of subject. "Is your gentleman here tonight?"

"Of course not!" Frances scanned the crowd. "We have a secret manner of corresponding, and we decided it would be too risky for him to come tonight, so long as my mother is nearby to watch me." Frances gestured with her head, and Clara saw Mrs. Wright on the other side of the room watching them. Frances lowered her voice. "You see? She is never far off. Right now, my intended and I are waiting for my cousin's wedding. My mother has taken charge of nearly all the planning. She will be so occupied the day of the wedding that it will be an easy business to make my escape!"

As Clara listened, her own heartache swelled and shadowed her perceptions like a storm cloud. "Listen to yourself, Frances. Are you sure you want to do this? Without knowing anything about this man—"

"I know him quite well." Frances pressed her lips into a frown and looked off to the side.

"Don't be upset with me, Frances. I only meant that *I* do not know anything about him. I don't know to what extent he can be trusted."

"Clara, you trust me, don't you?"

"Well, yes, but without really knowing him, I don't know how to advise you at all. He might be completely different from what you think." *Entirely different*, Clara thought bitterly.

"My dear Clara," Frances said, reaching out and giving Clara's shoulders a squeeze. "You don't need to advise me. Not now. I have no doubt he is the man I want. Just keep being my friend."

Clara tried to muster a smile. "That is my intention. It's just that—"

"Excuse me, ladies." A gentleman now stood before them clearing his throat.

When Clara looked up to see who spoke, heat rushed down her face all the way to her toes.

While she merely stared, Frances exclaimed, "Mr. Shaw! What . . . what are you doing here?"

Clara's insides swirled and boiled. It was her first time seeing Mr. Shaw since receiving his love letter. The very idea of dancing with him now, so shortly after the disaster with Mr. Thayne, made her head spin. She would never be able to keep her balance.

"Forgive me for catching you unaware," he persisted. "You were, no doubt, in each other's confidences, and I have intruded. However, I could not resist the opportunity to ask for a dance."

Clara stared numbly at the hand he offered, not to her, but to Frances, sparing Clara no more than a sideways glance.

Was it possible? Frances had her eyes fixed on him and was turning red! Clara was baffled. Frances looked around and stumbled on her words. "I . . . I beg your pardon. Why are you . . . I mean, I wasn't expecting to see you this evening."

Mr. Shaw displayed a teasing grin, making Clara cringe inside.

"Do you hesitate, Miss Wright? Surely we are friends."

Frances looked at Clara with wide eyes, but Clara could no more discern the meaning of that expression than change how her encounter with Mr. Thayne had gone. She silently watched as Frances took his hand and followed him to the dance floor.

Mr. Shaw never gave Clara a second glance.

Clara sat by herself, jilted for the second time that evening. Ever since Mr. Thayne's letters, she had hardly given Mr. Shaw a thought, but she hadn't considered he might lose interest in her. Was it possible his pride was hurt? Perhaps because she never replied to his letter, he made a point not to dance with her. If so, why did he have to choose such a wretchedly inconvenient time to prefer Frances?

And Frances, so tuned into Clara's feelings a minute ago, was too caught up in her own emotions to notice Clara's humiliation. Why did Frances blush so deeply? Why did Mr. Shaw look so sure of himself? *Was it possible . . . ?* Clara started piecing together the evidence . . . His presence had clearly flustered Frances. *Could it be that Frances and Mr. Shaw . . . ?*

It didn't make any sense, and yet . . .

She sat for a long time, not knowing what to do with herself. The constant shuffle of finely slippered feet in her downcast gaze reminded her that she was still within the public's scrutiny. If only the curtains could conceal her the rest of the night. She could not trust herself to contain her hurt should another gentleman dare approach her in this state. Dancing was out of the question.

Clara was fretting over what to do when Rose passed by the window seat and found her. Taking her aunt's hand, Clara slowly stood. "I . . . I'm not well, Aunt. I feel ill. Could we please go home?"

Clara gave no response as Rose bid her good night. She sat on the edge of her bed completely numb, repeating to herself that she was the wrong girl. Mr. Thayne had never meant to write to her. She was the wrong girl. How stupid she felt! How ridiculous she must have looked to him! What a disappointment she must have been. Her mortification was sharp.

And to be rejected again in her moment of pain! Not just by Mr. Shaw but by Frances as well! *So easily forgotten,* Clara lamented. *So easily left behind.* To think Frances might be engaged to a rake! And, worse, planning to elope with him.

In the lateness of the hour and the darkness of the house, problems spun tighter and tighter around themselves. The secret her father and Louisa were keeping, her father's bouts of illness, Frances secretly engaged to Mr. Shaw, Mr. Thayne not wanting her. If she wanted to be thorough, she could add to the list stubbing her toe on the stairs and shivering under the cold draft from her window.

Nothing was as it should have been, and there was nothing she could do. It was such a contrast to the light hope that had sprung inside her only hours earlier, all because of a letter, one deceptively innocent letter from Mr. Thayne that had snowballed into letter upon letter . . . upon love letter. *How stupid to trust in a letter!* Especially when she had known the dangers. *Nothing but false promises!*

Clara then noticed Mr. Thayne's last letter sitting on her desk. Intending to toss it in the fire, she snatched it up and thrust it threateningly above the flames, but her hand hesitated, holding the letter tight. She couldn't let it go. Perhaps it was never meant for her, but his words had taught her more about love and how it felt to be loved than any London ball ever had. Instead of burning the letter, she wedged it under her mattress and sunk into bed, weighted by the memories of the ball and each letter that had led up to it.

Rolling onto her stomach, she pushed her face in her pillow to swallow the sounds of sobbing. She couldn't tell when the tears ran out, only that when sleep finally came, she was completely empty.

Chapter 28

$\mathcal{C}$lara sat at the desk by the sitting room window for the benefit of the natural light. With her paint box, paper, and brushes before her, she decided to try her hand at a watercolor painting. Drawing alone had provided no comfort that morning, as her hand too easily drifted toward sketching the scenes that were burdening her mind. Her hope was that the focus required to paint would leave no room in her thoughts for memories of the previous night.

She began by lightly sketching out a simple scene, a woman from the back standing alone with her head tilted heavenward. Clara's hand sped across the paper, fully adept at laying out the figure and lines, but as she attempted to add the paint, she was unable to achieve the colors and effects she wanted. The watercolors bled across the paper in unpredictable patterns, and her brush shook in her hand whenever she leaned in to add detail. What was worse, she realized that painting was not providing the relief she wanted.

The blue paint reminded her of the forget-me-nots from Mr. Thayne and the way he had looked at her, or rather, the way he had avoided looking at her. And the water dripping from her brush all too accurately reminded her of the tears she had cried. She simply could not paint any longer.

Pushing her paints to the side, she looked out the window and blinked back the tears. The streets were unusually quiet. A lone little robin hopped on the ground and shuddered in the cold. Clara's heart reached out, wanting to scoop up and warm the little bird, but that's when she noticed a man walking purposefully close and approaching the door. Was it —*Oh, no! Why would he come now?* She stood up and looked around the room, not sure what she was looking for.

Aunt Rose, sitting across from Clara asked what bothered her, but before Clara could say anything, the butler was announcing Mr. James Thayne and showing him into the room.

Mr. Thayne's footsteps were slow as he entered the sitting room, but he stood tall and wished the ladies a good afternoon. Clara heard his words but hardly acknowledged them. Looking off to the side, she gritted her nerves and refused to be interested in his visit.

"Why, Mr. Thayne!" began Rose. "We were not expecting to see you again so soon."

"Yes, well, I—" Mr. Thayne cleared his throat.

Clara risked a glance at him. He looked just as uncomfortable as he had the previous night, but he looked directly at her this time. In the seconds their eyes met, Clara was certain that the blush on her face betrayed the feelings she didn't understand.

"I've come to apologize for my behavior last night and—"

Rose interrupted, "Oh, there is no need, Mr. Thayne!"

"Thank you, but I believe there is. If I may, I would like a brief word with Miss Everton." He looked determined despite Rose's efforts to put him at ease.

Clara couldn't bring herself to say anything. Instead, she looked away.

"Certainly," Rose replied. "I will be just down the hall if you two should need me."

Clara considered asking her aunt to stay, but Rose was too quick. Alone with Mr. Thayne, Clara mustered the nerve to look him in the eye again. They stood in front of each other, silent just long enough for the awkwardness to thoroughly settle in. Clara made up her mind not to be the first one to speak.

Mr. Thayne cleared his throat again. "Miss Everton, before you say anything, I must apologize . . . for everything. I can't imagine what you must be thinking. I'm not sure how much you know—"

"I know everything. And I accept your apology," she replied, clipping her words. "It was an honest mistake."

"Truly an unfortunate one!" He ran his hands through his hair. "The truth is, I am also here to make amends for my mistakes. I am aware of the impression it gives a young lady for a man to write such letters to her. Naturally as our correspondence increased, I realized you might have expected me to make you an offer. Although I have thought better of it since last night, I certainly want to preserve my honor as well as yours. So, it is with an honest heart that I request your hand in marriage."

Clara heard Rose gasp from all the way down the hall. Was this really happening? There was no question in Clara's mind what she should do. She looked at him, carefully considering her words.

"Sir, it is honorable of you to offer me your apologies, but you need not offer more than that." She held her hands clasped in front of her and tried to stand tall despite his being almost a whole head taller.

"Clara," he said, then stopped. It was the first time she had heard him use her given name. "I am sincere in my offer. Judging from our letters, I still believe we will get along well and eventually grow fond of each other."

Clara bit the inside of her cheek. If he was judging from their letters, he would have known she felt much more than fondness. But no longer! To be reminded of those letters, especially her most recent, was to add insult to injury. She would lose her temper if she was not careful.

"Be that as it may, you have thought better of it, as you just told me."

"Please, I didn't mean—"

"I hold you under no obligation. You are free to seek out Miss Watson or any other lady who suits you."

"Miss Everton, please—"

"I could never marry a man who thought he had to attach himself to me out of obligation."

Mr. Thayne looked off to the side before meeting her eyes again. "Obligation or not, it would still be my choice. I knew that writing letters to an unmarried lady came with risks. I'm ready to accept responsibility for my choices."

Clara tapped the corner of her mouth. "How very noble of you. And what of my choice in the matter?"

"Are you not at all worried about being disgraced if others discover we have been corresponding without being engaged?" Mr. Thayne remained calm as he spoke.

"No, I am not." Clara determined to show him a taste of her own pride. "I also knew I risked society's judgments, but a clear conscience is enough to bolster me against those. I never risked the possibility that I would be constrained to marry you!"

"Miss Everton." Mr. Thayne sounded like he was getting tired. "I too could withstand the *ton's* gossip and slander, but I would not consider myself a gentleman if I put my own wishes before your honor."

Clara exhaled slowly to ease the tension in her head. Her answer would not change, but at least now she knew he never meant to take advantage of her. It was a small consolation. He remained a gentleman, even if a foolish one. So she determined to act like a lady, even if a broken one.

"Well, that is very good of you, Mr. Thayne. I believe you have fulfilled that duty. Thank you for stopping by. Our maid will show you out. Good day." With that, Clara left the room.

Chapter 29

Was it wrong of Thayne to feel so relieved? He left Clara's house utterly embarrassed, slightly jilted, and thoroughly free. He had done his duty to Clara and walked away with a clear conscience. He could now focus on other pursuits, other honey-colored, amber-eyed pursuits.

"You are free to seek out Miss Watson . . ." Clara's words resounded in his mind.

Miss Watson. Thayne had pictured her face many times over the past few months, thinking that she was Miss Everton. He still thought her quite beautiful, but oh, how she had scowled at him when he called her Miss Everton! He had made the mistake of calling a lady the wrong name before, but this was enormously worse. Had he ruined his chance with her? How could he gain her favor when he had made such a fool of himself? Despite his efforts to live without regrets, regret had found him regardless.

Without thinking about where he was headed, Thayne started walking toward his old friend's jewelry shop. He checked on Mr. Cornell every time he was in town, using a pocket watch that tended to break as his excuse to visit. The elderly man often seemed lonely and reminded Thayne of Mr. Andrews, only gruffer.

Thayne walked into the shop and took in the handful of people who stood off to the side, admiring the jewelry on display. Two women in the back seemed to be arguing with Cornell. Thayne only saw their backs, but they were talking loud enough for everyone to hear.

"You can't be serious!" the younger of the two women exclaimed. "This necklace has been in my family for years!"

"It is a beautiful necklace, Miss," began Cornell in his husky voice, "but I am certain the pendant already had that scratch across the emblem when you brought it to me. As you can see, the clasp is fixed."

"This is the first time I am seeing this scratch!" The lady's voice grew louder. "The clasp may be fixed, but the necklace is worse off than before. I won't pay you!"

The other woman, whom Thayne thought might be the younger lady's mother, reached out and placed a hand on her arm. "Now dearest, can we really be so sure the scratch wasn't there before? It is quite old after all, and we only asked him to mend the clasp. Don't you think not paying him is a bit harsh?" The mother examined her glove hardly sounding like she cared.

The younger girl's hand clenched to a fist on the counter. "No, I don't! It seems only fair to me that if he can't fix this scratch, he shouldn't be paid."

Cornell scrunched his brows, examined the pendant under his loupe, and answered, "If I try to fix that scratch, it will disturb the whole emblem on the front."

The girl turned to her mother, her face hidden behind her hat. "I don't know why we come here. He's not as skilled as they say."

Thayne noticed other customers casting worried glances around as they witnessed the girl's complaints. Cornell noticed too. He scratched his head and tightened his frown as he looked at the necklace yet again.

Thayne considered what he could do. It would be impolite to interrupt, but the young lady was already making a scene. He strutted up to the front, stood next to the ladies, and gave Cornell a pat on the arm from across the counter.

"How are you, friend! I've come for my watch, which I do not doubt is in better shape now than when I dropped it off." Thayne made sure his voice carried. "There is no one else I would have trusted with it!" He then pretended to notice the ladies for the first time. Taking off his hat, he said, "Forgive me. It appears I am interrupting."

Thayne flashed a friendly smile in hopes of breaking the tension, but his smile froze. The young lady before him was Elizabeth Watson, and she was fuming.

Miss Watson opened her mouth, but her mother spoke first. "Let's not allow this unfortunate mishap to delay our errands. Come along, Elizabeth."

Thayne took in every detail as Miss Watson scooped up her necklace and gave both him and Cornell the same disdainful look she had given Thayne the previous night at the ball. Without bothering to pay Cornell, the ladies marched out of the shop with their noses in the air.

Cornell shook his head and walked to the back of the shop where he produced Thayne's watch. It gleamed as if new, just as Thayne knew it would. The men exchanged a few amiable words, but Thayne kept thinking about the scene he had just witnessed. Any desire for a second chance with Elizabeth Watson was snuffed in that moment.

When Thayne exited Cornell's shop, he saw Miss Watson with her mother across the street talking with another lady. It wasn't long before her proud glare focused on him. Thayne nodded his acknowledgement and walked on with his hands behind his back.

To think how close he'd come to corresponding with Miss Watson instead of Miss Everton. It was amusing, really, to think how muddled everything had become. At least it was over. Thayne would not dwell on it. He told himself he was no longer attached to Miss Everton or Miss Watson.

The question now was where to go next? He no longer had a reason to stay in London, but the pull of home hadn't reached him yet. How could he go back to Felton Park with nothing but disappointment over what he had lost?

His resolve to forget all that had happened was already breaking. The past few months had been too good to be true. He had lost Miss Everton and Miss Watson in less than a full day's time, an impressive failure, even for him, but his real regret was losing the girl he had pictured time and time again as he read those charming letters. That girl didn't exist. So, as he walked, he thought about those letters.

Chapter 30

Clara woke late, dressed slowly, and reluctantly went to breakfast. *Why bother*, she thought. What was the point when everything reminded her of Mr. Thayne and his letters? Why bother doing anything when she was the wrong girl? It was only for her aunt and uncle's sake that Clara plodded into breakfast that morning.

Rose sat waiting at the table, smiling too brightly, Clara thought, like the sun shining harshly in her eyes.

"Hello, dearest! How lovely you look this morning!"

Clara thanked her aunt and sat. Rose gestured to the fresh rolls on the table along with apricot preserves and rose hip tea that was already poured. Clara's stomach made an indifferent rumble.

Rose cleared her throat and patted Clara's hand. "I know things haven't gone well the past few days, dear, but your uncle and I have just received an invitation that I think will make you feel better."

Clara took a sip from her tea before looking up. This was going to be a long day. She didn't want to be a rain cloud to her aunt and uncle, but she could not imagine going to any social engagement where she might possibly cross paths with Mr. Thayne. With the weather turning colder, all that was left was sitting quietly around the house trying to read or draw while her aunt and uncle tried to cheer her up.

Rose persisted. "My cousin Lady Welton and her husband, Sir Douglas Welton, have invited us for Christmas!" She spoke as if she had just delivered the best news imaginable. "They are jolly folk, very hospitable. They will be hosting a number of guests and relations, so there will be opportunity to mingle with a different, but surely amiable crowd. I think it would be a most pleasant way to spend the holiday. Their estate is quite a ways north in a place called Brindley, but it is grand and very charming. What do you say, Clara? Shall we accept?"

"It sounds lovely, Aunt Rose, but . . ." The thought of Christmas in the country, with no possibility of running into Mr. Thayne, was a great relief, but it wasn't home. "Is there not some way I can return to Milton Manor to spend Christmas with my father?"

Rose's smile wilted. "Your aunt has written." Rose looked down and took Clara's hand. "Your father is ill again. Louisa also, though she claims to still have strength to tend to your father with the doctor's help."

Clara covered her mouth. "Then I must return . . ."

"I'm sorry, but no. Louisa asks that you stay with us while they recover. You know how much they worry."

A tear slid down Clara's cheek. "I do, indeed, but surely . . ."

"Clara," Rose said gently, "Louisa and your father were not the only ones who feared losing you to influenza those many years ago. It will ease *all* our minds to have you with us for the holidays."

Clara slowly nodded.

Rose left her chair and gave Clara a brief hug. "I will write to my cousin straightway to let her know we are coming."

Clara sat on her bed, wishing she were already on the carriage to Brindley with her aunt and uncle instead of debating whether or not she should bother descending the staircase to receive Mr. Shaw. *Let him visit with Aunt Rose if he's determined to stay*, she thought, but after several minutes, Rose convinced her to come down.

When Clara entered the sitting room, Mr. Shaw stood and smiled as if they shared a secret. Clara might have thought him handsome were it not for his smugness and the fact that he had ignored her at the ball despite having once sent her a love letter.

"Miss Everton," he stated with pleasure. He gave a slight bow and took off his hat.

"Hello, Mr. Shaw," she answered without feeling.

Rose called for refreshment.

"We always seem to meet at the wrong time," Mr. Shaw remarked. "I hear you are to be traveling to Brindley tomorrow."

"Yes, that is so." Clara gestured for him to have a seat.

"The Weltons have invited us for Christmas," Rose added as she sat down, folding her hands in her lap.

A maid came in and placed a tray of small cakes on the table. Clara was not hungry, but Mr. Shaw took three.

"How is your family, Miss Everton?" he asked.

Clara stared at him, debating whether to say anything about her father's illness, but she decided a simple answer was best. "I believe they are well, thank you." She tried to follow Rose's example and sat with her hands neatly folded. "And how is your family?" She asked merely because he had asked. She knew nothing about his family.

Mr. Shaw smirked. "They are well enough."

The great clock could be heard from the hallway ticking away the minutes as Mr. Shaw reached for another cake. Whenever he wasn't chewing, he looked at Clara with a shameless half-grin. Last season, that grin would have made her heart pound, but it had long since lost its appeal.

Finally, Mr. Shaw cleared his throat. "I thought you might be interested to know . . ." His grin for Clara faltered, and he looked at Rose, "that we might be distantly related."

Clara blinked several times. Had she heard him correctly? After ignoring her at the ball, he had the nerve to visit under the pretense of family?

Rose raised her eyebrows. "Is that so, Mr. Shaw? How have you discovered it?"

"Well," he began, "it has come to my attention that my mother is very likely to be distantly related to Mr. Everton. Naturally, when I found out, I wanted to pay a visit and become better acquainted with you."

Clara rolled her eyes. She really hoped this was not the man who had captured Frances's heart.

"How thoughtful of you," Rose replied. "My husband will want to hear all about it when he gets home. He is expected any minute."

"I would like to stay and share every detail with you." Mr. Shaw's confident half-grin returned as he stood up. "But I must be on my way. I couldn't impose upon your kindness longer than necessary, not when you are making preparations to travel." He picked up his hat, took one last cake from the tray, and nodded particularly at Clara. "I hope we meet again soon."

His attempts at charm only made Clara more fervently wish him gone. She nodded to him as he bowed and turned toward the door. Rose bid him a good afternoon and left the room, mumbling something about misplacing her needlepoint. The maid returned to gather up the tray and plates, making several clatters as she tidied up. Still, Mr. Shaw lingered at the door.

When no one was looking, Mr. Shaw leaned close to Clara and whispered, "I wish I could stay longer. I hardly have time to be here, but I had to see you before you left."

Clara took a step back, confused by the intensity in his voice. How could he possibly mean it? "I don't understand you, Mr. Shaw."

"Surely you got my last letter?"

"I don't know." Clara folded her arms as she regarded him.

The maid gave them both a timid curtsey as she passed by with the tray.

Mr. Shaw continued, "It's fortunate I came then, so I could tell you in person how much I long to be near you."

"Hmmm." Clara wanted to simply reject him and tell him how inconsiderate it was of him not to recognize her at the ball, but the only words she could form were, "I hardly know you."

"I hope to fix that," was the last thing he whispered before briskly stepping out.

Chapter 31

Clara leaned back and allowed the rhythm of the carriage to soothe her like a baby being rocked in a cradle. She was leaving her problems behind. The distance between her and Mr. Thayne was increasing by the minute.

Distance was a good thing, she told herself. Yet, part of her wanted to halt the growing distance and make amends with him before it was too late. That part of Clara was small and buried deep, but like an itch, it was difficult to ignore.

Clara had been travelling with her aunt and uncle for only a few hours and was trying to pass the time without thinking about James Thayne, but it was proving difficult. Rose was embroidering tiny blue forget-me-nots on a cushion, and William was reading a newspaper that Clara knew Mr. Thayne enjoyed. Looking for something else to hold her attention, Clara sighed and looked down at the reticule in her lap. There, sticking out at the top, was the corner of a letter. *Oh, yes!* She had forgotten all about it, having hastily stowed it there. It was from Aunt Louisa and had arrived only moments before Clara and her relatives stepped into the carriage to leave for Brindley. Louisa's letter would likely be the best distraction from Mr. Thayne that Clara would find, and she was eager to learn whether her father and Louisa's health were improving. She opened the letter and read.

Dear Clara,

Have you any idea how much I have to say to you, my dear? I am not sure I did the right thing encouraging you to run off to London so quickly. Rose has written to me about what happened with Mr. Thayne. I can imagine what a mix of emotions you must be feeling right now. Take comfort in knowing the hurt shall pass. It always does.

Since you are, no doubt, fretting over your father's health, I wish to reassure you that he is recovering, and I am quite well. It eases my mind to know you have a comfortable place to spend the holidays while we regain our strength. Your father sends his love.

The main reason I write is to tell you a story that is long overdue. Forgive my clumsiness in conveying it to you, but this is the easiest way for me to tell it. Starting has always been the hardest part for me, so I will write as plainly as I can.

When I was young, I was pretty and carefree. My father was too poor to ever give me a season, but one year, when I was about your age, a wealthy friend invited me to accompany her to London. That season gave me a penchant for frivolity. I lived for nothing but parties and dancing. I paid more attention to dresses and shoes than I did to the people that were close to me. Please forgive me! I'm embarrassed to say it!

Fortunately for me and despite my faults, I could be tender and caring when I wanted to be. I met a very kind, handsome man. We were growing quite dear to each other, and I was sure he was planning on making me an offer of marriage. Before he ever had a chance, however, we had a disagreement of some sort and quarreled. For the life of me, I cannot recall the details, only that we were very upset with each other.

I waited for him to apologize, but he never did. In fact, the only time I ever heard from him after that was through a letter explaining that he was going to make a future for himself in India. By the time the letter came, he was already on his way. I yearned to make amends, but I had no way of contacting him. He left no address. No one had any information to share. All I was left with was a sharp pain inside. I won't tell you how much I cried.

By the time I was ready to open my heart again, I realized I had grown old, and there was no one to open my heart to. Then I found a place in my brother's family, watching over you, my little niece, with great concern and love. My new chance for happiness became you finding happiness. I vowed to do whatever I could to steer you toward finding someone just as wonderful as the gentleman I once loved.

I suppose I write all this to tell you that I encouraged you to go to London because I believed it would help you and this secret gentleman, who is not so secret anymore, forge a deeper connection. I do not know whether I was mistaken to send you that way, but the truth has come out, as it always does.

I want you to know that the truth really is not as terrible as it must seem to you now. I am sorry it has taken me so long to trust you. I believe you will find happiness in your own way and in your own time, but I could not sleep peacefully if I did not share with you this one thought, that Mr. Thayne deserves another chance.

When Mr. Thayne came to Milton after you left for London, I sensed in him a strong affection for you. Whatever his mistakes, it is you he has fallen in love with. He has read your letters and has learned enough about you to know that you are just the woman he wants. He is drawn to the very essence of who you are. I am certain of it. He just hasn't realized it yet. This all must be a shock for him too.

I encourage you to give him a second chance once he has worked through his feelings. Mark my words, he will come for you. Best of luck, Clara!

> *Your loving aunt,*
> *Louisa*

Clara took several deep breaths. She was grateful, at least, to learn that Louisa and her father were well, but Louisa's letter was far from comforting.

Mr. Thayne had gone to Milton? Had Clara read that part correctly? In her home, talking with her family? It was an incredibly devoted thing for him to do, but Clara's heart stung at the thought. It only served to remind her that he was a singularly wonderful man, and she had lost him.

Oh, why did she have to read Louisa's letter now? Would nothing distract her from thoughts of Mr. Thayne? It was no use! He was everywhere. Why should she fight it? What was the point in trying to avoid her own mind? She stopped struggling and imagined everything she could about his visit to Milton. What did he think of her home? Did her father like him? Had Louisa shared embarrassing stories from Clara's childhood?

As Clara pictured Mr. Thayne walking the halls of Milton Manor, she realized something. If she had remained at home, she would have been present for his visit. Her heart would have broken in front of her family after confessing that she had written to a man she hardly knew. If ever there was a silver lining to be grateful for, it was that she had missed such awkwardness!

Clara read her letter through again, this time thinking of Louisa. *Poor, dear Louisa!* Clara never would have guessed about her past romance. It explained why Louisa had never married. She had been thwarted in love at a young age and never recovered. The man she loved had run off to India without giving her a chance to mend things. How her heart must have broken! Aware of the pain they now shared, Clara suddenly missed Louisa dreadfully and wished she could give her a hug.

So, she did the next best thing. She gave Rose a hug.

"Goodness, child!" Rose started, then patted Clara's back as she choked back a sob. "Is there yet more heartache?"

"Sorry, Aunt." Clara sat back up and shook her head. "It's just that I've received a letter from Aunt Louisa and . . ." Clara didn't know whether she had permission from Louisa to share all the contents of the letter. Some parts were too private. "Louisa thinks . . ." Clara sniffled. "She thinks I should give Mr. Thayne a second chance."

Rose rubbed Clara's back. "Don't you think you should?"

"It's not that simple, Aunt. I can't give Mr. Thayne a second chance if he doesn't want one. Louisa seems certain he will, but I can't be so sure."

Clara hid her face in Rose's shoulder and cried. When Clara finally looked up, Rose didn't seem to know what to say and gave a pleading look to her husband who was still reading his paper. Rose cleared her throat, but when he didn't react, she whacked him on the shoulder from across the way.

Uncle William grunted, lowered his paper, and said, "Yes, yes. I was paying attention! Mr. Thayne. Disappointment. Something about Louisa?"

"Oh, for goodness sake, William!"

"I don't know what this has to do with Louisa," he began, making Clara smile, "but I've known Thayne for years. He is one of the best men I know, takes after his late father. Thayne is an honest sort. He just needs time. He'll come to his senses. Once he grows attached to someone, he is very loyal."

"But Uncle, I'm not the one he grew attached to. It was that other girl, Miss Watson-whatever her name is," Clara grumbled.

"Clara," he pointed at her, "that makes no sense. He may have mistaken you in appearance, but aren't you the one who wrote to him? Aren't you the one who enchanted him so much that he wrote back again and again?"

"Well, I suppose, but—"

"No buts about it." Uncle William sat back and resumed reading his paper.

Clara was somewhat soothed as Rose continued to rub her back. "I think your uncle makes a lot of sense, dear, but even if Mr. Thayne is not the one, you are a remarkable young lady. No mix up or misunderstanding could ever change that."

Clara was grateful to have such an aunt and uncle. It was for her sake they were travelling to Brindley in the first place, and Clara loved them for trying so hard to cheer her up. For their sakes, she would try to enjoy herself.

As the carriage rambled on, she wondered what she would have done all those years ago if she were Louisa. Would she have closed her heart? Maybe. Wasn't she trying to close it now? Even with her family's encouragement, how could she let herself hope that Mr. Thayne would still want her? It was a foolish wish. Clara had no way of knowing whether he would ever want her again.

The carriage jolted as she tried to put her thoughts together. She didn't want to go on hoping for something that might never be. There had to be another way to find peace.

As the carriage rolled over a particularly large bump, Clara made two decisions. First, she would be happy regardless of whether Mr. Thayne ever took an interest in her again, and second, she would not let pride stop her from finding love.

Chapter 32

*S*haw reclined along the sofa with his arm hung across his eyes. He was running out of time. The year was nearly up and he wasn't engaged yet. He had to be engaged, at the very least, before he could hope to stand any chance of being in his father's good graces again.

Confound his father's good graces! The sting of being rejected by the only girl Shaw had ever loved was still too fresh. It was too soon to consider another relationship. His father didn't know that, of course, but Shaw would never tell him. Shaw hadn't told anyone what had happened last year, not even Harris. Remembering was painful, more painful than he was ready to admit. He usually shoved the memories deep, but this time, as he laid on the sofa too worn out to put up his usual defenses, he let the memories flow.

It was summertime last year in Colchester. He was to spend at least two months with his great aunt who was very ill. He had grumbled when his father insisted on him going to keep the old woman company. Shaw was the least suited for the job, but any displeasure he felt was swept away when he met Blaire, beautiful Blaire, who was daring, boisterous, and made him feel alive. They were often thrown together in the same social circles and were simply drawn to one another. It wasn't long before they formed an attachment and spent every moment they could together.

One morning in particular, Shaw prepared to call on Blaire with a special purpose in mind. He took extra care to wear his best jacket and apply fresh scent to his shirt. He never fussed over his hair, especially since she liked it when his locks fell wherever they wanted to. So, after a quick tousle with his fingers, he was ready. He walked briskly down the path, aware of how his blood raced in anticipation of making his heart so vulnerable. He had no idea what he was doing, but it felt like the next step.

He approached her house and was met by her two younger sisters who giggled when he passed. He hated when they did that, but this time, it made him laugh too. They would soon be old enough to be out in society, and then they would see what it felt like to be teased for having a suitor.

When he was shown into the main parlor, he waited longer than usual. He assumed Blaire was simply taking extra time to dress and primp. She always took pride in her appearance. But the clock kept ticking, and he was kept waiting. He almost lost patience, but he refused to taint the day with unpleasant feelings. Instead, he shook out his nerves and used the quiet moment to review what he wanted to say.

When she came in, he stood up expectantly, but her eyes, hard and haughty, were as sobering as a bucket of cold water over his head. Shaw swallowed hard. Had something happened? Eager to help and reassure, he sat next to her on the sofa and leaned in close as he usually did, but she looked vacantly across the room and held her hands in her lap.

"Blaire, what is the matter?" he asked.

She spoke quietly. "Mr. Shaw, it would be best if you respectfully addressed me as Miss Haddington."

Was that all she had to say? They had long dispensed with such formalities, especially when alone together. Was she merely jesting? Or did her father not approve? Shaw saw no reason why her father wouldn't but supposed it was possible. Shaw knew he wasn't exactly a model gentleman, but wasn't he a decent fellow?

He asked again, "Blaire, please, tell me what is wrong."

She looked down at her hands. "Nothing is wrong."

Did she expect him to believe that? With words so hollow? "Blaire—"

"Miss Haddington!" This time she was firm, angry even.

Shaw gaped at her. He couldn't fathom what this was about. He had never seen her like this before, not with him. His arms itched to reach out and embrace her, to comfort her and fix whatever was wrong.

"Miss Haddington," he replied calmly. "What can I do to help you feel better?"

She shook her head and claimed, "I feel perfectly well."

Shaw chose to believe her this time, wanting her words to be true, and remembered what he had come for. He considered his next step and debated within. Something was clearly wrong with Blaire, but surely his surprise would be just the thing to pull her out of this dejection. If things went well, they would both walk away the happiest couple in England.

"My darling, Bla—Miss Haddington!" He spoke earnestly. "In the short time I have known you, my affection for you has grown stronger than I have ever known it to grow for anyone."

"Please—" she interrupted, but once Shaw had begun, he was determined to finish.

"Our time together has been short, but it is enough to convince me that I would be happy if the rest of my life were spent with you. Will you accept my hand, Blaire?"

Shaw took her hand and held it tight.

She pulled away.

"I am engaged to Mr. Hunt." This time, she looked Shaw in the eye, slowly at first but with such forced confidence, he knew it must be true.

His heart dropped to his stomach. He stood up so fast he nearly tripped over his own feet. He couldn't speak, and she said nothing else.

Then her mother came in.

"Did my daughter tell you the news?" Mrs. Haddington's proud voice pounded the truth in his brain like a hammer driving a nail into brick. "He will be able to provide for her more comfortably than any gentleman I can think of."

So, this was about money. Shaw couldn't believe it. His inheritance should have been ample enough. No, this was about more than money. This was about greed.

His mind raced for reasons Blaire should marry him instead. They were so much alike. They laughed at the same jokes. They . . . as he was about to speak, Blaire's sisters came in still giggling, one pointing her finger at him and the other covering her mouth. Shaw now realized they were laughing at him.

"Blaire!" His tone revealed a passion and hurt he wished he could hide.

He looked questioningly at her, but she shrugged her shoulders and looked off to the side. How could she remain so cool after all the time they had spent together? After that stolen kiss . . . She must have known what his intentions were. Her coldness, almost tangible now, finally pierced him. Bitterness and hurt welled up inside, terrifying to face, but the only defense he knew. How could she! He clenched his jaw, determined to fight her coldness with heat! With one last look at everyone, he cursed them all and stormed out.

He could hardly remember what else had happened that night, only that he lost all his money and fueled his anger with recklessness.

Shaw's reverie was suddenly disturbed by the clacking of carriages passing outside. He rubbed his forehead, sensing he had been in some sort of stupor. As he rolled over, thinking it mattered little whether he stayed awake or fell back asleep, he bumped his head on the wooden part of the armrest.

The jolt brought him back to the present moment with painful efficiency. He cursed the armrest, pounded it with his fist, then cursed Blaire for her disloyalty. She had married someone else for money. Now money was the only reason he had to marry, which to him was another way of saying he had no reason at all.

Still, he had his pride to consider. Even if he inherited the Everton estate, he would not let Philip strip away his birthright. Shaw would cling to what was rightfully his. A marriage to placate his father was the only way.

He rolled over once more and weighed his options. Elizabeth Watson was interested in him, but Shaw wouldn't risk entangling himself with her until he understood her reasons for marriage. Clara Everton was pretty and pleasant and seemed the least scheming of the women he knew. She didn't come with a grand fortune, but he was probably going to inherit her property in any event. Shouldn't that give him the upper hand somehow? He was certain Clara had been interested in him last season, but her interest seemed to have diminished since then. *Pity*, he thought, considering his need for haste.

He would simply persuade her to say yes anyway, and if he followed Harris's advice, which was the best he had at the moment, he would need to make it impossible for Clara to refuse him. But how? If she were spending the holidays with the Weltons in Brindley, he would need a reason to intrude on their hospitality.

Shaw stretched his head from side to side and massaged the crick in his neck. Just a little more pressure . . . and then he saw it! The way to secure Clara! Like rain cascading downward, a scheme descended on him so suddenly, so clearly that he saw all the necessary steps fall into place to overcome the obstacles. He knew what he had to do. He would go after Clara and put an end to his troubles, but first, he determined, rolling back his shoulders, it was time to pay another visit to Barnes.

Chapter 33

The Weltons' estate was larger than any Clara had ever seen before. From the carriage, she could see deer bounding through orchards, frozen ponds sparkling beyond the road, and vast fields lightly sprinkled with snow. Then she caught sight of Brindley Hall. Situated on high ground, Clara had an excellent view. One central block of house stood planted in the middle of extended portions of exaggerated hallways and more square sections of house. Clara thought it looked like one beautiful mansion had its arms around another. She wrapped her arms around herself, partly for warmth and partly to hold in her anticipation.

The sun was dipping behind the hills, changing the sky from pale pink to shadowy indigo. Very close now, the carriage entered a narrow path lined with trees. The wheels muffled over old, damp leaves that spread before them like a carpet.

Soon, the carriage rambled to the main doors where servants stood ready to receive their guests. As Clara stepped out, enjoying the use of her legs again, footmen began collecting trunks and ushering her inside before the flitting snowflakes had time to melt on her cheeks.

Inside, she stood with her aunt and uncle in a long, marbled entry hall with vaulted ceilings and detailed paintings depicting scenes from mythology. The finery and scale were grander than what Clara had observed in London but were balanced with enough space and light to awe without burdening one's senses. Clara might have fancied herself spirited into a fairy tale were it not for the cheerfully approachable couple who came tromping down the staircase with arms held wide.

"Bless my soul, Rose! Is it really you?" A woman who Clara assumed was Lady Welton took Rose's hand. "It's been too long! You don't know how glad I am to see you!" Clara could see tears brimming in Lady Welton's eyes as Rose returned the embrace.

Clara liked the way Lady Welton reminded her of Frances, only older, her eyes laughing and the corners of her lips constantly tilted up. Clara could also perceive the family resemblance between Lady Welton and Aunt Rose, which added to the sense of kinship Clara felt toward her.

The gentleman standing next to Lady Welton, presumably Sir Douglas, welcomed Uncle William by vigorously shaking his hand and patting him on the back. Sir Douglas's youthful face and healthy glow contrasted with his greying hair, boasting of a spirit and strength that defied age.

Clara felt her own spirits rise with her hosts' enthusiasm. Until they turned their attentions to her.

With a closed-lip smile that hinted of pity, Lady Welton took her hand. "My dear, you must be Miss Clara Everton. I've heard that you are in need of some cheering up."

Clara's eyes widened. *Oh, no!* Aunt Rose must have hinted something of Clara's disappointments in her reply to Lady Welton's invitation. Clara hadn't expected the Weltons to know details about the catastrophe with Mr. Thayne.

As if perceiving her thoughts, Lady Welton added, "Now don't look so worried! Rose here hasn't betrayed any confidence. She only mentioned that you were feeling a little down and could benefit from a pleasant holiday." She patted Clara's hand warmly. "This is just the place to be cheered up. It's delightful to meet you!"

"Thank you for your kindness, Lady Welton," Clara said, only somewhat relieved, but with real sincerity.

"Come," Lady Welton waved them up the stairs. "I'll walk with you."

They followed two maids upstairs to a small sitting room that connected the bedchamber meant for Clara to that of her aunt and uncle. Clara peaked in her room, pleased to see that the Weltons had thought of everything for her comfort, from extra blankets and pillows on her bed to warm drinks and biscuits on the table. The maids stood ready to help Clara and Rose dress for dinner and dancing, which was to take place later that evening to welcome the guests.

Before Lady Welton left Clara and her relatives to the privacy of their chambers, she added, "Don't be too long. There will be some fine eligible young gentlemen here tonight who can cure any heartache quickly enough or, at the very least, make you forget it!"

Clara bit her cheek.

Lady Welton continued, "There will also be some ladies here who will make pleasant company. Mrs. Watson is coming with her daughter, Elizabeth, about your age I'd reckon. I imagine you two will get along well, and . . ."

Clara lost attention for everything else Lady Welton said after that, but it wasn't for lack of trying. She just couldn't get past the reference to Elizabeth Watson. Rose looked questioningly at Clara but had probably not caught the meaning of it all. Clara closed her eyes and hoped it was just another girl who also happened to be called Elizabeth Watson. Surely it was a common enough name, but as Clara went to her room to dress for the evening's festivities, she had a feeling she was not going to escape the tangle of a mess she had fallen into with Mr. Thayne. With luck, this Miss Watson wouldn't know a thing about the whole misunderstanding.

But Clara's instincts told her otherwise.

Clara wore her blue silk dress accented with lace. It was one of her finer dresses, and she liked the way the cool material hung from her figure and brought out her eyes. With one last look in the glass, she braced herself, breathed deeply, and exhaled slowly. It was time to meet a house full of guests, one of which was the girl who had actually caught the attention of the one man Clara had come to care for.

She descended the marble staircase slowly, holding her head high and running her hand lightly on the cool lacquered wood of the rail. She promised herself she would not immediately dislike Elizabeth Watson, even if Mr. Thayne did prefer her.

At least there were other people for Clara to meet as well. Earlier, she had taken a wrong turn in the unfamiliar house intending to find her aunt, but instead, she met Thomas and Emma Bailey, a brother and sister who were the nephew and niece of Lady Welton. They appeared close in age to Clara and had also recently come from London. After exchanging a few words of welcome, they kindly reoriented Clara so she could find her relatives.

Not long after, Clara met Rose and William at the bottom of the stairs and crossed the main hall where they were greeted with the sights of a holiday ball and the sounds of rising conversation and tinkling glasses. Musicians and neighboring gentry were gathering to dance and ring in the holiday season. Holly boughs ornamented doorways and fireplaces. Red ribbon swirled around banisters and columns like icing on cake, and evergreen sprigs tied with gold string hung in the windowpanes. Clara breathed deeply again, taking in the fresh pine scent, and renewed her resolve to enjoy herself. In the commotion of all the heartache and embarrassment she had lately been dosed, she had forgotten it was almost Christmas.

Rose and William were quickly swept up by the Weltons who began introducing them to other guests. Clara hung back to make her own observations and study the new faces at her own pace. She kept to the perimeters of the room, not yet ready to enter the tumult of the party, when her sights caught hold of one face she would never forget.

There by the fireplace, standing tall and effortlessly attractive, was James Thayne. Clara suddenly forgot how to breathe and held her stomach tight. Confusion and uncertainty bore down on her so heavily that she couldn't walk or take her eyes off him. What on earth was he doing there? Had he always been so handsome?

He was talking with Mr. and Miss Bailey and smiled often. He tilted his head occasionally and showed all the signs of an attentive listener. Clara could hear them laughing. Seeing him so unexpectedly close yet so beyond her reach left her mind throbbing and her chest aching.

When last they met, Mr. Thayne had looked completely embarrassed. Now, among friends, he carried himself with confidence. Clara watched the creases around his mouth curve up in harmony with the clean lines of his cheek and jaw. The light from the fire flickered in his hazel eyes, and he continued to smile as he talked. Clara imagined he had looked that way when he wrote to her about . . . but never mind!

It hadn't really been her he was writing to. Mr. Thayne had intended those letters for someone else.

Just as the memory settled along with the inevitable disappointment, Mr. Thayne looked her way and their eyes met. His composure was lost for only a second, hardly long enough for anyone to notice unless they were watching for it, which Clara was.

With little time to collect her thoughts, she realized Mr. Thayne had excused himself from his friends and was striding toward her. She turned from side to side as if there might be someplace else to go, but of course, there wasn't. Mr. Thayne was coming, and she would have to face him. Her breathing became shallow, and the closer he got, the more she fidgeted with her fan, pulled on her glove, and pushed loose curls away from her eye.

"Miss Everton." Mr. Thayne bowed, his eyes eager but unsure. "I . . . I had no idea you would be here . . ."

He paused, waiting, but Clara had no words to fill the space.

He began again, "I assumed you would still be in town, and well . . . I also assumed you would prefer that we not keep meeting in society, so I accepted an invitation in the country. Here."

"Yes, well . . ." It took a few heartbeats, but Clara swallowed her timidity and straightened her back. She would not allow this man to put her off balance. "Lady Welton is my Aunt Rose's cousin. I was invited for Christmas."

"Then I must beg your pardon for intruding on your visit. I honestly didn't know."

"As I told you last time we met," Clara was certain she detected a slight grimace from him, "there is no need to apologize. I certainly hope you enjoy your time here. Now if you will excuse me . . ."

"Miss Everton?"

"Yes, sir?"

"When the time comes, may I have the first dance?"

Clara almost lost her balance. In their letters, hadn't they once promised each other a dance? She could feel the blush rise to her cheeks and deepen as she tripped over her words. "Oh. All right."

Once Clara comprehended that she had just agreed to dance with Mr. Thayne, she scolded herself for letting him catch her off guard. He bowed and walked off, looking over his shoulder at her a second and third time. She merely looked away, wishing she had not followed him with her eyes, but her eyes instinctually sought him out again and again.

The thought of dancing with Mr. Thayne made her want to run and hide, but part of her undeniably wanted it, if only to prove to him that she was desirable. She wanted him to regret his actions and feel his loss, but she also wanted to pretend like their first awkward meeting had never happened. Perhaps this dance could be a new beginning.

She discarded the idea as quickly as it came, reminding herself that still wanting Mr. Thayne was naïve and misguided. It was only a small part of her that still wanted him anyway, and she would work on extinguishing it.

"Miss Everton, it's a pleasure to see you again. Are you enjoying yourself so far?"

Clara hadn't heard the question at first but then realized Mr. Bailey was addressing her. After an awkward pause, she said yes, everything was lovely.

"Are you acquainted with Mr. Thayne? You two appear to know each other."

Clara stuttered out her answer. "Oh, yes. I suppose, yes. We were . . . introduced in London."

"Only introduced?" Mr. Bailey looked over at Mr. Thayne who was again looking at Clara from across the room. Mr. Bailey raised an eyebrow, cleared his throat and said, "Then I hope you will be my first dance partner this evening."

"Oh. Thank you, but I'm afraid I just promised the first dance to Mr. Thayne."

Mr. Bailey's smile faltered but quickly recovered. "Well, the second then?"

Clara finally took a good look at him. He was not quite as tall as Mr. Thayne, but he carried himself well. His pale blonde hair was short and straight and his features young and smooth, as if he had recently grown into his role as a gentleman, but his voice was strong, and his light grey eyes looked intelligent. Clara promised him the second dance.

As she spoke to Mr. Bailey, she noticed that Mr. Thayne kept glancing her way. At one point, a smile flickered in the corner of his mouth, and she realized he must have thought she was stealing glances at him too. Her face reddened, and she began searching the room for something else to look at when two little girls with dark blonde hair and pink ribbons ran in, the older in pursuit of the younger as they weaved in every direction through taller guests' legs.

"Stop! STOP! Make her stop!" the littlest girl cried out with just as much delight, Clara thought, as distress.

Grunts from the men and exclamations of "Oh, my!" from the older ladies could be heard throughout the ballroom.

The younger girl kept running until she stopped behind Mr. Thayne and grabbed his legs. The older girl skidded on the floor as she caught up and planted herself directly in front of Mr. Thayne, essentially trapping him, while trying to catch her younger playmate who dodged from side to side.

A middle-aged woman with a brown messy bun and a wiry build came marching into the room with a look that communicated pure frustration. Her high-pitched voice was stern but pleading. "Emily! Mabel! Come back to the nursery at once!"

The littlest only clutched Mr. Thayne's right leg more tightly. She then sat on his foot, wrapped both her hands and feet around his leg, and tucked her face in. "I won't!" came her stubborn but muffled cry as the other girl snatched at her hair.

Clara observed shock and annoyance on several guests' faces, but Clara loved the chaos. She did not often have the chance to be around small children, but when she did, she relished their pure, unrestrained spirit. She noted that Mr. Thayne did not seem bothered by the interruption either.

"Perhaps I can be of service," he said with a slight bow. "Which way to the nursery, Miss Stanley?"

Clara watched as Miss Stanley, who she assumed was the governess, pinched the top of her nose and pointed toward a door in the back of the room.

"Right," said Mr. Thayne. With a look of cheerful resignation, he proceeded to take large steps with the younger girl still attached to his leg. His smile widened as the child's protests turned to laughter. The other girl watched and skipped alongside them until she pounced on Mr. Thayne's other leg. Clara laughed as he stumbled a little with the surprise attack. He looked down at the two girls, then proceeded to walk with large, swinging footsteps as Miss Stanley guided the way.

Soon, Lady Welton was profusely apologizing for the scene, though Clara saw no need for her to do so. The girls' timing had been perfect. Their interruption had loosened the knot in Clara's chest and cleared her thoughts. With a laugh, Lady Welton explained that Emily and Mabel, ages six and eight, were her granddaughters who were staying for the holidays under the supervision of their governess while their parents toured Europe. Though sweet and affectionate, the girls were apparently difficult to manage. Lady Welton predicted that the guests would become well acquainted with them during their stay at Brindley.

Clara certainly hoped so. Their presence promised to make her stay more enjoyable, though she reminded herself not to discount the other guests. She braced herself for the moment she would meet Miss Watson, but the moment never came. Miss Watson was not there. She and her mother were late in their travels and would be arriving in the next day or two.

Then, like a simple arithmetic problem, the sum of Clara's troubles was clear. Miss Watson and Mr. Thayne would both be there. At the Weltons'. Under the same roof. And Clara forced to watch them together. It was too much. Clara hastily excused herself and stepped into the hallway to hide as she processed her plight. Barely alone, she slumped against the wall. Her hand instinctually covered her heart to secure it from the coldness that was creeping all over. What had she done to make fortune her enemy? How had such a fateful trap been sprung?

With all her hopes once again turned upside down, Clara decided her only option was to beg Rose and William to take her back to Milton. She could collect her belongings and call for the carriage in mere moments, making a tidy escape.

When she stepped back into the ballroom, she saw her aunt and uncle standing right where she had left them, talking and laughing with the Weltons. Rose and William looked so happy. She knew they would convey her to Milton if she insisted on it, but she did not want to add "ruining her generous relatives' holiday" to her list of regrets.

No, she could not be so inconsiderate and selfish as to ask them to inconvenience themselves again on her whim.

She resigned herself to stay. *What a holiday it will be*, she lamented. She would simply have to find ways to pass the time and distract herself from further heartache. *Perhaps I shall hide in the nursery with Emily and Mabel.*

Clara's attention was suddenly called back to the festivities as Sir Douglas gave the signal, and the musicians tuned their instruments. Mr. Thayne had not yet returned from the nursery to claim his dance with her, so she chose a place along the wall to watch the others. Perhaps she would be spared the embarrassment of having to dance with Mr. Thayne.

Mr. Bailey approached her instead. "You're not dancing," he stated with a raised eyebrow. "I can only assume that your partner, who seems to be missing, could not expect you to sit out the first dance. So perhaps I may—"

"Her partner is right here!"

Clara turned around to see Mr. Thayne advancing with triumph in his grin. His hair and cravat, however, were messy and crooked as if they had been tugged at by little hands. Mr. Thayne ran his fingers through his hair and offered Clara his hand. She would have liked to see what other games he had played with those girls before leaving them in the care of Miss Stanley, and somehow, lost in the thought, Clara forgot to dread dancing with Mr. Thayne. In fact, she reached out most willingly and took his hand.

They walked side by side, close enough for Clara to tell he was slightly winded from hurrying back to the dance floor. Curious and full of questions, Clara stole several sideways glances at him and noticed he did the same. As they took their places among the couples, Clara had no choice but to meet his eyes head on. Perplexed by his attentions, she stood very still and tried to breathe regularly.

Like rain, the music trickled lightly at first, then simpered and swelled until it flooded the room and urged the couples to give way to the melody. Clara knew the dance well, but her movements were calculated and choppy. She was usually graceful on the dance floor, but with Mr. Thayne standing so close, she could hardly concentrate on the rhythms. Instead, her attention became ensnared by the warmth of his hand as he firmly held hers. Try as she might, she could not ignore how his thumb caressed her fingers each time their hands clasped. Was he doing that on purpose?

Finally, the effort to resist was too much. Casting worries aside, Clara tuned into his touch and tried to believe in the hope in his eyes. Her doubts were suspended for one heavenly moment, but as she and Mr. Thayne separated to spin around another couple, the spell was broken, and she startled at how eagerly Mr. Thayne took hold of her hand again. Her reservations returned, and she became painfully aware of how earnestly she had been watching him and how tightly she had been holding his hand in return. She loosened her grip and again focused on the steps.

There were moments when Clara thought Mr. Thayne was going to say something, but he never did. The quiet between them, felt even amidst the music, became too unnerving to endure.

"Those girls seem like quite a handful," Clara ventured.

"Yes!" Thayne laughed, looking grateful she had spoken. "They certainly are spirited."

Clara agreed and nothing more was said for a time. As she spun around, she saw her aunt and uncle watching them. Aunt Rose covered her mouth with her hand, and Uncle William stood dumbstruck, but only for a second. Soon, he wore a huge grin. Then he bent forward and shook with low rumbling laughter. When he stood up, Rose whacked him in the arm with her fan, though she was chuckling too. Clara knew Mr. Thayne could not be oblivious to the scene those two were making, and she missed a step.

Mr. Thayne cleared his throat. "Miss Everton . . ." The music suddenly gained tempo and everyone spun. Clara listened attentively as she faced him again. "I would like to know whether you prefer I leave Brindley for the time being."

Clara didn't know what she had been expecting to hear from him, but this was not it. "I'm not sure I understand you."

"Well," he continued, "I fear my presence here makes you uncomfortable. Truly, I came not expecting to see you, and I do not wish to upset your holiday." His eyes wandered over to Rose and William.

Clara stiffened. "Are you so certain it is your presence making me uncomfortable or could it be that my presence is offending you?"

He opened his mouth, but no words came out. He and Clara separated and circled around the other couples. When they rejoined, he answered, "I mean you no offense, and your presence here is quite the opposite of offensive."

Clara grudgingly liked how the right side of his mouth tilted up sometimes when he talked.

Mr. Thayne continued, "It would please me to stay. I only offer as a gentleman to put my own wishes aside to make your visit more pleasant."

"I see . . ." Clara considered his words. He wanted to stay but would leave if she requested it. She was convinced he was trying to be kind, but did he really mean it? She was sorely tempted to test him, but her pride would not let him leave on her account. "And what exactly are your wishes?"

"To stay here with you," he stated simply.

Clara missed another step. Had she heard him correctly? Her heart sped up. What could he mean by it? After their last disastrous exchange, she couldn't imagine he was sincere, but everything in his look suggested he was. For another brief, blissful moment, Clara allowed herself to hope that James Thayne's heart might genuinely turn to her.

Yet, it felt too easy. She couldn't believe his feelings were changed so suddenly. Did he really think that one dance was enough to regain her affection, let alone resolve the hurt he'd caused her?

Then Clara remembered another reason why he might be there. "What about Miss Watson? Should you not also like to be here with her?"

This time, Mr. Thayne missed a step. "I was unaware she would be a guest here. Truly, I came not knowing who any of the other guests would be. Miss Everton, there is so much to say . . ." He trailed off. Squeezing her hand and looking directly in her eyes, he said, "I only consider myself fortunate to have another chance with you."

"I'm not sure I care to give you a second chance." She regretted it the second it was out of her mouth.

She saw him flinch.

"I suppose I deserve that," he acknowledged, stirring in her a strange mix of longing and regret. Warmly, he added, "But I'm not afraid of a challenge."

Clara almost smiled, but no matter how much she wanted to believe him, her pain was not so easily forgotten. She would be more cautious this time.

As the last notes of the dance eased to a silence, Clara dipped into a curtsey and rose to find her aunt, but Mr. Thayne begged her attention a little longer.

"Miss Everton? Do I assume correctly that I remain here with your approval?"

It was only one short holiday. Clara could manage with him there for a few weeks. She would be grown up about all this. She would not have him leave on her account.

"Yes," she answered clearly. There was so much she could say, but it was time to dance with Mr. Bailey. She smiled and hoped Mr. Thayne would understand she was being polite.

Thayne made his decision right then. He was going to spend his holiday doing everything he could to earn Clara's affection. She was right for him. He could feel it, and this was his opportunity to prove to her that he was right for her too. It would be inconvenient, to say the least, to have Miss Watson wandering around as a guest, but maybe that would allow Thayne another avenue to prove to Clara how much his heart had changed.

He had spent the last few days reviewing the letters he and Clara had exchanged. Reading through them again, this time with a clearer understanding of who she was, stirred all the same feelings as before. Only this time, those feelings ran deeper as he learned to see her face behind those words. By the time he got through all the letters, his regret of losing her had thickened and stuck inside him.

Then to have her show up like this! What had he done to deserve such a blessing! He was a fool for ever letting her get away. And when he saw her standing there across the room? Fear and hope and anticipation had boiled up faster than he thought possible. He would not, absolutely could not let this chance with Clara pass by.

When he had left her standing there at Mrs. Chelsea's ball less than a fortnight earlier, he thought his disappointment would be too difficult to overcome. Yet, the initial shock had worn off, and he began to see that it was not Clara that had disappointed him. He had just felt like such a fool for mixing up Miss Watson and Clara in the first place. Duty had driven him to make Clara that tepid marriage offer, but pride had turned him into a coward who ran away.

As he watched Clara dance with Mr. Bailey, he chose to be humble. He would admit his fault. He would reject his pride. He would do anything for Clara. He would even make a fool of himself again so long as it was for her this time. Seeing her spin, graceful and glowing, made him keenly aware of what he wanted.

His old friend, William Martin, also an unexpected though pleasant guest at the Weltons', came up to Thayne and gave him a jovial slap on the back.

Martin was still laughing as he shook his head and said, "We came here to get away from you! Ha ha!"

Thayne merely watched Martin make his wheezy laugh, the one that indicated he was much too entertained by this coincidence.

Sir Douglas joined them and put his heavy hand on Thayne's shoulder as if he were already in on the joke. "That was terrible, Thayne! I've never seen two people so obviously smitten with each other so awkward while dancing! Shall I offer you some courting tips?"

Thayne shrugged off their hands, "No, thank you. Not necessary. Wait. Two people so obviously smitten with each other?"

Sir Douglas replied matter-of-factly, "Of course! You saw it, didn't you Martin?"

This started Martin laughing again as he nodded his head.

Sir Douglas added, "It is fortunate it happened so fast. I hear that girl has recently experienced a heartache of some sort. No doubt, she will recover quickly with you around, eh, Thayne?"

This comment pierced Thayne to the core. He knew the exact cause of Clara's heartache. He drew his brows together and answered, "I hope so."

As Thayne paced the floor in his room that night, his emotions were in flux. Oh, what Clara must think of him! How he had treated her! At least she hadn't asked him to leave. No doubt, endearing himself to her again would require finesse. In such a small circle of people, his advances would not go unnoticed, but so be it. He wanted Clara. He could not risk hiding even the smallest amount of affection he now felt for her. Now was no time to fuss over propriety. Thayne sat down and planned his next move.

Chapter 34

$\mathcal{C}$lara opened her eyes feeling more rested than she had in weeks. Out her window, a pale, cloudy sky hinted of snow but gave no indication of how late she had slept. The maid had not yet come in to stoke the fire, so Clara huddled in her blankets feeling luxuriously lazy. With nothing but breakfast to concern herself with that morning, she waited until her dreams drifted from memory and then stood to stretch. Before leaving her room, she changed into a simple green morning dress and wrapped her hair up without much concern. Then, grabbing a cream-colored shawl, she wandered to the library, hoping for a quiet hour of reading before breakfast.

Clara should have known that her aunt, who was familiar with her habits, would be there waiting. As soon as Clara entered the library, Rose took her by the shoulders. "Oh, Clara! I had no idea he would be here! I promise you, I didn't!"

Clara hugged her aunt, too refreshed by sleep to let anything bother her. "I know you didn't."

"Well, what should we do?" Rose clasped her hands and prodded Clara with all the questions she didn't get to ask the night before. What was Mr. Thayne doing there? Did Clara mind that he was there? What would she do? What would she say? What would she wear? Somewhere between Rose's questions and apologies, Clara kissed her on the forehead and informed her that she was hungry.

Clara was trying not to think about James Thayne as she walked downstairs and sat at the breakfast table. She tried not to think about how they had danced together and how he had said he wanted to stay at Brindley to be near her. No, she would not think of it. Instead, she would focus on the spread of breads, ham, and fruit preserves laid out before her. She really was hungry.

Lady Welton was the only person sitting at breakfast when Clara and Rose arrived. After a warm greeting, she smiled broadly and invited them to eat. Clara chose a seat and reached for a warm piece of bread, tempted by the buttery smell it emitted, but froze when Mr. Thayne was suddenly at her side settling into the seat next to her and wishing her a good morning.

He held a small bough of holly in his hand. "Flowers are scarce this time of year, but I found this outside and thought it the next best thing." He twirled it in his fingers, letting the berries show off their vibrant hue. "I thought it might brighten your room."

Clara reached for the gift, their fingers close.

"Thank you," she said, cautious not to be too delighted by the unexpected gesture.

A few strands of hair fell across her eyes as she likewise twirled the holly bough. Why hadn't she done more to tame her hair before coming down to breakfast? Twirling the holly in the opposite direction, she noticed a tiny glint of white peeking out from the green this time. Her hand paused. A small piece of paper was tucked into the holly. Clara looked up at Mr. Thayne, who ever so slightly smiled when their eyes met. She nonchalantly smoothed back her hair as she lowered the holly into her lap where no one would see her remove the note before laying the holly next to her plate.

Mr. Thayne reached for his serviette and greeted Rose and Lady Welton. Both ladies gave Mr. Thayne an affectionate, maternal look as they wished him a good morning. Once Rose and Lady Welton started eating and fell into their own conversation, Clara risked a glance at the tiny note in her lap.

Accompany me on a walk? There is something I would like to show you. —JT

"What would you like to do today, Miss Everton?"

Clara jumped at Lady Welton's question.

"Oh, well . . ." she considered, "I . . . thought I might go for a walk." Clara scrunched her brows together, hardly believing she had just said that. From the corner of her eye, she saw Mr. Thayne smile behind his teacup.

"In this weather?" Lady Welton exclaimed. "Mr. Thayne, you must accompany her and ensure she stays warm."

Before he could answer, Emily and Mabel ran in with just as much spirit as the previous night.

Mabel shouted, "I get first choice of the jams because I'm the oldest!"

Emily spoke louder. "No, I get first choice because I'm the cutest!"

"Girls, please!" cried Lady Welton. "Where is Miss Stanley?"

The girls replied with giggles and gave each other knowing looks.

Lady Welton closed her eyes and mumbled to herself, "I shall call myself lucky if Miss Stanley does not quit before Christmas."

The girls bumped into the back of Clara's chair as they ran past her crying, "James!" After several pushes and nudges, the girls managed to share the chair on the other side of Mr. Thayne.

"Good morning, ladies!" he said with exaggerated deference. "I would like to introduce you to my good friend, Miss Clara Everton." He leaned back and gestured toward Clara.

Clara smiled, but the girls eyed her warily.

Miss Stanley came into the room, out of breath and scowling. She sharply clapped her hands twice. "Back to the nursery, both of you! The jam is just as good up there as it is down here, but if you do not come this instant, there will be no jam for you at all!"

Mabel and Emily solemnly nodded and gave Mr. Thayne a hug before joining Miss Stanley. Emily called out, "Don't forget your promise!"

"Never!" Mr. Thayne cheerfully called back. Then, with a more serious expression, he added, "Don't forget yours!" The girls nodded vigorously, curls bouncing, and primly followed Mrs. Stanley out of the room.

"Your promise?" Clara asked Mr. Thayne.

"Yes," he answered. "I promised I would join them for theater tonight but only if they behave for Miss Stanley today."

"Theater?"

"Play theater," he clarified with a wink.

"That is very kind of you, Mr. Thayne," Rose commented.

Mr. Thayne thanked Rose and looked straight at Clara. Nervous from his attentions, she shakily picked up her cup and gulped down several mouthfuls of hot chocolate. The smooth liquid slid straight down her throat and warmed her up too quickly, and with a face that was red from more than just the chocolate, she met his eyes.

Mr. Thayne said, "Now, about that walk?"

Thayne was immensely relieved when Clara agreed to join him. All morning he had feared she would decline. He had completely underestimated the courage it would take to unapologetically court Clara when, at any moment, she could turn her nose at him. Asking her to dance the night before had been an impulsive act, driven by sheer desire and unhindered only because he was desperate to show her he was sincere. Bolstered by the fact that she did indeed dance with him and had even smiled at him, he promised to put his whole heart into this.

He would have been completely content walking with Clara if only he knew what she was thinking. Courting Clara would take time, but his instincts told him that this holiday at the Weltons' was crucial. It was the only time he had to make things right with her. It would be too easy for them to go their separate ways after that. He had a few weeks at best.

He watched Clara out of the corner of his eye and listened to her feet hit the gravel. Her breath came out in white wisps while loose strands of hair flew around her face. He memorized the way her cheeks flushed in the cold, bringing out the pink in her lips.

"Are you warm enough, Miss Everton?"

"Yes, thank you."

She glanced at him briefly, and he forgot what he was going to say next. Her eyes were such a bright, deep blue with silvery grey flecks and lashes that spread around them like petals on a flower. She had a tiny mole under the corner of her right eye that sat atop her cheek like a tear. The more Thayne noticed little details like that, the more he was drawn to her. First impressions and embarrassing mishaps were growing dim in memory. All he saw now was this radiant young woman he wanted to know better.

Clara asked, "Are we going anywhere in particular, Mr. Thayne?"

"Indeed. I thought we might go to the stables. There is someone there I would like you to meet."

"Oh." Her tone was positive but hesitant.

Thayne tuned into her every movement, the tilt of her head, the lightness in her step, and considered the things he still needed to say, the things he should have said when he made that awkward proposal in London. Fighting against the tightness in his throat, he spoke quickly. "I never meant to hurt you, you know. I am so sorry."

He could see the tension in Clara's eyes before she looked off to the side. Her voice was quiet as she spoke. "I'm sorry for the disappointment you felt when you realized it was me."

Ouch. Thayne received her words like a jab to his ribs. "I do not feel any disappointment now." He watched her expectantly, watching for any change in demeanor, any sign that she believed him.

"I'm glad to hear you say it, but you have no idea how much it hurt, even if it was all a misunderstanding. I felt like such a fool standing there listening to you and my uncle—"

Thayne groaned. "You heard that?"

She looked down and nodded. "Every word. I was the wrong girl."

Thayne would have smacked his head against a tree trunk just then if one had been close enough. He had been so stupid in London, as Clara knew all too well. He needed her to know how he felt now. Emboldened, he put his finger on her chin and gently guided her face up to meet his eyes. He nearly melted to finally know how soft her skin was, but he kept his voice steady. "I now know for certain that you are not the wrong girl."

Clara's gaze pierced him to the core. She looked hopeful but delicate, and he hoped she would trust him. He wanted her to know how grateful he was that her uncle had directed him to her, even if it had started out as a mistake. He wanted to tell her that the Clara he had become acquainted with through letters had enchanted him, but being in her presence was much more potent.

Just as Thayne was organizing his thoughts into words, all the hope in Clara's face dissolved and she turned away.

"It still hurts," she whispered.

Yes, it does, he thought. If his hurt was even a fraction of the pain he had caused her, he could leave no room for her to doubt him.

When the stables came into view, Clara increased her pace and stepped directly onto a patch of ice and lost her balance.

Thayne didn't even think. His reaction was instant. He reached out just in time, firmly wrapping his arms around hers to catch and steady her. She quietly thanked him but stared into his face like a scared animal. He was afraid he had done something wrong and was about to apologize, but her eyes relaxed and she didn't move away. His first thought was to pull her close. For just a second, he felt as if she might want him to, but it was too soon for that. Clara needed to know first that she was important to him. He would take his time and wait until there was no doubt whether they should reach for each other.

He let go, slowly, and let her lead the way.

The warmth of the stables hit as soon as they crossed the threshold, and the familiar smell of animals mixed with hay and damp earth was everywhere. They greeted a nearby stable hand and approached the horses.

"Awww," Clara gushed as she walked up to a midnight-colored horse and began rubbing its nose. "Aren't you a handsome horse!" She looked around for something to feed it. "This makes me miss Rabbit!"

Thayne relished her uninhibited smile. He stepped close and rubbed the horse's neck. "Miss Everton, allow me to introduce you to my good friend, Knight."

She beamed at Thayne and then spoke to the horse. "I feel as if we are already friends."

Clara found a carrot in a nearby feeding trough and held it to Knight's mouth. She continued to rub his head and neck as she whispered more compliments. Thayne envied all the attention his horse was getting, but he could have stood there with Clara all day.

After talking to Knight, she remarked to Thayne, "I can see why you feel like a knight on such a fine horse. He is even more beautiful than I imagined from your letters."

Thayne could see her suddenly stiffen. It was the first time she referenced something he had written to her about. She cleared her throat and looked down.

Thayne could only guess what she was feeling, but he wanted to make one thing clear. "Miss Everton, those letters were for *you*. I didn't know it at the time, but I now believe that they were always meant for you. I'm glad, so immensely glad they went to you."

Thayne wasn't always the best with words. It was one of the reasons he had favored writing in the first place. He hoped that, at least this time, he had said the right thing.

Clara looked up at him with a half-smile. "I'd like to believe that."

As Clara fed and brushed the horses, she struggled to stay upset with Mr. Thayne. Like ice melting in the sun, her resolve was thinning under the heat of his earnest eyes. She told herself that he had merely caught her in a good mood and knew from her letters that being in the stables would put her at ease. It had nothing to do with his kind manner or thoughtful gestures, and it certainly had nothing to do with his dark hair or hazel eyes or confident smile. If anything, Mr. Thayne was just being civil. Any special attentions beyond that she would choose to ignore.

She closed her eyes and vowed to be more careful.

Clara had nothing against Mr. Thayne's horse, however, so she continued to dote on Knight. When she noticed his water was low, Mr. Thayne went to search the yard for the stable hand they had seen earlier. Clara walked over to a light brown speckled horse that looked envious of all the attention Knight was getting. She said hello and held her hand out for it to sniff and nuzzle. As she picked up a brush, she heard the wood creak beneath heavy boots. *Mr. Thayne has returned,* she thought, with the hint of a smile.

"Miss Everton!" spoke a different, more formal voice. "What a pleasure it is to see you here. Are you fond of horses?" Mr. Bailey stood in the middle of the stalls with his hands behind his back. His fashionable riding jacket looked like it never got dirty.

"Yes, Mr. Bailey. I enjoy their company."

Mr. Bailey tilted his head back and chuckled, startling Clara. Had she said something amusing? As he came closer, she could smell freshly laundered clothing and some spice that she could not quite identify. It was pleasant but clashed with the earthy smells of the stables.

"I am having my horse prepared for a ride," he stated. "Even in such cold weather, I find riding very invigorating. Would you join me?"

Clara was about to explain that she was there with Mr. Thayne, but there was no need. Mr. Thayne walked in at just that moment.

"What a splendid idea!" Mr. Thayne said as he clapped his hands together. "What do you say, Miss Everton? Shall we join him for a ride?"

With narrowed eyes, Mr. Bailey enunciated his words. "Mr. Thayne. As usual, your timing is impeccable."

Mr. Thayne replied with a nod and a grin.

Truthfully, Clara didn't want to go for a ride, not with Mr. Thayne, not with Mr. Bailey, and definitely not with both of them. She wanted to go back to the house and get cleaned up. The almost comfortable moment with Mr. Thayne was broken, and Clara remembered that Elizabeth Watson was still coming.

"Actually I—" Clara began but was stopped short by a sudden quaking filled with screaming, neighing, and crashing. Somewhere in the far end of the stable, metal clanked to the ground. Clara's muscles tensed and the hair on the back of her neck prickled. Though the crash lasted only a second, the neighing continued and was soon followed by deep groaning.

Turning toward the noise, Clara saw the stable hand lying precariously close to a skittish grey horse that was rearing and stomping just beyond its stall. The man was shielding his face with his arm while trying to pull himself away with the other. When he tried to use his legs, he cried out in pain and rolled to his side, revealing a face smeared with blood.

Mr. Thayne rushed to the stable hand's side and struggled to gain hold under his arms, presumably to pull him out of the horse's reach. Clara's mind raced as the horse continued to kick and stomp close to where they were. She remembered once seeing her father calm an agitated horse with slow movements and soft words. Perhaps she could do the same with this horse. She walked slowly toward it, holding out her hand and talking in soothing tones.

"Easy, easy," she repeated.

After several seconds, the horse stopped stomping and began sniffing her hand. Clara wondered whether it liked the smell of her lavender soap. Soon, she sensed Mr. Thayne slowly coming to her side.

"That's it," he whispered.

The horse was letting Clara and Mr. Thayne rub its neck. Clara could feel the horse's heartbeat slowing and the tension in its neck relaxing. Mr. Thayne gingerly took the horse by its bridle and walked it back into the stall. When Clara stepped away, the horse whinnied as if in complaint, but once Mr. Thayne exited and closed the stall door, the horse quietly turned to its hay.

Now that the horse was no longer a danger, Clara hurried to the stable hand, who was still groaning on the floor, and bundled up her scarf to prop under his head as an improvised pillow. He was trying to speak, but she couldn't understand him. Mr. Thayne knelt next to Clara and began blotting the injured man's face with a handkerchief.

"Bailey, go send for the doctor!" Mr. Thayne cried.

Mr. Bailey didn't budge. He hadn't moved from his original spot throughout the whole ordeal, though he did look paler than usual. Instead of running for the doctor, he stumbled back and shook his head. "I . . . I was about to ride . . . sh—should have been more careful with my horse . . . He—he'll be fine . . ."

Mr. Thayne ignored Mr. Bailey's ramblings and took Clara's hand in both of his. In a firm but calm voice, he said, "Clara, please. Go send for the doctor."

Clara instantly stood up. Mr. Thayne looked fervently in her eyes and pressed her hand before letting go. With a heart that raced for many reasons, she left the stables and ran back to the house, avoiding slushy puddles and patches of ice. Somewhere in the back of her mind, she registered the fact that Mr. Thayne had held her hand and called her by her Christian name. She had no time to reflect on it, however, because right now, she was needed.

When she arrived at the house, she grabbed the arm of the first person she saw, a maid who was dusting. "Man injured," she panted. "Just now in the stables. We need a doctor!"

Miss Stanley and Lady Welton walked by just as Clara finished instructing the maid, so Clara repeated her message again. A doctor was sent for, and Clara had a moment to catch her breath. Sir Douglas was also called, so he and another servant went out to the stables to see what was needed. Clara waited to see how else she might help, but within moments, she was alone in the hallway with nothing to do but hope the injured man would be all right.

After getting cleaned up, Clara spent the next few hours sitting restlessly by the fire in the drawing room with the other ladies. She held a pencil and sketchbook but hardly drew at all. She was waiting for Mr. Thayne to come with news, but there was no sign of him.

The stillness of the drawing room pressed on Clara until Miss Bailey began a frantic song on the pianoforte that prompted her into movement. Clara left her chair to examine books, paintings, and eventually, the scenery through the windows, which proved to be the most calming. Soon, she left the drawing room to follow the windows in the hallway, mentally mapping where she was inside in relation to the gardens outside. As she turned a corner, the view changed from the manicured gardens to dormant vegetable beds and a hot house, and just beyond, the stables. They looked just as they did that morning, but Clara's view locked on a person standing out there.

Perhaps she was mistaken, but no. Mr. Thayne was standing at the edge of a copse chopping firewood. What he was doing out there? Surely there were other servants to take care of such chores. She watched him pick up a new log and properly position it before swinging down hard. The wood split, and Mr. Thayne stood up and wiped sweat off his forehead with the back of his arm. He must have been working for some time to be sweating in the cold. It looked like strenuous labor.

Clara watched as he positioned another log, raised the axe, and swung again. She was entranced by the repetition of the task and the strength in Mr. Thayne's swings. There was not a single other gentleman she knew who would be willing to do servant's work like that, and she admired him for it.

Stop it, she told herself. *Stop liking Mr. Thayne!* How could she forget all the hurt after one morning with him? She scolded herself for being placated too easily, but in her defense, he was effortlessly charming. Mr. Thayne was not exactly what she had pictured when they had exchanged letters, but she liked the real version better. She liked his facial expressions and the genuineness in his voice, and each time he said her name in those deep timbres, the more she wanted to hear him say it.

Clara backed away from the window, feeling her hold on her heart slipping. Try as she might, it was hard not to like him. She meandered back down the hallway, pausing to look at small details like the design on a curtain or the arrangement of flowers in a vase.

What if Mr. Thayne really did care for her?

No! she told herself. She could not let her feelings run ahead of her this time.

Just outside the drawing room, she took several deep breaths to help the last itches of uncertainty ease into a quiet acceptance. She had a loving family, a comfortable home, and an excellent opportunity to relax and enjoy her holiday. It was enough.

As Clara turned the handle and pushed open the door with the resolve to contain her heart, she heard new voices mixing with the familiar, and she knew that all the guests had finally arrived. Lady Welton was introducing Mrs. Watson and her daughter, Elizabeth.

Chapter 35

lizabeth curtsied to Miss Bailey and Miss Everton, looking each girl in the eye to discern whether either were her equal. *Doubtful,* she thought, but for the sake of appearances, Elizabeth would follow her mother's example and put on a pleasant face. *Be patient and smile,* she told herself. Meeting all the ladies was a necessary, if tedious, requirement as a guest, but with that out of the way, she would be free to focus on the single gentlemen who would hopefully join them soon.

Elizabeth noticed her mother listening to Lady Welton with a polite but somewhat vacant expression. Having seen that look before, Elizabeth knew exactly what her mother was thinking. How long did she have to sit in a room full of ladies she didn't know before she could excuse herself? They had only been there an hour, and already her mother was retreating to the seclusion of her own affairs, leaving Elizabeth to socially fend for herself.

Elizabeth tried to remember why Lady Welton had invited them to Brindley Hall in the first place. It had something to do with Sir Douglas and Elizabeth's father having some connection. Had they been childhood friends? Had they traded properties? She forgot the details, but when the invitation arrived, her unsociable father immediately cited business as his excuse to remain at home. Elizabeth's mother, however, claimed it would be a splendid opportunity to spend time together and make new friends.

Rubbish.

Elizabeth knew her mother had only accepted the invitation to separate her from Mr. Davril. At the time, Elizabeth thought her mother was being overly protective and old fashioned. Only now did she understand how right her mother had been.

Despite her initial reluctance, Elizabeth now saw the benefits of being at the Weltons'. A new crowd meant new opportunities, and Elizabeth needed new opportunities to improve her prospects. She had a feeling something good would come of this holiday, and she, more than anyone, knew how to make any circumstance work to her advantage.

As she sat down with her needlepoint in hand, she went over the names of each lady again in her mind. Mrs. Rose Martin and her niece, Clara Everton. *There is the competition*, thought Elizabeth. She could see it in Miss Everton's proud face, but did Miss Everton understand the art of attracting men the way she did? *Doubtful.* Though, with that clever brow and innocent smile, Miss Everton did strike Elizabeth as the kind of girl who could scheme if she wanted to. *No matter*, thought, Elizabeth. Miss Everton could never do it with flair to match her own.

Next, she turned her attention to Miss Bailey who was playing a complicated tune on the pianoforte. Elizabeth noticed several small slips of the finger and shook her head. None of the other ladies seemed to notice, but then again, Elizabeth didn't expect them to. Most ladies lacked the education and opportunity she had been raised with, so she couldn't reasonably expect them to have as refined a taste as she had. *What is the point in playing without the men around, anyway?* she thought. *A wasted effort.* No competition would come from that quarter.

Miss Bailey's playing was interrupted by two young girls running into the room laughing about some joke they had played on their governess.

"Hahaha! Locked in! She's locked in the nursery!" laughed the older girl to no one in particular.

"Goodness, child!" shouted Lady Welton. "What are you talking about?" She stood up so fast she lost balance and had to lean back on the sofa for support.

"Mabel snuck the key out of her pocket this morning!" explained the younger girl, relishing the attention.

Elizabeth could not stand it when children lisped as this little girl did.

"Emily!" the older girl, presumably Mabel, scowled. "You weren't supposed to tell!"

"Oops!" Emily giggled. "At least I didn't tell them how we locked her in."

"You did it on purpose!?" Lady Welton's jaw dropped. "What have you done?"

"Emily!" Mabel shot her sister an angry look.

"Bless my soul!" cried Lady Welton. "In front of our new guests too!" With her hand on her cheek, she turned to Elizabeth and Mrs. Watson and apologized for the disturbance.

Elizabeth smirked. She could admire a good prank. These girls reminded her of herself at that age. She had played quite a few tricks on her governess, and truth be told, she still enjoyed seeing the governess fume afterward. Perhaps she would have the pleasure of seeing this Miss Stanley react once the girls had freed her.

Elizabeth could hear Miss Everton say, "Girls, what will Mr. Thayne say when he finds out? Didn't you want him to play theater with you tonight?"

The girls looked crestfallen with this reminder. Lady Welton took advantage of the calm moment to question them and beg them to return the key. When Elizabeth felt like she had gleaned her full share of amusement from the scene, she returned to her needlepoint.

As Lady Welton ushered the girls out, a tall, handsome and vaguely familiar man walked into the room. His build was lean and muscular and his clothes struck the right balance between simplicity and style. It was hard to pinpoint his exact age, but he looked like he was at the beginning of his prime. Elizabeth wondered what his yearly income was.

Sir Douglas, who Elizabeth had greeted earlier, came next, followed by another younger gentleman who cocked his brow and wore a self-satisfied grin. Elizabeth determined right then to outwit him in a game of cards or chess. If she were feeling indulgent, she might let him win a round or two before putting him in his place.

It was a shame there were not more men to choose from. Neither of these two were particularly striking, but Elizabeth preferred the one who looked familiar. He seemed more mature, more gentlemanly, the kind of man she could feel secure with. Where had she seen him before? Probably at a ball, but that didn't help.

Elizabeth sat straighter as Sir Douglas led the men over. Pointing to the younger gentleman first, he said, "Allow me to introduce my nephew, Mr. Thomas Bailey."

Mr. Bailey gave a polite bow and cocked the other brow. *Oh, this will be entertaining!* thought Elizabeth. He looked ripe for teasing, so she fluttered her eyelashes back.

"And this is my good friend, Mr. James Thayne." Sir Douglas indicated the other gentleman.

Mr. Thayne kept a straight face, bowed politely, and looked off to the side. No, not just to the side, observed Elizabeth, but at Miss Everton. *Miss Everton! Oh, that's it!* The memory descended suddenly on Elizabeth like a summer storm. Mr. Thayne was the man who had approached her at the Chelsea ball as if he knew her and had called her Miss Everton. *Interesting*, she thought. Elizabeth gave him a special smile and put the memory in safe keeping. She would need to observe everyone more closely to know how to proceed with her goals, especially Mr. Thayne.

Chapter 36

As Mr. Thayne stepped closer, Clara doubted that the growing warmth she felt could entirely be attributed to sitting by the fire. She didn't mean to look up at him from her drawing quite so quickly, but his deep forest green jacket set off the green flecks in his hazel eyes in the most startling way. She was still getting over the fact that he was much more handsome than she had imagined when they were writing to one another. She silently noted that he came to her instead of Miss Watson. Perhaps she would find it in her heart to forgive him after all.

"Good evening, Miss Everton." He asked how she had spent her afternoon, whether she was all right after all the excitement in the stables, and she inquired after the state of the injured stable hand. Mr. Thayne explained that the stable hand, whose name was Henry Cook, had received a fierce kick to his leg, causing significant bruising, but nothing appeared broken. Mr. Cook's head had also sustained several scratches and bruises when he hit the floor. Although the man would be off his feet for several days, the doctor was confident he would recover well.

Mr. Thayne leaned closer as he finished. "Thank you for remaining calm and sending for the doctor, Clara."

She felt a deep blush spread across her face at hearing her name again spoken with such familiarity, but hearing it in Mr. Thayne's deep tones made her want to hear it again. She was about to ask why he was out chopping wood, but she was interrupted by Mr. Bailey and Miss Watson walking over.

Mr. Bailey put on a simple smile. "We are about to play cards. Four players would be ideal. Won't you join us?"

"How kind of you Mr. Bailey," answered Mr. Thayne, "but I'm afraid I am already late for another engagement. Miss Emily and Miss Mabel are expecting me for a night of theater, and I was hoping Miss Everton would join me."

Clara didn't take long to decide. She preferred just about anything to playing cards. "I wouldn't want to disappoint those darling girls."

She excused herself and accompanied Mr. Thayne without a hint of regret. In the hallway, Clara listened to her footsteps click in rhythm with his on the tiled floor. She pressed her lips together, unsure whether to release the smile she felt.

"Thank you for saving me from a tedious card game," she offered.

"I've never been fond of cards." Mr. Thayne winked. "But I should be thanking you for spending more time with me."

Mr. Thayne reached out like he wanted to take Clara's hand, but he let the gesture fall incomplete, barely brushing the side of her hand instead. She wasn't sure whether he meant to do that, but she marveled how such a small, soft touch had such a rippling effect on her.

She cleared her throat. "Do you really think the girls have behaved well enough today for this kind of reward?"

Mr. Thayne laughed. "Certainly not, but I'd be willing to wager Miss Stanley would like a rest anyhow."

"Poor overworked woman!" Clara declared.

Mr. Thayne agreed, and for a time, nothing more was said. Their steps continued to click together as he led her through a part of the house she had not yet seen. There were paintings of exotic animals and landscapes and paintings of children at play or sitting among family. The bright blue curtains that lined the windows were pulled back just enough to reveal a heavy sun casting rays of light along their path. At the end of the hallway, past a large door left ajar, was the children's nursery.

Clara immediately noticed the cheerful decor. The whole room was a miniature version of the downstairs sitting room only more colorful and full of dolls, puzzles, picture books, two rocking horses, and in one corner, a brilliantly painted toy theater. The girls were sitting together at a small table, eating biscuits and talking excitedly. Clara and Mr. Thayne stood by the door, waiting to be noticed. Emily was the first to make eye contact, but it didn't take long before both girls were running over, squealing loudly enough for the whole household to hear.

Within moments, Emily had Clara by the hand and was leading her to the theater, explaining the role she should play and generally instructing her in the ways of make believe. Mabel was doing the same for Mr. Thayne.

Playing theater with the girls turned out to be a much more active sport than Clara had imagined. The girls jumped on the ground, jumped on Mr. Thayne, jumped on her, ran around the room, threw dolls in the air, and often giggled and screamed as they performed impromptu stories about fairies and princesses.

At one point the girls insisted that Mr. Thayne and Clara put on a play for them. With no time to agree or object, the girls set to work preparing them for their new roles. Mabel decided that Clara's upswept curls did not look enough like a princess's hair. Before Clara realized what was happening, Mabel's fast little hands had pulled enough pins from her bun to send her wavy, chestnut hair rolling down her shoulders. Emily, not to be left out or outdone, reached for a brush and added several silk flowers. Clara obliging sat as the girls yanked on her hair, each trying to grab her fair share, each with a different style in mind.

Once the girls were satisfied and Clara was no longer distracted by all the pulling, she noticed Mr. Thayne's gaze on her. His look was intent and penetrating. With her hair loose and messy, she felt completely bare. Determined not to show it, however, she held his gaze with her own. Though her heart swelled with the effort not to look away, she relished his ardent eyes. Every speck of green, each line of gold and brown sent light and heat all through her. In that moment, the connection between them grew. Clara wasn't exactly sure what it meant, only that it was intimate, and her feelings for him were unmistakable.

"This is boring!" complained Mabel, popping Clara's thoughts like a bubble. "They need to tell each other they love each other already."

"What?" asked Mr. Thayne, looking startled.

"Yes!" agreed Emily. "Make the prince climb up the princess's tower. They need to say they love each other so they can get married."

Oh. Clara realized the girls were talking about the prince and princess puppets they had shoved into her and Mr. Thayne's hands. Mr. Thayne cleared his throat and moved his prince over to the wooden tower. He then made his prince climb the tower to be near Clara's little princess puppet. Clara held her princess tight as she tried to focus on it, but her eyes kept straying to Mr. Thayne's face. The setting sun cast a warm glow on his skin, and his hand was very close to hers as they sat by the toy theater.

Still holding his prince, he looked straight at Clara and said, taking deep breaths in between, "My princess, I . . . I simply adore you."

Clara heard those words and forgot everything else. There was something about the way he said it, something in his voice that went beyond a game, something that was meant just for her.

She tried to think. Was she supposed to say something too?

Emily and Mabel started laughing. Clara forgot she had an audience.

Mabel shouted, "Tell the prince you love him too!"

Clara exhaled and smiled at the girls and then at Mr. Thayne. "Of course. My dear prince, my heart is yours."

The girls cheered. "Hurray! Now they can get married!" The girls didn't wait for Mr. Thayne and Clara to do or say anything else. They took the puppets and started chattering away while setting up for a new play.

Clara still had her thoughts focused on Mr. Thayne when a door swung so quickly it hit the wall and made everyone jump. Miss Stanley came out of her room and announced that it was time for bed and to say good night to Miss Everton and Mr. Thayne.

"Awwww!" pouted Emily and Mabel.

"No arguing. Come quickly!" clapped Miss Stanley.

Emily and Mabel gave several good-night hugs before Clara and Mr. Thayne waved goodbye and closed the nursery door behind them.

As they walked together in the hallway, Clara hummed softly to herself and tried not to feel too self-conscious as she rearranged her hair back to a more presentable state. Mr. Thayne picked up on her tune and began harmonizing with her. Clara hadn't even realized she had been humming, but she finished the song and allowed herself to enjoy the moment, just as she had when she was the princess in the toy theater. When she finished twisting up her hair, she smiled at Mr. Thayne.

"I think you missed one." He stepped close and reached for her curls.

Clara held very still. As he hovered close enough to embrace, his breath fell to her cheeks, and she caught the faintest scent of freshly cut pine and mint. His eyes strayed to her face, and a few seconds later, he stepped back holding a small silk forget-me-not. He twirled it in his fingers a few times, then offered it to her.

"Is it safe to say we are friends now?"

Clara would have taken the flower, but his question made her pause. It was the same question he had asked in one of his letters. She put her hands behind her back and began walking again.

"I'm not sure," she stated pensively. "What do you think?"

Mr. Thayne matched her pace. "I really hope so. What can I do to convince you?"

Clara thought about it. "Well, first, you must make me laugh."

He raised an eyebrow. "What about when we laughed just now with the girls?"

Clara shook her head. "That doesn't count. Those girls would make any situation entertaining."

Mr. Thayne nodded. "All right. I accept your challenge. What amuses you?"

Somehow, Mr. Thayne got Clara talking about her father and Louisa and how they teased each other. She talked about Frances and what an excellent friend she was. Clara forgot about Mr. Thayne's original question and started telling him all about her life in Milton, about drawing, about picking blackberries by the pond. She told him about a time when, as a young child, she fell out of her rowboat and panicked before realizing she was only a few feet from the bank and could easily stand. He laughed freely at everything she said, and before she knew it, she was laughing too.

"Does this count?" he asked. "You *are* laughing."

Clara shook her head. "Not at all. I did all the talking."

Mr. Thayne nodded. "I see. Then it is my turn to talk . . ." He went into detail about his life at Felton Park. He described how to find a particularly large tree in his orchard that grew the best apples. He told her about an old forgotten passageway between his bedchamber and study that he sometimes liked to use. He told her about a time when he had visited the Weltons' as a young boy and put a frog in young Bailey's bed.

Clara laughed. She couldn't help it. Mr. Thayne knew how to tell a story, how to bring out the suspense and humor. "All right. I admit it. You made me laugh."

Then Mr. Thayne's stomach rumbled loud enough for Clara to hear, and she laughed again.

"Pardon my stomach," he said. "It is far too outspoken."

She smiled. "Well, it deserves a chance to be heard, especially after all the work you put it through this afternoon. You must be famished." Clara thought of Mr. Thayne's strong arms chopping wood.

He turned his head quickly at her with raised eyebrows but said nothing.

She admitted, "I was looking out the window and saw you chopping firewood earlier today."

"Yes, Mr. Cook was worried, even in his injured state, about getting his work done. He didn't want to add to any of the other servants' work, what with it almost being Christmas. He looked so agitated, and he was in no state to stand, so I volunteered to help him."

"That was very kind of you," Clara said.

"Oh, it's nothing," Mr. Thayne said as he scratched the back of his neck. "I don't keep more servants than absolutely necessary at Felton Park because I like the independence. I try to share the work when time allows, which keeps me in good health and reminds me to appreciate the people around me." Clara thought she detected a hint of embarrassment as he added, "I realize there are men in my station who would think it improper of me to engage in such rough work, but my servants never complain."

The corner of Clara's mouth rose. "Would you like to know what I think?"

He flashed a look that was both debonair and playful. "That I am incredibly strong and handsome?"

She almost agreed with him but maintained her original thought. "That you are just being *humble* again."

She could tell by his smile that he had caught the reference to his first letter. He bumped her shoulder with his and once again offered her the tiny silk flower he had untangled from her hair. This time, with their fingers briefly touching, she took the flower.

Chapter 37

"Up, dear, up!"

Clara bolted awake as someone poked her in the side. Disoriented, she looked around the sitting room and realized she must have dozed off on Rose's shoulder. Clara's sketchbook sat in her lap but her pencil had rolled to the floor. Reaching for it, she noticed that Miss Bailey had stopped playing the pianoforte and the other guests were all looking around at one another. Had something just happened?

A piercing scream from outside cut through the room.

Clara instinctively looked for Mr. Thayne, a habit she had only recently developed. It had been five days since the morning they had walked to the stables together and played theater with Emily and Mabel. Since then, Mr. Thayne always found a slice of day that was just for Clara. An hour discussing favorite books, an afternoon making Christmas ornaments from pinecones and ribbon, an evening reviewing her drawings. It didn't really matter what they did together. His attentions were distinct, and her barriers were crumbling. However, Clara wasn't entirely sure whether he meant to court her or simply be her friend. She thought it entirely possible that the extra attention was merely his way of making up for how he had treated her in London. If only she could be certain of his feelings.

A tiny voice screamed out again, this time in long wails.

Clara saw Mr. Thayne on the opposite side of the room leaning out an open window with his head tilted up. "Mabel! Don't move! I'm coming." He threw off his jacket and ran out of the drawing room.

"I'm coming too!" Sir Douglas gave Lady Welton's hand a brisk kiss. "We'll get her down safely," he added before racing out after Mr. Thayne.

Clara jumped from her seat and ran to the window to look outside with the other guests. The cold air pricked her face as she leaned out. Was Mabel all right? What had happened? Clara couldn't see anything distinct in the dark, but she most definitely heard crying.

It couldn't be, she thought.

Following the sounds with her eyes, she saw the ghostly image of Mabel, barefooted in her nightdress, desperately clutching the branch of a tree at least three stories up. Mabel's cries billowed like her nightdress in the wind. Clara could see where the tree's branches scraped against the nursery window, which must have provided the avenue of Mabel's initial escape. Pale curtains fluttered out like hands half-heartedly beckoning Mabel back. Enough light came from the window to reveal a broken branch dangling at an awkward angle just above the one that Mabel now clung to. Clara shuddered to think how narrowly Mabel had missed a fall to the ground. Though her face was hidden, the terror in her sobs was clear.

Lady Welton nudged against Clara to lean further out the window. "Hold on, Mabel. Hold on!" Clara put her arm around Lady Welton as she cried. "I can't let anything happen to her! I can't!" She shook her head vigorously. "What will her mother say? Oh, and her father! My precious grandchild! What can I do?"

Rose came to the other side of Lady Welton and put an arm around her waist.

Clara leaned out a little farther when she saw Mr. Thayne reach the tree. He rolled up his sleeves despite the cold and started climbing. Clara could see his arms flexing as he pulled himself higher and higher into the branches.

Sir Douglas arrived moments later and positioned himself under Mabel with arms outstretched. "Mr. Thayne is coming up, Mable, and I'm here below. You'll be all right!"

Inside, Clara could hear Mrs. Watson. "That governess should be instantly removed after this. If I were you, Lady Welton, I would march right up to her and—"

"Mother!"

Clara turned to see Elizabeth Watson give her mother a scathing look.

"Lady Welton, I'm sure Mabel will be all right," Elizabeth said firmly before walking away from the window and staring at the floor.

Clara considered Elizabeth. She never could tell what Elizabeth was thinking, but Clara suspected something troubled her. Whatever it was, Clara doubted Elizabeth would ever say anything about it to her.

Clara leaned out again to see Mr. Thayne's progress. The winter air numbed her face as she strained to see in the darkness. Mr. Thayne was moving cautiously but steadily higher. At one point, Clara heard a branch crack as he tested its strength. She bit her lip and kept her eyes intently on him as if her gaze were holding him up.

"Hurry, James, please!" cried Mabel. It might have been the wind, but Clara thought she could see Mabel trembling.

"Almost there, Mabel." Mr. Thayne spoke reassuringly even under the strain of climbing.

Mabel tried to turn her head toward him, but she started to slip. "Help!"

"Hold still, Mabel!" he commanded, unable to hide the panic in his voice. Just a few more branches up, but he still had to angle himself closer to reach her. With his torso facing the trunk and his right hand on a branch, he extended his left arm out. "I'm here, Mabel."

She only wailed, "I can't let go! I can't let go!"

The branches were thinner higher up. Mabel was holding one of the thickest branches available at that height which left Mr. Thayne fewer options. He slowly tested the branches around him. Somewhere in the darkness a cat mewed and leaves rustled on the ground.

No matter how close Thayne managed to get, it would be a difficult reach for Mabel. Her arms were no doubt about to give. Clara heard another branch crack, though neither Mabel nor Mr. Thayne had moved that time. Clara held her breath as Mr. Thayne swung himself closer so that he was also holding Mabel's branch. One foot was secure, but his other foot needed a few attempts to stabilize. He was now right under Mabel.

"Mabel, your grandfather is below, and I am right here. Climb down on me just as if my arm were another branch."

The wind carried Mabel's whimpering all the way to the sitting room. Clara held her breath.

"You can do it," Mr. Thayne encouraged. "I won't let you fall. Now, deep breaths."

Clara exhaled, taking his instruction to heart. With one hand holding tight to the branch, Mr. Thayne reached out and took Mabel's arm. Her whimpering stopped, and soon, she was able to climb onto him, wrapping both her arms around his neck and her legs around his waist.

"Good girl!" shouted Sir Douglas from below. "Good work, Thayne!"

Mr. Thayne and Mabel were still high up, but Clara knew they would be all right now. As each measured step brought them closer to the ground, her muscles unclenched and the entire room of guests sighed in relief. Clara's mind cleared, and, with Lady Welton's approval, she asked the maid to bring blankets and herbal tea for Mr. Thayne and Mabel.

Clara and the others hurried to the entry hall to meet Sir Douglas and Mr. Thayne who carried a very sober looking Mabel in his arms. Lady Welton pushed through everyone and was the first to get her arms around Mabel.

"Naughty, naughty girl!" she cried, not sounding a bit unhappy as she pulled Mabel out of Mr. Thayne's arms and held her tight. "What on earth were you doing up in that tree?"

Mabel frowned and whimpered through shivers. "I was . . . pretending to be . . . a princess in a tower."

"Ha!" Lady Welton nervously laughed as she held Mabel in a crushing embrace. "Naughty, mischievous, beautiful girl!"

Two maids entered carrying blankets and tea. Lady Welton directed them to the sitting room and told Mabel she could warm up by the fire. Clara could hear Lady Welton mumbling the whole way how she was never going to let go of Mabel again. Most of the others followed them back to the sitting room as well.

Clara, however, lingered in the entry hall, not quite knowing what she would say to Mr. Thayne but wanting to say something. He stood by the staircase looking incredibly exhausted, and, in her moment of hesitation, Elizabeth Watson, who Clara hadn't noticed was still nearby, stepped forward and began congratulating Mr. Thayne on his heroic rescue.

Clara looked down and turned away, wishing she could stop her ears from hearing Elizabeth's bloated praise. "So brilliant! I can't tell you how impressed I am. I—"

"Aha! There you are!" Sir Douglas returned to the entry hall, cutting off Elizabeth's efforts. "Don't hog all the attention, now, Thayne. I was out there too! I didn't sit around like Bailey always does. I was ready for action!" Sir Douglas slapped Mr. Thayne on the back and suggested he join him and his wife and granddaughter by the fire. Sir Douglas didn't wait for an answer but wished the ladies good night and walked back to the sitting room.

Clara didn't know what to do. Elizabeth looked determined to stay and spoke as if Sir Douglas had never interrupted. "I've never seen such bravery, Mr. Thayne. I hope you and I can—"

"Forgive me." Mr. Thayne placed his hand on his chest. "Thank you for your kind words, Miss Watson, but I must excuse myself. I'm rather tired. Now that Mabel is safe, I would like to retire for the night."

"Of course." Elizabeth sounded a bit defeated but kept her voice sweet. "You deserve to rest. Good night." She gave a slight bow, which Mr. Thayne returned before slowly walking up the stairs. Elizabeth's eye briefly met Clara's on her way back to the sitting room.

Alone in the large entry hall, Clara rubbed her arms for warmth and wondered what had happened in that tree. It was more than Mr. Thayne saving Mabel. It was seeing him risk himself for someone else. It was seeing him vulnerable, open to a fall, and she couldn't help but remember how he had once taken a risk on her. She had taken a risk on him too, meeting him letter for letter, until all she was left with was a broken heart.

Was it possible to try again? She wanted to, but only if she knew he wouldn't hurt her again. Yet, the uncertainty of waiting for him to love her, of holding back until she was sure, was its own kind of risk.

Hoping it wasn't too late to express her admiration for what he had done, she turned to call after him before he was gone.

"Mr. Thayne! Oh!" She stumbled right into his arms.

Had he returned for her?

Mr. Thayne steadied her, just as he had when she'd slipped outside the stables, sending waves of warmth through her skin.

"Oh, James! You startled me! I didn't hear you!" She laughed nervously and realized she had spoken without thinking. Her face flooded with embarrassment. "I . . . I mean Mr. Thayne." She put her hand on her chest, willing her heart to steady. "That was a very good thing you did tonight. I just wanted to say that I'm relieved you and Mabel are all right."

His hands slowly released her arms. "You were not just concerned for Mabel? You were also concerned for me?"

As she looked in his eyes, she knew that if he were injured, it would hurt her too. "Of course, I was."

Mr. Thayne took a step closer. "That means so much to me. Good night, dear Clara."

Chapter 38

Thayne descended the stairs slowly that morning, each movement stiff and awkward. His whole body ached from climbing the tree. He considered himself to be in good health, but retrieving Mabel the previous night had required all his strength. Hopefully, he could pass a quiet day with Clara.

"Thayne!" Sir Douglas and Martin greeted him at the bottom of the staircase. Bailey walked a pace or two behind. Martin said hello to Thayne with a slap on the back.

"Ahhh!" Thayne winced. He swung his arm and rolled his shoulder to loosen the muscles.

The men all laughed.

"Forgive me, Thayne!" Martin said cheerfully. "I only wanted to tell you that Sir Douglas has a surprise, something that will help you single men with your lady troubles."

Bailey's back straightened. "I am not having any trouble with the ladies."

"Oh, no?" Martin chuckled. "Are you trying to tell me that spilling tea on Miss Watson was part of your plan to woo her?"

Bailey's nostrils flared.

Thayne suppressed a laugh. Spilling tea on Miss Watson must have happened while he and Clara were playing theater with the girls. *Poor Bailey,* he thought to himself. *Always trying so hard but never quite getting it right.*

When the men entered the drawing room, Thayne saw Clara on the far side by a window, occasionally looking out as she worked on a sketch. Sunlight illuminated her hair and face, and he pictured the moment Emily and Mabel had unraveled her hair and added silk flowers. Clara's hair was longer than he had expected but also softer. The girls had made a mess of it, but even so, Thayne kept picturing Clara's smooth skin against the waves and how her eyes dared to meet his in that moment. It was strange to think there had ever been a time when he did not know her face. Now, he had every feature memorized.

With the men still standing together, Sir Douglas begged everyone's attention. Clapping his hands, he announced, "I have a surprise for everyone. It is aimed at our unmarried guests, but I assume it will be enjoyable for all." He elbowed Mr. Martin who answered with a grin of his own. "It is a Christmas tradition we do every year. Somewhere on this estate, both indoors and out, are three carefully placed kissing boughs."

Thayne saw Clara look at him. Was she thinking about those kissing boughs? He certainly was. Then he noticed Miss Watson regarding him. He shot his eyes back to Sir Douglas.

"As each young lady knows," Sir Douglas winked, "accepting a gentleman's kiss from under the kissing bough will bring her good luck. So I recommend that any lady who is caught not refuse."

"Goodness!" cried Mrs. Watson and Miss Bailey in unison.

"To every person here whether young in age or young at heart, beware the kissing boughs, and good luck!" Sir Douglas chuckled and turned to face the men. In a quieter voice, he jested, "I hope our younger gentlemen are not too dense to know what to do next." He cleared his throat and put his hands in his coat pockets, clearly pleased with himself.

Martin, with a gleam in his eye, gestured to the men. "Don't think that I won't be looking for those kissing boughs. I plan to make Rose feel like a young bride again this Christmas." He bowed and went to join his wife by the fireplace.

Bailey, full of smugness, turned directly to Thayne. "Don't be surprised when Miss Everton warms up to me after I catch her under one of those kissing boughs."

Thayne felt the heat rumble in his chest, but he would not allow Bailey to rile him up over such things. "Are you so sure of yourself, Bailey?" he crisply replied.

Bailey smirked. "My chances are as good as yours."

Thayne pushed his lips out in a frown. "Only if you actually find a kissing bough. Even then, your chances are still doubtful. A kiss won't make Miss Everton like you."

Bailey stuck out his chin. "Ah, but three might."

"Three will be enough to send her running to me," Thayne scoffed.

Bailey pinched his mouth harder. "I intend to find all of those kissing boughs, and I'm going to make sure that you don't find any."

The heat rumbled again in Thayne, but he was still in control. Why did Bailey want to turn this into a competition? Thayne shook his head and breathed out his nose. "For your sake, Bailey, I hope that none of the ladies are holding a cup of tea when you try to kiss them."

Thayne wasn't worried, but he did feel a greater resolve to find those kissing boughs first. He was fairly confident he already knew where one of them would be. He had spent Christmas at Brindley Hall before. Then again, so had Bailey. There would be no time to waste, and yet, Thayne did not want to lead Clara into a kiss unless he felt certain she wanted it.

As Thayne crossed the room to Clara, he nodded to Lady Welton and Mabel and Emily who were flipping through picture books and making Christmas ornaments. After Mabel's recent stunt, the Weltons had promised to spend more time with their granddaughters, giving Miss Stanley a much-needed respite. Emily and Mabel waved vigorously to Thayne as he walked by. Next, he nodded to Miss Bailey who perpetually sat at the pianoforte. She returned the nod without ever pausing in her playing.

When Thayne reached Clara, he hesitated by the bookshelves. She looked so intent on her drawing, erasing lines and adding new ones, and he began to regard her skill as a type of magic he shouldn't interrupt. Her paper displayed a forested landscape like Milton's that blossomed beneath her touch. Thayne watched her add the outlines of a man and woman holding hands. The woman distinctly reminded him of Clara, something about the curve of figure and style of hair, but he could not be so certain about the man. Was it too optimistic to hope it was himself? There was not yet enough detail to make such a strong conclusion.

She hadn't yet noticed him, so he continued to watch her draw. He was captivated by the way such small adjustments to the drawing made such an impressive impact. It reminded him of the progress he was making with Clara. Small things like smiling and laughing together were healing the rift of his earlier mistake. Although, sometimes he still caught Clara with a worry or hurt pressing upon her brow that flung him back to a place of doubt. What if Clara only considered him a friend? What if she hadn't forgiven him completely? Truly knowing her feelings was trickier than he had anticipated. He wanted to be the man in her drawing, but what he really wanted was encouragement.

Lost in these thoughts, Thayne scanned the book titles on the nearby shelves, wondering which ones Clara might like.

"Mr. Thayne?" Miss Watson appeared next to him. "Having troubling finding something to read?"

As she stepped uncomfortably close, he stepped back at least two feet.

"How are you, Miss Watson?" he replied, trying to sound formal. He didn't care to know what motive had brought her over.

He risked a glance at Clara from the corner of his eye and saw she had stopped drawing. Her pencil hovered irresolutely over the man and woman. She was probably listening.

"I am quite well, Mr. Thayne, but you look troubled. You seem not to have heard my first question. I know you must have many things on your mind . . ." She paused and looked narrowly at Clara. "So, I thought I would come keep you company."

"Is that so?" Thayne kept his eyes on the books taking another two steps away from her.

She took two steps closer.

"Oh, you need not be so cold with me. I know where your interests lie." Again, she looked at Clara. "Though I must say, it saddens me to think I missed an opportunity to become better acquainted with you just a short while ago. I have been thinking . . ." She leaned against the bookshelf and looked more directly at Thayne. He persistently searched the books instead of asking what she had been thinking. He didn't want to take her bait.

"I have been thinking about our first awkward introduction. I don't doubt you recall the moment I refer to. You called me Miss Everton and said something about meeting in person."

Thayne started to sweat, and the only reply he could think of was, "I was not myself that night."

She smiled. "You seemed perfectly well to me."

Thayne kept tracing his finger along book titles, trying to regain focus. He didn't want to be bothered with Miss Watson right now.

"Ah, well," she sighed. "Anyway, I began to think. You are obviously quite taken with Miss Everton." Thayne could detect a hint of dislike in her voice. "So I had to ask myself how you could have possibly confused her with me." She was clearly amused. "Is it possible, Mr. Thayne, that I once meant something to you?"

What a question! Thayne was thoroughly annoyed and had no desire to explain things to her. He gave her a cold look, but she merely seemed pleased he was looking. He returned his attention to the books and replied, "I hope I did not cause too much of an interruption to your party that night."

"Oh, not at all! I did not bring it up to seek out your apology. Rather, I wanted to make my own apology."

"I beg your pardon?" He paused to look at her again.

"I was impolite to you that night, and I was quite rude at the jewelry shop, which I also assume you remember."

Mr. Thayne nodded in appreciation of the acknowledgement.

"I want to make amends," she said. "As a token of my friendship, I offer you the first dance of the evening tonight if you are inclined to ask me." She smiled triumphantly and put her hands behind her back, swiveling on her feet while she waited.

This was the last thing Thayne wanted! He was sure Clara was listening, and though he did not want to be ungentlemanly to Miss Watson, he would not say anything that might give Clara reason to doubt his feelings.

"How kind of you, Miss Watson, but I am afraid you are too late."

For the first time since talking to him, her smile faded. "Oh?"

"I was about to ask Miss Everton to be my dance partner tonight." Thayne looked at Clara and back at Miss Watson. "As you correctly observed, I am quite taken with her."

Miss Watson frowned and examined her fingernails. "No matter," she replied before sauntering off to another part of the room.

Thayne, both embarrassed and emboldened, took the chair closest to Clara's and cleared his throat. "Surely you heard all that?"

Clara answered without looking at him. "Yes."

He needed more than that so, keeping his voice light, he tried, "Is that all you have to say?"

"Well," began Clara, adding a few more lines to her drawing, "you have not asked me anything else. What more should I say?"

"Say you will be my dance partner."

Now she looked at him. "For the first dance?"

"And every dance after that." Thayne knew it was a bold request, nearly as bold as writing to Clara in the first place, but he wanted to send a clear message to Miss Watson and everyone else in their party. Clara was the only one he wanted. He just had to make sure she felt the same way.

Clara responded with one of her most classic smiles, beautiful and sweet, and playfully suspicious. In that moment, Thayne was all the more certain that Clara's uncle had done him a huge favor the night he mistook Clara for the girl Thayne had been enamored with. It was the mistake that set things right.

Thayne almost forgot he was waiting for an answer when Clara said, "Surely, you do not want to dance all night."

Chapter 39

Clara wore a lavender muslin dress that night with clean lines and minimal lace. Rose complained about the simplicity of the gown, but that only meant Rose did not suspect Clara of having alternative plans for the evening. Clara didn't feel badly about missing a few dances that night, especially since the Weltons suggested dancing every other night. Her plans were innocent, but she did wonder whether they might bring her and Mr. Thayne under one of the kissing boughs.

While she waited in the drawing room for dinner, Lady Welton asked, "How are things progressing with Mr. Thayne? You seem cured of your broken heart, and he must be close to declaring his feelings for you."

Clara's whole face warmed up as Lady Welton winked at her and exchanged knowing smiles with Rose. *So they have been talking about us.* Clara tried to keep her voice natural. "You are kind, Lady Welton, but Mr. Thayne and I are still becoming acquainted."

"Rose, is that true?"

Lady Welton and Rose walked across the room whispering to each other.

Soon, Sir Douglas, Uncle William, and Mr. Thayne walked in, slapping each other on the backs as they always did when talking. Mr. Thayne looked intently at Clara for just a moment before returning to the men's conversation.

Eventually, Miss Bailey came in followed by Mrs. Watson and Elizabeth, who did not appear to be in very high spirits.

Clara noticed Elizabeth watching Mr. Thayne from the corner of her eye, and though he never returned her furtive glances, Clara couldn't help but worry whether he might eventually succumb to Elizabeth's persistent flirtations. Was Clara letting her guard down too quickly? What if he lost interest in her after the holidays? Was it too much to hope he would pursue her when she returned home?

With these questions stewing, Sir Douglas and Lady Welton invited everyone into the dining hall. Clara relaxed a bit when Mr. Thayne sat to her left, but when Elizabeth sat to her right, Clara suddenly felt like she was trying to warm up in front of a drafty window. All the while, strange looks were coming across the table from Mr. Bailey, some amorous, some brooding, and she wasn't always certain whom he intended them for.

Emily and Mabel also joined the party as a special treat with Miss Stanley sitting stiffly in the middle of them. Miss Bailey sat next to her brother and calmly nodded as the elder guests rambled on about favorite dogs, the weather, and what a pleasure it was to see the younger guests enjoying themselves. Clara, always aware of Mr. Thayne on her left and Elizabeth on her right, mostly ate and smiled and wondered what her face looked like as she tried to do both at the same time.

When all had eaten, Lady Welton stood up and announced, "Let us proceed to the main hall. I know the younger guests are never satisfied until we have dancing."

Sir Douglas and Lady Welton invited everyone to follow them into a small adjoining ballroom. Miss Bailey ambled toward the pianoforte with a downcast gaze and several sideways glances. Clara realized that Miss Bailey was the only one without an obvious dance partner. Did that explain why everyone expected her to provide the music? If Clara wasn't useless on the pianoforte, she would have volunteered, but perhaps Elizabeth could take a turn.

While Miss Bailey shuffled through her sheets of music, Sir Douglas pulled Mr. Thayne to the side, wanting his opinion on some matter Clara hadn't caught. As she waited for Mr. Thayne, a cool, slender hand gripped her arm.

"Miss Watson!" Clara started, but then, remembering Miss Bailey, she asked, "Do you play the pianoforte?"

Instead of answering, Elizabeth leaned close and whispered low. "Clara, I know you are planning something with Mr. Thayne."

How did Elizabeth know? Clara thought Elizabeth was across the room when she and Mr. Thayne were plotting. "It is an innocent diversion, I assure you, Miss Watson. Now if you will excuse me—"

Elizabeth tightened her grip. "Please call me Elizabeth."

Clara looked around hoping that Mr. Thayne would finish with Sir Douglas.

Elizabeth continued to press Clara. "I don't doubt your plans are harmless, but I ask that you remain with the party for the evening. Please save your plans with Mr. Thayne for another time."

"Elizabeth, why should you ask that we remain?"

"Clara," she whispered, her eyes full of implications, "it will look very inappropriate if you leave together."

Clara stood straighter. "You obviously do not know me, Miss Watson. I do not wish to appear inappropriate, but I see no reason why I should accommodate your request."

Urgency and panic filled Elizabeth's voice. "Please, I do not feel well tonight. I'm not sure I can dance much at all. Besides, the Weltons are going to notice your absence from the dance floor as will your aunt and uncle. Please . . ."

Clara noticed that Elizabeth was very pale.

"Please stay and keep me company. If you stay and dance, the others will not mind as much if I sit out. Please, I do not wish to worry my mother."

Clara was tempted to feel concern for Elizabeth, but she hesitated.

"If it makes you feel better," Elizabeth added, "I promise I won't try to dance with Mr. Thayne."

Clara's pride bristled. "Such promises are not necessary, Elizabeth."

Elizabeth actually looked offended. Clara stiffened and was about to pull away until she saw the sparkle of a tear sliding down Elizabeth's cheek.

Clara sighed heavily. "Let me tell Mr. Thayne there has been a change of plans."

Looking around, she saw that Mr. Thayne had just finished speaking with Sir Douglas and was walking toward her. Meeting him halfway, she explained Elizabeth's request.

"Are you disappointed?"

He cocked an eyebrow and raised a corner of his mouth. "I still get to spend time with you tonight, don't I?"

Mr. Thayne was becoming very skilled at making Clara feel desirable.

Finally, Lady Welton gave the signal, and the music began. Clara danced with Mr. Thayne, and Elizabeth managed to dance with Mr. Bailey, though she was not as graceful as usual. The older couples also danced while Mrs. Watson stood near Miss Bailey at the pianoforte, occasionally pointing at the music sheets.

As the couples weaved around each other, Clara remarked to Mr. Thayne, "I'm not sure what Elizabeth wants with me tonight, but I'm sure you and I can make arrangements for our secret engagement tomorrow." Clara realized what she had said two seconds after she said it. What a choice of words! Worse yet, it had come out louder than she had intended in an effort to be heard over the music.

"Secret engagement?" laughed Sir Douglas, leaning closer. "Ha ha! Your secret is safe with me!"

Clara looked bashfully at Mr. Thayne. He didn't seem to mind Sir Douglas's jest, but he didn't say anything either. When they finished the dance, Mr. Thayne squeezed her hand and promised to find her later. He then walked off in the same direction as Sir Douglas.

Clara rested only a minute before Elizabeth was at her side again, noticeably fatigued. "I know what you must think of me," she said.

Clara shrugged. "I don't know you well enough to have an opinion."

Elizabeth ignored Clara's coldness. "Well, I—Oh, my!" she breathed out, gripping her stomach. "I need some air."

Clara was surprised by the strength of Elizabeth's grip as she both leaned on and pulled Clara out to the terrace with her. Clara was beginning to regret agreeing to keep Elizabeth company. It was terribly cold outside. Clara shivered and hugged herself, but Elizabeth drank in the fresh air.

"Elizabeth, the air is quite bracing, but I can't stand more than a minute out here. It's freezing!"

Elizabeth opened her mouth to say something, but then she buckled over and vomited into a bush.

"Elizabeth!" Clara patted her back and felt a surge of guilt for questioning her motives. "You need a doctor!"

"No!" Elizabeth actually sounded frightened. "No, I am not sick. I just ate something that disagreed with me. That's all. The fresh air has helped. I feel better already. Please, don't say anything about it. Walk with me inside."

The rest of the merriment was cut short after that. Clara told Mr. Thayne how Elizabeth had become ill outside. Elizabeth begged Clara not to draw attention to it, but Clara was worried about her. Elizabeth was in no condition to stay up late dancing.

Clara began arguing with her, but before they could agree on what to do, Mr. Bailey came over and gave Elizabeth a flourishing bow.

"Miss Watson, I am overcome by your ravishing beauty tonight. May I have the pleasure of another dance?"

Panic stricken, Elizabeth looked to Clara. *Goodness!* thought Clara. *Can't he see she's turning green?*

"Forgive me, Mr. Bailey," Clara began, taking Elizabeth's arm and wrapping it in her own, "but I must ask you to excuse Miss Watson this time. She and I have private matters to discuss which I'm afraid cannot wait." Elizabeth curtsied to Mr. Bailey who walked away frowning.

"Mr. Bailey!" Clara stepped away from Elizabeth and gestured him toward her. "I happen to know that Miss Elizabeth is very fond of ginger tea. Would you mind having some sent up to her bedchamber? I'm sure she will appreciate your thoughtfulness."

"Of course." Mr. Bailey bowed and walked off.

Clara then begged Aunt Rose to distract everyone, perhaps with a game of charades, as she and Elizabeth left the party. Without a larger guest list, the dancing never lasted long anyway. Rose looked confused but agreed to help.

Once everyone was gathered to guess the meaning behind Rose's elaborate pantomimes, Clara and Elizabeth quietly retreated.

Clara let Elizabeth lean on her arm as they walked. The chill on the stairs reached her neck and made her shiver. Elizabeth, however, needed to stop and fan herself. Why did she so firmly object to the idea of a doctor? Did she just need rest? Perhaps, but Clara suspected Elizabeth was troubled by more than illness.

They walked along in silence until they reached Elizabeth's room. Clara helped Elizabeth to her bed and sat in a nearby chair. Though Elizabeth looked worn out, her eyes were keen.

"You lied," she said softly.

"About what?" Clara asked.

"About having private matters to discuss."

Clara shook her head. "I was not lying. I was hoping you would tell me what really ails you."

Elizabeth scratched her arm. "How did you know I'm fond of ginger tea?"

"I guessed, but I did notice you request it at breakfast." Clara stared at her, debating how hard to press for answers.

Elizabeth looked down at her feet and started to cry. The last of Clara's doubts dissolved with those tears. Elizabeth truly needed help. Clara went over and put a consoling arm around her.

"I can't—I'm not—I'm—" Elizabeth stuttered through sobs.

There was a small knock. A maid walked in carrying a tray with a tea kettle and two cups, which she sat on a table near the bed. "Your tea, miss." She curtsied and left.

Clara poured the tea, and for a while, neither girl spoke. Clara looked around the room and saw some of Elizabeth's things scattered about, an open journal, a pen left in ink, a few dried flowers on the open page. Something about that paper and ink, enlivened with Elizabeth's words and thoughts, made Clara see herself in Elizabeth. There Elizabeth sat with heartaches and burdens, perhaps wondering who she could trust, and Clara knew how she felt.

"Elizabeth, I know we have never confided in each other before, but are you certain you are only ill?"

"Oh, Clara!" Elizabeth put her cup down and shut her eyes tight. "I—"

"Elizabeth?!" Mrs. Watson burst through the door, making both girls jump. Elizabeth quickly blotted her eyes with a handkerchief and sniffled.

"Why did you leave, Elizabeth? I don't believe for a second that you and Miss Everton have anything to discuss." She sat on the bed next to Elizabeth and started rubbing her back. "Are you ill? Ah, yes, I can see it. Your eyes are all swollen. Very unbecoming. This isn't like you. Let's see if we can get you feeling better, love." She finally acknowledged Clara with a look that seemed to ask, *What are you still doing here?*

Clara stood to leave.

In quiet, expressionless tones, looking off to the side, Elizabeth said, "Thank you for your kindness, Clara."

Elizabeth did not look grateful, but Clara thought that might have been due to the nausea or the presence of Mrs. Watson.

"You're welcome," Clara answered and left, unsure what to think.

She stepped back into the hallway and walked slowly, running her fingers along the wall's wooden trim. It was early for bed, but too much weighed on her mind to return to the party. Instead, she wandered at random, walking upstairs and down, pausing occasionally to stare at a painting or sculpture while her thoughts were elsewhere. Her moment with Elizabeth had tested her compassion and pressed against her insecurities in ways that were new to Clara. Should she have done more for her?

Eventually, she came to a vacant sitting room she had never seen before. It was smaller than others but struck her as more inviting with one overly cushioned sofa placed directly before the fire. Though the flames had died and let in the chill, embers still glowed like rubies within the grate, enticing Clara to sit and find relief in the solitude.

Like ocean waves, thoughts began to wash over her, some gentle, some rough and unexpected. She thought of her mother, her father's poor health, quarrels and laughter with Louisa, Mr. Platt's threats, secrets with Frances, rumors of Mr. Shaw, and so on, but somehow, she always returned to Mr. Thayne. His hazel eyes. His hair the color of rich earth or wet tree bark. She thought of his natural smile, big and inviting, his thoughtfulness, his attentiveness, the way he appreciated her talents, the way he called her Clara. It all spoke to her. Maybe that was why he was different from other men. There was something about James Thayne that fundamentally connected with her.

As Clara ran her finger along the sofa's silver trim, a wintery draft reached her neck, and she saw the reason for the extra chill in the room. A window had been left open, leaving the curtain to flutter with the wind.

Clara crossed the room to secure the window, but as she pushed back the long curtains, she saw her mistake. Where she thought a row of windows had been, behind curtains that reached the floor, were large double doors, one of which was slightly ajar. Clara was about to close it, but she heard footsteps outside and peeked her head out.

"Clara?"

She froze. Mr. Thayne was leaning against the stone balustrades of a small, rectangular balcony. In the moonlight, his eyes looked deep and soft. Clara had never seen him look so at ease. She, however, looked around, wishing for a coat or blanket to throw around herself. With thoughts of him so recently blazing, she felt like all he had to do was look, and he would see everything.

"I thought you had retired to your room," he remarked.

"No. I have not." She considered running back to her room now, however.

"Come take a look at the lake." He gestured for her to join him. "The view is magnificent."

Clara faltered. She wanted to stay but wasn't sure she should be alone with him on the balcony of a dimly lit room.

As if reading her thoughts, he said, "Listen," and pointed down. "We're not alone."

Clara hadn't noticed it at first because she was too struck with his presence, but as she listened, she recognized Uncle William's voice. She couldn't make out his words, but Rose and the Weltons were laughing in response to something he had said. Clara and Mr. Thayne were directly above the party.

"Perhaps I can join you for a minute."

She stepped out and looked at the lake as he had suggested. It looked like frozen glass dusted with powdered sugar. The sky was a dome of clouds, cool and close, strangely aglow for such a late hour. She felt an icy tickle on her nose and realized it was lightly snowing.

"It's beautiful," she agreed.

"Beautiful in so many ways," Mr. Thayne sighed and looked at Clara as if he were no longer talking about the view. "Oh! Here." He quickly removed his jacket and wrapped it around her.

Even with her stomach fluttering, Clara managed a calm tone. "What are you doing out here?"

He shrugged and looked up. "Thinking."

"Do I get to know what you are thinking about?"

His face turned pensive. "I've been thinking that you still have not answered my question."

"What question is that?" Clara couldn't think of what he was referring to.

"The other day, I asked if we are friends now."

Ah, yes. "But I did answer."

"Oh, no. You only admitted that I made you laugh."

Clara bit her lip. "Mr. Thayne, I already told you in a letter that we are friends."

Mr. Thayne shifted on his feet. "I wouldn't mind hearing it from your lips. So much has happened since the letters."

Clara felt that familiar ache again. "I wish I knew. I mean, being friends is not—" Clara was about to say *not enough. Being friends is not enough.* But did he feel that way? Why was this question so important to him?

Mr. Thayne shifted again and scratched the back of his neck.

She exhaled. "Mr. Thayne, I see no reason why we can't—" But she couldn't finish her sentence. Why was she feeling so tongue-tied? She shook her head. "I wrote to you under no misconceptions. I discovered you as you wrote to me. But you wrote thinking I was someone else. I'm more curious to know whether *you* think we are *just* friends." *Just* friends. Would he catch the emphasis?

"Clara—" He started to speak but exhaled instead.

She still felt a thrill to hear him speak her name unburdened by formalities, but the thrill was snuffed as embarrassment colored his face and awkwardness wedged its way in. Clara shook her head. She had been alone with him for too long. She hastily said good night and turned to run out.

"Clara, wait!" Mr. Thayne called, reaching for her arm, but never making contact.

She paused and slowly turned to face him.

Emotions battled across his features. "I don't know why this is so hard. I wish you would just tell me what you think. I tell you everything—"

"Hardly!" she inserted.

Mr. Thayne looked away and ran his fingers through his hair. "This doesn't have to be complicated. If you could only admit your fault sometimes. If you knew what I've been through . . . I mean, I realize it's not your fault that Mr. Platt intercepted your letter, but—"

"What did you say?" Clara gasped as if the wind had been knocked out of her. "Mr. Platt did what?"

Mr. Thayne talked as if he were thinking out loud. "But if you hadn't rejected me in London perhaps we could have worked out our differences by now and—"

"You can't be serious!" Clara interjected. "Tell me this instant what Mr. Platt's involvement is."

Mr. Thayne stopped pacing and looked at her. "I never heard back from you after I sent my last letter asking when we should meet. Then I met Mr. Platt in Milton and discovered he stole the last letter you wrote to me."

Clara felt the color drain from her face. "You never received my last letter? The one where I poured out my . . . where I confessed how much I . . . how dear you . . . He took it? Oh, my! It was a very personal letter!"

Mr. Thayne looked more perplexed but less disgruntled. "A letter like that never would have escaped my notice."

Clara explained, "I spent hours on that letter. There was so much to say." She paused for a breath and watched it escape as quickly as it had come. "I suppose it no longer matters . . . I wanted to meet you, but I wasn't sure whether you should come to Milton. I didn't know how to tell you that and still tell you what you meant to me." Color rose back to Clara's face too quickly, making it burn.

Mr. Thayne paused and suddenly his eyes were dancing. He covered his mouth but Clara had already seen his smile. Did he have no compassion for her embarrassment?

"Forgive me," he said. "It's just that I specifically went to Milton because I didn't get your letter."

"And then to London! You went straight to London. To . . . to see me?" Clara concluded. "Oh, James, I'm so sorry!"

This time, Mr. Thayne made no efforts to hide his smile.

"What?" she asked.

"I like it when you call me James."

Clara felt snowflakes melt on her cheeks. "Well, that is your name, isn't it?"

"Of course it is," he grinned. "I like hearing it from you, Clara." His voice grew gentle but strong. "It sounds best when you say it. You shouldn't call me anything else."

Clara's heart quickened. "What did you say to Mr. Platt when you discovered his interference?"

"I planted him a facer." Mr. Thayne shrugged. "And I threatened to put him in the clutches of a certain ruthless moneylender. Mr. Platt won't be bothering you again."

It was a lot for Clara to process. She closed her eyes. She hardly knew how to thank Mr. Thayne. Before he even knew who she really was, he had stood his ground to protect her.

Mr. Thayne . . . James, looked steadily into her eyes. "So, does this mean we're friends?"

Clara's heart snapped back shut. Why did he have to ruin a perfectly good moment with that same silly question?

"Why is that such an important question to you?"

He stepped closer. "Why are you so set on avoiding it?"

They stood facing off, close enough for Clara to feel his breath on her face. Somewhere in the quiet that followed, an owl hooted and a breeze whistled its unrest. Clara didn't know why she kept avoiding the question. Maybe it was because it was the one thread that could unravel all her hopes. *Just friends.* Just when she thought Mr. Thayne would confess real feelings for her, he insisted on demoting it all back to friendship. Day by day, he had nudged her into the comfortable security of attachment, only to be tossed back to cold uncertainty with this deceptively plain question.

There was one thing, at least, she was certain of. "It is not my fault things are complicated."

"That isn't what I meant," he faltered. "Please, I—"

"Perhaps I will answer your question when you finally tell me what 'being friends' means to you."

Mr. Thayne shook his head as if disappointed. "Clara, when are you going to take a risk? Do you never open your heart?"

The silence that followed nearly crushed her. "I just did," she cried. "Just as I did with my first letter to you, and every letter after that!

And look what happened! I'm trying. I really am, but when everything is going well, my heart gets trampled!"

Mr. Thayne looked away, but even from his profile, Clara could see a struggle of emotions passing over him. When he looked back at her, he spoke quietly but with effort. "I can't predict the future, Clara. I can't promise everything will be perfect, but you'll never know what I'd do with your heart unless you trust me."

She closed her eyes tight. His words, sharp with honesty, penetrated more deeply than he understood. She wanted to stay, to take a risk, but her wounds were too raw to let her trust as she wanted to. Before he could see her wet face, she turned and ran all the way to her bedchamber.

After shutting the door, she fell to her bed with a sad realization. She was letting pride stop her from finding love.

Chapter 40

As Shaw exited Mr. Barnes's office, he smiled smugly to himself, feeling as if he had outsmarted the world and already gained his fortune. He held an official statement that plainly outlined evidence of his right to inherit the Everton estate once Mr. Everton was dead.

Obtaining the statement had not been easy. When Shaw first made his request, Barnes had gaped at him. Then he denied any knowledge of Mr. Everton's affairs, but Shaw made it clear that he knew Barnes was searching for an heir. Barnes was still reluctant to provide an official statement, suggesting there were still matters to research, family lines to investigate, and so on, but Shaw thought that was nonsense. It was more likely Shaw's father had paid Barnes to keep quiet about the Everton estate. *Well, ha!* Shaw had found out about it anyway and could play the same tricks. A few extra pounds was all it took to persuade Barnes to draft the statement, which would add validity to Shaw's claim when he next approached Clara.

Shaw praised his own cunning as he shuffled along, whistling as he went. Barnes had put him in a good mood, despite his insistence that Shaw meet his daughter. Shaw didn't need to worry anymore about who he would marry. He had exactly what he needed to convince Clara to say yes: a claim on the home she loved. He was the only surviving male heir of the Everton family, and he would claim her too, securing his own rightful inheritance in the process. He would live his days in comfort, and as for Philip, well, Shaw hoped for his sake that he was good at manual labor.

Shaw laughed to think of his perfect brother, who his father had always loved best, working for his bread. It was hilarious, the best sort of revenge! Philip could become a professional beggar for all Shaw cared.

The pompous, annoying, no good—

Shaw clenched his teeth and impulsively kicked a brick wall.

"Ow, ooh, ow!" he exclaimed as he hobbled on the sidewalk.

Two middle-aged women scoffed their disapproval as they walked by.

Shaw brushed off his jacket and reminded himself that he didn't care a whit what others thought, not those old maids and definitely not his family. He was going to outsmart them all. With a fresh pain in his foot and an old grudge on his shoulders, he headed for home. It was time to pack his bags and leave for Brindley.

Chapter 41

*I*t was Christmas Eve. Thayne was gliding on the ice, puzzling over the ladies in general. Miss Watson had dropped her simpering airs lately and, instead, usually looked uncomfortable or upset. Though she claimed to prefer the cold to remaining indoors with her mother, she complained about the snow, her skates, and how ridiculous it was that anyone else could enjoy the ice. Miss Bailey didn't talk much and was usually by herself. Sometimes Thayne forgot she was even there.

And then there was Clara. Thayne had his eyes on her most of the time. This was her first time skating, and she frequently stumbled. She sometimes grabbed her aunt's shoulders and the two would spin and laugh. Clara smiled the whole time, even when she fell, and whenever she smiled at Thayne, he forgot how cold it was. Her eyes shined like little rays of sun breaking through winter clouds, and she looked graceful even when losing her balance. He couldn't decide whether he wanted to skate with her or simply watch her.

Watching the men skate was not nearly as entertaining. Mr. Bailey skated back and forth as if he were pacing or brooding. Sir Douglas and Mr. Martin were on their skates but might as well have been off them. They remained still and talked, just as if they were standing in the drawing room.

Thayne started practicing figure eights as he considered Clara. He hated how awkward things had ended the other night on the balcony. Why didn't he just tell her they were friends? Because he knew he wanted more, but also because he wanted to know if Clara really had forgiven him. Still, why didn't he just tell her? Thayne could kick himself for being so stubborn. It was understandable for Clara to still question his feelings, especially after all that had happened, but today, he was determined to settle this "friends" question once and for all.

As Thayne watched Clara and Mrs. Martin complete another lap around the pond, Clara slipped and fell. Tiny flecks of ice stuck in her hair and sparkled in the sun. She shook her arms and skirts free of other ice remnants and slowly made her way to a fallen log at the edge of the lake. She smiled despite her fall and sat down, hugging her knees to her chest.

The ice scraped next to him, and there was Martin.

"If I were young and in love," Martin said meaningfully, "I would not risk letting another man sit next to the lady I admired." He gestured with his head toward Bailey who was also looking at Clara.

Thayne took the hint. He slapped Martin's shoulder and pushed off.

In those brief seconds gliding toward her, Thayne felt completely aligned. His desire for Clara steadied him. The seconds slowed and his awareness heightened. Her face glowed rosy with exertion, and the tiny mole under her eye sat like a gem. Her hair was a mix of chocolate and cinnamon in the sunlight, and her smile a blooming crescent brimming with unspoken ideas. He loved everything about her. As he sat next to her, he was certain he loved her.

Placing a hand on the log, he sat close enough to catch her soft floral scent and feel her stray hairs brush his cheek when the wind blew. His thoughts were turning, putting ideas together like gears in a clock. Despite the awkwardness of the other night, things were working now, and it was best not to think too hard about what to say.

"How do you like skating Clara? You are doing quite well."

"Thank you," she replied. "I enjoy it, but I have trouble balancing for more than a few minutes."

Thayne watched her closely. Was it true? The awkwardness of the previous night was not affecting her easy manner. "It is not so very different from dancing. Would you allow me to take you around?" Thayne stood up and lowered his arm toward her. She reached up but hesitated.

"And how many turns around the pond shall I take with you? Will we create scandal if we take more than two turns together?"

He shook his head, loving the playfulness in her voice. "That is not a fair comparison. A turn on the ice takes but a few moments while the cotillion may last a solid half hour. I would not feel satisfied if you did not at least give me that much."

Thayne soaked up Clara's laughter.

She stumbled and clung to his arm as she stood up and found her center. "I would give you half an hour, but I don't think I'll last that long."

No matter, Thayne thought. His plans would take them off the ice anyway. They pushed off and began gliding. He wouldn't have minded if she needed him to catch her more often, but his arm was enough to keep her balanced. He tuned in to the light pressure of her hand and how she held tighter around the curves. Thayne caught Martin nodding his approval at them.

"Clara," Thayne said, "there is something I've been wanting to show you. I wasn't sure the time was right before. It's not far from here. Perhaps now, the time is right." He spun around to face her, searching her eyes as they searched his.

"All right."

Thayne led Clara to the edge of the pond where they unstrapped their skates from their boots.

Fighting the nervousness that pounded inside, he gestured with his head toward a small path and tried to look confident. The trees, though bare, were slightly thicker and the path smaller, so they were able to slip away without drawing too much attention to themselves.

Clara shivered one last time before accepting Thayne's jacket. She felt badly about depriving him of it when it was so cold out, but then she saw he wore an extra one underneath. Hugging his jacket close, she breathed in his scent and soaked up the extra warmth. She was grateful he didn't seem upset about the other night. In fact, he was extra solicitous, persistent even, about seeing to her comfort. At times like these, it was hard to imagine ever doubting that he liked her. So why had things been so awkward the other night?

"We won't be far from the others," he reassured her. "Just beyond these trees overlooking the valley."

They could still hear the others scraping their skates on the ice and occasionally laughing, though the sounds were muffled by wind. A few snowflakes flitted through the air as they walked down the path.

Thayne explained, "This place is special to me for many reasons. It was here, for example, that I decided to keep a journal. Every Christmas I write down goals for the upcoming year."

"A lovely tradition," Clara remarked.

"I would like to show you the exact place that tradition began."

They passed a few trees as they rounded the bend and came to a spot that overlooked a vast winter landscape. In the distance, they could see tiny cottages with snowy rooftops, soft hills on the left, and an icy river on the right. She could just barely hear the wind whistling through leafless trees. The scene reminded Clara of a dream she once had. She took it all in before turning around and seeing that Mr. Thayne now sat on a bench a few feet back under a large tree. Its thick, bare branches provided just enough protection to keep the bench free of snow.

Clara sat next to him and regarded the view. "It's very peaceful," she commented. "You said this is where your tradition of journal writing began?"

"Yes," he smiled sheepishly, "but before I get to that, I was wondering . . ." He paused and sucked in a nervous breath. There was something very endearing about that look on Mr. Thayne. "I want to be sure that you have truly forgiven me. I think you have, but I believe it is best to ask."

"Have I forgiven you?" Clara repeated to herself. She truly thought she had already forgiven him, but why had her pride flared so strongly the other night? Was it possible her forgiveness was incomplete? He *had* broken her heart . . .

Mr. Thayne shifted in his seat. "I hate to think about how I treated you only a few weeks ago. My behavior in London was downright shameful. If I could go back and change it, I would."

The sincerity of his words poked and pulled at the last splinter of pride remaining in her chest. There was no need to hold onto past hurts. No need at all. She let the splinter fall and forgave him completely. "Yes, Mr. Thayne."

"James," he whispered.

"Yes, James," she said softly. "I have forgiven you."

"Thank you," he exhaled. "All I have wanted since coming here and seeing you was to be friends again, just as we were when we wrote letters to each other."

"I see," Clara looked over the small valley. Mr. Thayne's words were kind, but they were not what she wanted to hear. "Then there is still something I would like you to clarify for me."

"Oh?" Mr. Thayne sounded cautious.

She had to be careful. *No more pride*, she promised. She kept her tone light. "As *friends*, would we go fishing together and play cards?"

"Of course not," he said with a gleam in his eye. "Neither of us like cards."

She managed a half-smile before looking away.

"Clara, I do want to be friends again." He spoke soft and low.

She turned back to face him, but she could feel her hope wilting and knew she didn't hide it well.

He tilted his head closer. "Because I have learned that friendship is the best foundation to build something deeper on."

Clara made a breathy laugh as his words sunk in. She didn't know whether to elbow him for teasing her or hug him for caring for her. Would there ever be a time when she could reach for him whenever she wanted?

"I'm sorry for the other night."

"So am I."

She didn't know how long they sat without a word being spoken, but it was a comfortable silence, made all the more refreshing by their apologies. Before long, Mr. Thayne continued his story.

"So now I will tell you what is special to me about this place. I was thirteen years old. My father was friends with Sir Douglas. My family used to come here every other year or so. I would often come to this bench to be alone. As you can see, it is a convenient place to sit without being observed."

Clara could still hear the muffled sounds of the others talking and skating, but sitting on the bench with Mr. Thayne felt intimate.

He pointed to a small path further down the hill that she had not seen before. It probably stood out against green grass in the spring and summer, but in the winter, it was hard to distinguish from the rest of the bare, frosted ground.

Mr. Thayne cleared his throat. "One time, I came here with my notebook to draw. I never had your talent, but I liked to occasionally sketch a scene. I saw my mother and father walk down that path. They didn't know I was up here. I saw my father hug my mother and tenderly kiss her. I already knew they loved each other, but it was the only time I ever saw my father so gentle and affectionate. I wanted to be just like him."

Clara sat close enough to feel his arm brush against hers when he shifted.

"In that moment I wondered what it would be like to be in love." He took a deep breath. "I took my notebook and instead of drawing, I wrote down a goal: kiss a girl under this tree."

Clara swallowed. "An interesting start to your Christmas tradition."

"A simple enough goal, but as a young boy, not quite a man, I had no idea how to make it happen." Thayne smiled and rested his elbow on the back of the bench as he turned toward Clara. "Since discovering that you and I were both to spend our holiday here, I have thought about that goal." He paused. Was Clara's heart speeding up? "You should know this about me. When I set my mind on something, I pride myself on having the determination to see it through." His eyes began tracing every feature of her face until they stopped at her lips.

Clara tugged at the scarf around her neck and shivered. "Is that so, James?" she whispered, still adjusting to the sound of his name on her lips. She could see herself reflected in his eyes. When had he leaned so close?

"The reason I brought you here . . ." He trailed off and looked up.

Clara followed his eyes and saw something hanging from a tree branch. She never would have noticed it had he not pointed it out. It was a Christmas kissing bough. She held her breath. She would be calm and collected, she told herself, no matter how fast her heart was trying to go.

"Did you put that up there yourself?" she asked.

He gave a short laugh. "In truth, it wasn't me. However, I can't deny I expected it to be there. The Weltons hang it there every year."

Clara sat completely still as Mr. Thayne reached up to cradle her cheek. As his thumb brushed her skin, her blood coursed faster and the warmth of his touch set her aglow like a candle newly lit. She saw the intent in his eyes, and her wanting grew. His hand shifted ever so slightly, and she waited, certain the kiss was coming. But then he held still like that for so long, she worried he might not kiss her, which, in that moment, seemed the worst possible fate. Without thinking, she took his lapel and gave a gentle tug. It was all the encouragement he needed. Mr. Thayne smiled, gave her cheek another thrilling brush, and leaned in. His lips, warm and soft, eagerly met hers and soaked up the rose balm she wore. Clara breathed in and marveled at how fluently his lips moved with hers. Each heartbeat, each small tilt of the head kept the kiss changing and the anticipation hanging, until his hand moved to the back of her neck, and their lips reluctantly parted ways.

With the kiss complete, Mr. Thayne gently rested his forehead on hers and inhaled deeply. She kept her eyes closed and enjoyed the warmth of his breath on her face. Relaxing into the moment, Clara ran her hand down his stubbled jaw as she eased back. Looking into his eyes, she didn't know what to say. Every idea fell short. The moment was too strong for words, but the silence couldn't last.

Mr. Thayne was the first to speak. "I think we just became more than friends."

Clara's smile spread wide. "I can admire a man who sees his goals through."

Chapter 42

Clara rested on her bed spinning the kissing bough from a string she held. She enjoyed the way it spun until the string grew taut before spinning in the opposite direction. After Mr. Thayne had kissed her, he jumped up and pulled the kissing bough from the tree to give to her as a keepsake of the day they became more than friends. She happily took it, though she didn't need a keepsake to remember that moment.

After their kiss, Clara and Mr. Thayne snuck away as they had hoped to the other night when Elizabeth became ill. Clara had prepared a basket with bread and candied nuts to give to Henry Cook, the stable hand who had been kicked by the horse. He lived in a small cottage on the Brindley estate not far from the lake where they had been ice skating. Clara wanted to see how he was doing, but she would only go with Mr. Thayne. Mr. Cook's leg was still swollen and extremely bruised, but he cheered up at the sight of visitors, especially visitors with a basket of treats. Clara noticed how highly Mr. Cook regarded Mr. Thayne, thanking him over and over for helping with his chores after the accident. He also thanked Clara for remembering him. The rest of the visit was short and pleasant.

As they walked back to the house, Mr. Thayne surprised Clara with an apple tart he had saved for her, which she willingly shared with him. Soon, she was telling him about Christmas at Milton Manor, how Louisa had a special family recipe for plum pudding, how everyone exchanged homemade gifts, how the whole house smelled like cinnamon and pine, and how they always ate apple tarts. Clara loved how closely Mr. Thayne listened to these details that meant so much to her.

She smiled and shared a thought that had been stirring ever since their conversation on the balcony. "I still can't believe you went to Milton."

Mr. Thayne looked very pleased with himself. "If you are curious, I believe your father approves of me."

Mr. Thayne stopped walking and turned to face Clara. He took one of the strands of loose hair flying around her face and tucked it behind her ear. His thumb lingered on the same cheek he had touched earlier when he kissed her. He looked like he was about to kiss her again, and suddenly all Clara wanted was another chance to test how well those lips worked with hers. She knew, however, that without the liberty the mistletoe gave him, Mr. Thayne, being a true gentleman, wouldn't kiss her again unless they were engaged. *Engaged*? Did she really just think that? *Calm down,* she told herself. *One step at a time.*

With the memory fresh in her thoughts, Clara reached over on her bed to where she had thrown Mr. Thayne's jacket. She picked it up and breathed in its scent of fresh wood and mint. Then, draping it across her chest of drawers with the kissing bough on top, she laid back down and closed her eyes to rest before dinner.

A few seconds later, however, her rest was interrupted with a loud knock. A maid had a letter for her. Clara thanked her and took the letter. Bewildered, Clara broke off the wafer on the back and unfolded the paper. It was from Frances! How did she know Clara was at the Weltons'? Curious to know what news her friend would send, Clara read.

Dear Clara,

How are you, my friend? I hope you are enjoying your holiday in Brindley. I heard rumor you were a guest there for the holidays. Word reached me quickly as I am in a neighboring village not far from you. The servants in these parts all know each other, and they do talk! I begin to suspect who your secret admirer is, and I must say, I approve your choice! I was so glad to learn you were nearby. I set about to write to you straightway, for you are the only one I can confide in.

I am here for my cousin's wedding, but I am also to be married soon. At least, that is what my intended and I have been planning. You are still the only one who knows our secret, and I am worried! He was supposed to be staying at an inn until we found the right moment to run away, but I have not heard a word from him! My mother continues to watch me relentlessly, so perhaps he is simply waiting for the right moment. Still, I should have heard from him by now! I cannot imagine what his reasons might be. Oh, but that's not true! I can imagine the worst! Our plans have been thwarted before, but he always managed to send word. Now, he is completely silent. I worry he is injured or that his feelings are changed. I cannot bear the thought of him not coming. What am I to do?

I cannot properly express how frightening it feels to be this close to my future happiness but left in limbo. For the past year, all I have thought about is the day I shall become Mrs. Shaw. Yes, I reveal him to you now and hope you will understand. If you know anything of his whereabouts, please put my mind at ease.

Frances

Clara put down the letter and closed her eyes in disbelief as her earlier suspicions were confirmed. Sweet, good Frances, her dearest friend, and Mr. Shaw? It would certainly explain Frances's reluctance to admit who she was engaged to. It also explained why her mother did not approve, but how had Frances not seen his true nature? Admittedly, Clara had never been sure which rumors to believe, but she had seen firsthand the way he fluctuated between ignoring her and recklessly flirting with her. To learn he had been engaged to Frances the whole time! There was no question left in Clara's mind. Mr. Shaw was untrustworthy, and Frances needed help.

Clara clenched her fist around the note. Frances had not yet sealed her fate. There was still time! Clara could save her friend from a scandalous elopement and a future of heartache.

She hastily dressed for dinner and went to find her aunt and uncle. With their help, Clara was sure she could stop Frances from making a dreadful mistake. Meanwhile, Clara silently begged Frances's forgiveness for fervently wishing Mr. Shaw would not come.

Chapter 43

With an insuppressible grin, Thayne paced the drawing room as he waited for Clara to arrive for dinner. Each step he took sprang from a buoyant happiness that kept his feet from grounding. He had just kissed Clara! He was certain she cared for him! He felt like the richest man in England, and he now knew what he would give her for Christmas. Everything he had to offer, his hand, his heart, and a chance to build a life together.

His thoughts were suddenly interrupted by a hand on his shoulder.

"Easy now, Thayne!" said Martin. "What's gotten into you? You look like you're about to float away or wear a hole in the carpet."

Thayne turned and grinned. "Just in a good mood, Martin. It's Christmas Eve after all."

Martin took one scrutinizing look at Thayne. "You kissed my niece today, didn't you?"

Mr. Bailey shot them a glance from the corner where he was sitting. Martin could be so loud sometimes.

Martin continued, "Well, Rose and I also found one of the kissing boughs today. Don't think you can have all the fun!"

Mrs. Martin came up to her husband and slipped her arm through his. "William, are you teasing Mr. Thayne again? Come, now. It looks like the Weltons are inviting us to be seated for dinner."

"But where is Miss Everton?" Thayne asked looking around.

His question was soon answered. Clara briskly entered the room, her face all soberness. Thayne's grin faltered. What could be troubling her after such a wonderful day? It had been wonderful for her too, hadn't it?

He was walking over to talk with her, but before he could ask what was wrong, she just gave him a brief smile and went straight for her uncle. Thayne stood still, perplexed and aching, with his feet finally grounded. He would have done whatever he could to fix Clara's troubles, but she had walked past him and wedged herself between her aunt and uncle. *Don't worry,* he told himself. Most likely, they just needed a moment alone. He could still sit with Clara at dinner and ask about her troubles then.

Thayne followed everyone into the dining room, grateful, at least, that as Clara sat next to her aunt, the other seat beside Clara remained free. Right as Thayne went to take the seat, however, Bailey came out of nowhere and planted himself next to Clara. *Of all the moments for Bailey to interfere!* Thayne would have to be content with the seat across from her.

He watched Clara and the way her brows creased when she leaned close to her aunt and uncle to whisper, pausing occasionally to catch her breath, all while servants reached over and across to fill the table with trays of food. At least Bailey couldn't get Clara's attention in the midst of it all. It wasn't until his third or fourth attempt, from what Thayne could tell, that she finally acknowledged him with a slight nod before turning back to her aunt. *Just what he deserves,* thought Thayne.

When Bailey turned away from Clara and forcefully shook out his serviette, Thayne took it as a sign he had given up.

"How are you, Bailey?" Thayne asked.

Bailey glowered at him.

Miss Bailey came in and sat next to Thayne on his left. "Good evening, Mr. Thayne."

Thayne politely returned her greeting.

"It seems my brother is making an idiot of himself again," she whispered.

Thayne stared at her. It was the most expressive thing he had ever heard her say.

"Forgive me," she said lowering her head. "I only wish he could gracefully accept defeat. As I have."

She looked into his eyes, blushed deeply, and looked away.

Thayne looked at his plate and frowned. He didn't know if he had understood her correctly, but he had never suspected Miss Bailey of anything but quiet, sisterly affection for him.

"I—" He tried to think of something he could say.

"Please don't," she said quickly. "There is no need to say anything. I only wish you and Miss Everton happiness."

"Thank you," Thayne said, considering his next words carefully. "There was a time, a few years ago, when I had to accept defeat. It hurt for a while, but it taught me to fight for what I cared about most." He looked at Clara and then back at Miss Bailey.

She looked down at her plate and nodded. "I'll remember that."

Thayne was just about to take a bite of roasted venison when Miss Watson, the last to arrive for dinner, sat on his right. "Mr. Thayne! What a pleasant surprise it is to see a vacant seat next to you! I do hope nothing has come between you and our dear Clara. She seems positively put out!"

Thayne would give Miss Watson credit for one thing. She was observant. "Good evening," was all he said in return.

She kept her eyes on him and tilted her head, tapping the side of her chin as if considering him.

Thayne immensely disliked the idea of Miss Watson considering him.

As she then looked around, Thayne could see the moment her shrewd face lit with understanding. "Oh my, I believe I see it now. The problem is not between you and Clara, is it? It must be between you and Mr. Bailey!" She seemed highly amused.

Thayne cleared his throat and finally took a bite of his roast.

"That confirms it!" she stated with certainty. "But I know how we shall make him mad with jealousy. He tried to kiss me today, you know, but I only let him have my cheek."

Before Thayne realized what she was doing, she spread her fan out in front of her face and leaned close to Thayne's so that both of their faces were behind the fan. She then closed it with a flourish, started laughing, and playfully smacked her fan on his shoulder. This did get the attention of Mr. Bailey, who, Thayne supposed, was either very jealous or suffering from indigestion, but it also got the attention of

Clara, who gave them a puzzled look and went right back to whispering with her aunt.

Thayne looked sternly at Miss Watson. "I am not interested in making Mr. Bailey mad."

She shrugged her shoulders and took a sip from her glass.

Thayne turned again to his meal and took a roll from the nearest tray. Out of habit, he picked up the tray and offered it to Miss Bailey and then to Miss Watson. When she saw the rolls, her eyes grew large. She eagerly grabbed three, nearly making Thayne drop the tray.

Thayne watched her take a large bite out of one while still holding the other two.

"Please don't look so shocked!" she said after swallowing. "My stomach can't tolerate all this meat. That roast smells positively foul, and these rolls are the first thing to look the least bit appetizing."

"Ah, yes. You have been ill," he recalled, trying to sound sympathetic, but when she just grimaced in response, he said nothing more.

Thayne sat up straighter and dropped his fork when he saw that Clara had finally stopped talking to her aunt and uncle and was looking directly at him. She was composed, but he knew her face well enough to see the lines of worry and the slightest downward tilt of her mouth. If only he hadn't been too slow with the seating. He could have held her hand and offered comfort. Instead, he had nothing but sympathetic smiles to give across the table.

After a minute of eating, one of the servants entered briskly and walked over to Sir Douglas. Thayne couldn't hear what the servant whispered, but judging from Sir Douglas's reaction, the servant's message was unusual.

After some pensive nodding, Sir Douglas answered loudly, "So be it! Let him join us. We can't leave anyone out in the cold on Christmas, can we?" Then turning to address the entire group, he said, "It seems we shall have one more guest joining us this evening."

The servant exited the room and returned moments later with a tall fellow mumbling to him. "Whatever you have that's hot. It's dreadfully cold out there."

Thayne heard Clara take in a sharp breath. Before the servant could announce the newcomer, Clara gasped, "Mr. Shaw?!"

Who is Mr. Shaw? Thayne muttered to himself.

All eyes turned to Clara and then to the gentleman. The clanks of forks and knives halted as Mr. Shaw brushed past the servant and took an empty seat at the end of the table without any further introduction.

Whether Clara was embarrassed for prematurely announcing this fellow, Thayne didn't know, but the blush on her cheeks was deepening by the second. She was also fidgeting with her hair, biting her lip, and occasionally looking at her aunt and uncle who were also watching Mr. Shaw.

Thayne was careful to observe everything, the way Mr. Shaw smiled at each of the ladies, especially Clara, and the way he smiled at the men as if issuing a dare. All Thayne could say for certain was that he didn't trust this Mr. Shaw.

"Good evening, Miss Everton," Shaw said as his lip crept up in a half smile.

Thayne gripped his cutting knife. How dare Shaw single her out before the whole group.

"What umm . . . how did you . . ." Clara began mumbling when Shaw gave a small chuckle.

"I was travelling through these parts when the weather turned especially bad. There is a terrible snowstorm brewing out there." Shaw took the glass the servant had just poured for him and raised it high. "Sir Douglas, Lady Welton, I must thank you for allowing me to impose on your kindness and interrupt your supper."

"My pleasure." Sir Douglas then went over introductions for Shaw's benefit. When he came to Clara, he remarked, "It would appear you already know Miss Everton."

Shaw nodded and spoke directly to Clara. "You look surprised to see me."

Clara said nothing.

"I heard you might be staying here, but I'm only passing through. I'm actually on my way to meet some relations a few miles north of here. Oh, do I have a Christmas surprise for them!" He chuckled to himself.

Thayne caught Clara's eye before she nervously replied, "Well, I hope your journey has been well so far despite the cold."

"Mhhm," he hummed in response, having just taken a bite of meat.

Thayne saw a tiny bit of sauce dribble out the corner of his mouth.

Between bites, Shaw said, "You know, Miss Watson and I are also acquainted."

Thayne noticed Miss Watson stiffen in her seat.

Shaw added, "I was unaware I would have the pleasure of such lovely company here. Very fortunate, indeed. Perhaps I ought to get stuck in snowstorms more often."

Sir Douglas laughed politely at Shaw's attempt at humor.

Thayne looked around and thought it was his turn to say something, anything, especially if it exposed Shaw as a good-for-nothing.

"Bread?" Thayne held up the tray and cursed his lack of creativity.

"Right. Hungry. Smells delicious." Shaw slapped his hands and rubbed them together. A servant came and obligingly took the tray from Thayne and carried it down the table to Shaw.

Thayne saw Clara shift in her seat. "You heard I was here? Why would . . . um . . . ?" she trailed off, her cheeks still blazing.

"Does a man need a reason to visit his most enchanting cousin?" Shaw answered confidently.

Had Thayne heard Mr. Shaw correctly? He was Clara's cousin? Thayne liked this man less each time he opened his mouth.

"I beg your pardon, Mr. Shaw," Clara said, "but I believe you spoke of our *possible* relation as being fairly distant."

"The relation may be fairly distant, but I have no doubt you are fair." Shaw emphasized each word and waved his fork as he talked. "I won't impose on the Weltons' kindness for long. I plan to leave early in the morning."

Thayne wished he were close enough to hear what Clara mumbled under her breath just then. Instead, he heard Shaw's teeth grinding on nuts.

The meal carried on in silence for several minutes until Sir Douglas revived the conversation by asking Martin about his favorite outdoor sports. Then Lady Welton and Mrs. Watson began debating the best ways to care for mischievous children. Mrs. Watson was subtly hinting that Emily and Mabel needed a new governess. Miss Bailey said nothing, only nodded occasionally in one direction or another as if unsure which conversation she belonged to, and Elizabeth sullenly picked at her food. Mr. Bailey made another attempt to talk with Clara, but he eventually gave up and ate in silence. Thayne again regretted being too far away to talk quietly with Clara.

As plates were taken away and desserts were brought out, Clara stood up. "If you will all excuse me, I'm quite tired. Mr. Thayne, would you accompany me to the stairs?" Thayne's heart jumped to his throat at the mention of his name, evidence she wanted him.

He rose from his seat, eager to oblige, but Shaw inserted himself. "I hope I am not too bold in requesting the pleasure myself."

Thayne saw that Clara was uncomfortable with this suggestion, and he absolutely detested the idea. But when he began to protest, Shaw persisted.

"I really must insist. You see, I did not want to bring attention to it, but I admit that I planned on stopping here, snowstorm or not. I have some rather urgent but private news for Miss Everton."

What Thayne would have given to hear that news! He waited as Clara looked between him and Mr. Shaw. He didn't understand what she was trying to communicate with her eyes, but when she agreed to let Mr. Shaw accompany her, Thayne sank back to his chair, defeated. Clara bid everyone a good night and walked with Shaw out of the dining room.

If no one else had been watching, Thayne might have followed them quietly from behind. For a while, he grumbled to himself, stirring around the potatoes on his plate that no longer looked appetizing. *Then again*, he thought, dropping his fork to his plate, *who cares whether or not anyone is watching.* He stood up, excused himself, and marched out the door.

Chapter 44

Clara stepped along, sensing the imbalance and rigidity in her gait, but no matter how many times she brought calming images to her mind, Mr. Shaw's presence wound her insides like fibers in a rope. What news could he possibly have for her? She vowed right then and there that if it had anything to do with Frances, she would duel him herself.

Taking the long way, Clara led him through the lower east wing of the house to the stairs on the side farthest away from the dining hall. She hadn't thought her route through, exactly, only that she felt greater safety in walking with him than in standing still.

As they came to the end of the hallway and turned the corner that led to the staircase, Mr. Shaw took Clara's hand and spun her into his arms before she knew what was happening.

"Darling Clara!" he whispered dramatically, clasping his head to hers. "You can't comprehend how I've missed you!"

Clara positioned one hand on his head and another on his chest and focused all her muscle into pushing him away.

"How dare you!" she spat, taking as big a step back as she could. Clara shook off the daze of having been so quickly encircled and saw that there was real hurt in his eyes. What on earth was he thinking? She cleared her throat and calmed her tone. "Mr. Shaw, what are you really doing here?"

"I came to see you." He took a small step toward her, holding out his hand as an invitation this time. It troubled Clara to see him looking so innocent.

"You said you have a message for me?" She folded her arms and took another step back.

"Yes, of course. I do, but . . ." He looked around as if making sure they were alone. In a hushed voice, he asked, "Are you really so unhappy to see me? I still remember how you smiled at me at the end of last season."

Clara stuck her nose up. "Much has changed since then."

Mr. Shaw stepped closer. "Things can change again. I missed you, Clara. I was hoping to steal just one short moment with you tonight to tell you that."

"*Stealing* is certainly the right word. I can't fathom why you would presume to take such liberties with me."

Mr. Shaw looked down and twisted his face like he was ashamed. "You are right to censure me. I was too overcome. Please forgive me!" He took Clara's hand again, more gently this time and looked pleadingly in her eyes.

Clara pulled away, hating to entertain the possibility that he might be sincere, and started walking up the stairs without minding where she was going.

Mr. Shaw followed her closely. "Dear Clara," he whispered. "You underestimate your power to captivate."

She spoke over her shoulder. "Do you insist on following me, Mr. Shaw?"

"I really have missed you."

Clara reached the top of the stairs and walked faster.

"Can't you see how I care? There never seems to be a good moment to say it, but I was trying to when I last saw you in London."

"Mr. Shaw—"

"Clara, please. I came all this way for you."

It wasn't until she stood before a familiar door and put her hand on the knob that she froze with embarrassment. Wanting solitude, Clara had inadvertently walked to her bedchamber. The compromising state of her current situation chilled her from the inside out.

Mr. Shaw put his hand on hers and twisted the knob, swinging it open.

"Mr. Shaw . . ." Clara retracted her hand and stood to block the entrance. "Is that your message? That you wished to tell me you care?"

Her insides screamed a warning as she watched him lean against the doorframe. "Well, yes and no. Yes, but there is more."

She spoke slowly. "Then deliver your message and leave."

Mr. Shaw regarded her. "Very well. I will not keep you in suspense. I've written it all out for you to read in private, in case we were interrupted. There is much to consider but very little time." He stood straight and began patting his chest and sides, searching his pockets but apparently not finding what he was looking for. "Blast!" he whispered fiercely. "This is going to be more difficult without my note."

Chapter 45

Elizabeth leaned against the wall in the hallway holding her queasy stomach and a letter. She had excused herself early for many reasons. She was tired. So, so tired. She was afraid she might vomit again, and she desperately wanted to avoid that, especially in front of her mother.

Her main motive for leaving dinner early was to read a letter from Mr. Shaw. When he had stood to leave the table, he carelessly dropped an unaddressed note on the ground close to her chair. Had he dropped it by accident or was it intended for her? She was certain no one else had noticed, so she covered it with her shoe and slid it closer. Then, when no one was looking, she picked it up and excused herself.

Now, as she clutched the letter in the hallway and willed her stomach to settle, her curiosity was peaked. Why would Mr. Shaw be at Brindley at all if not for her? He had looked surprised to see her, but perhaps that was merely to keep up appearances. Still, if he had come all that way for her, why put up the pretense of delivering a message to Clara?

If he really had come for Clara instead of her, she vowed she would make him regret his visit.

Having no qualms about opening the unaddressed note, Elizabeth unfolded the paper. She desperately hoped for Mr. Shaw's sake as well as hers that his letter contained an exceptional explanation. She read,

Dear Clara,

How are you, my darling? I hope you are well, but I'm afraid your happiness is about to be shaken. I bring sad news. An impersonal messenger was called to deliver this very personal message, but I offered to deliver the news to you myself in hopes that I may soften the blow. Ever since I discovered that we are related, I have found myself thinking about you more and more, so please forgive me if my own personal desires to see you influenced my decision to come.

And now to get on with the difficult task. The sad news is this, that your father is dead. He had been growing ill for some time but grew much worse while you were in London until he ultimately passed. Word was first sent to your London address, but I stepped in, knowing you had already gone to Brindley, and offered to come to you myself. This terrible news was also made known to me because—oh, forgive me for adding burden to your suffering—your estate was entailed, and I was contacted as the rightful surviving heir.

Your father surely would have loved to look upon you one last time, but news of his precarious state travelled too slowly. My heart aches knowing that your heart must be broken upon reading this, but I retain one small comfort, namely that the inheritance falls to me rather than to some unfeeling soul who would instantly turn you out. I am not so unfeeling and could never do such a thing. If I had my desire, it would be to see you always at the home of your childhood and I there to share it all with you. Can you see it? I can spare you a difficult future if you will accept my proposal of marriage. I believe your father would be pleased, and you would continue to have every comfort you have grown up with.

I wish to settle the matter soon so you may have a home and a husband who will care for you. You know that I admired you long before this unfortunate news reached me. Please let me know your answer tonight. We need not wait. Given the swift passing of your father, it seems prudent that our union be swift as well.

I have arranged it all. You need only listen for my knock on your door tonight, and we can begin our journey.

Yours truly,
Owen Shaw

At first, Elizabeth trembled. Then she fumed. She crushed the letter in her hand and threw it against the wall.

Shaw had already written to Elizabeth declaring his love for her! Was she destined to become second choice to Clara again? Truly, Mr. Shaw must be a fraud and a complete idiot. Elizabeth doubted every word in his letter.

How could he! He had written love letters to me! To me! He should be here for me!

It would have been romantic, a surprise visit from a hopeful lover. But he had come for Clara. Would she think his actions romantic? *Doubtful.*

Elizabeth started imagining ways she could sabotage Mr. Shaw's visit, and for a moment, she was sorely tempted to consult Emily and Mabel on the subject. Oh, how her emotions ran wild these days! She took several deep breaths, trying to regain some clarity, and a new thought occurred to her. If Clara ran off with Mr. Shaw, Elizabeth would have Mr. Thayne to herself.

She retrieved the letter from the floor, smoothed out the wrinkles, and walked toward her room feeling suddenly calmer. She would still have to reconcile herself to being second choice, which would be nearly unbearable, but as she rubbed her belly, she reminded herself she did not have time to be particular. Instead, she should worry about how to make Mr. Thayne want her after Clara was gone. Elizabeth could show him, for instance, how fickle Clara had been, and that it was she who stayed.

Poor Clara!

The thought came unbidden, but Elizabeth could not suppress it. If Clara cared about her father at all, she would be devastated. Elizabeth could imagine Clara sobbing in her room wondering what was to become of her. Clara would not only be devastated. She would be vulnerable, and surely, Mr. Shaw would have thought of that.

What a rake, urging Clara into marriage after such a blow! What reasons could he have for such haste?

Of course, Elizabeth knew. Mr. Shaw was the kind of man who would take what he wanted, the kind of man who harbored the worst of intentions. Could she really let Mr. Shaw take advantage of Clara like that? Clara was in love with Mr. Thayne. Though Elizabeth had made her observations grudgingly, she had seen how tenderly Mr. Thayne looked at Clara and could tell how much he wanted to be with her. As envious as Elizabeth was, seeing them together was a reminder that love did not always come tainted, that perhaps even she could rise above her own unfortunate circumstances. Elizabeth had no strong affection for Clara, but she knew she could not live with herself if she let Clara fall prey to a liar as she had.

No. Elizabeth would not allow it. She would confront Shaw about it directly and watch his discomfort confirm his guilt.

Or better yet, she thought mercilessly, she would catch him in his own snare.

Chapter 46

Clara sank to the floor and shook with spasms. Her father dead? How could it be so? How had she not seen it coming? Because all this time, she had turned a blind eye to how sick he really was, never comprehending a day when the world would not sustain him. Her dear father, who had encouraged her to go to London, to be happy, to enjoy herself. Gone.

Guilt and fear smothered Clara. Her father gone, and she not there to hold his hand and kiss his cheek one last time. And poor Louisa! Alone at Milton Manor without any other family to comfort her.

And the final blow? Clara's home was not her own anymore. It belonged to Mr. Shaw now. He even had a statement from the solicitor. She was still numb to his proposal, his shocking, earth-shattering proposal that felt more like a rug being pulled from her feet than the chivalrous rescue he painted it to be.

She loathed herself for not saying no right away. Granted, she was stunned and crushed under the weight of such misery, but she remembered her father's words. *All the luxury in the world means nothing if you don't love the people you are with.* Clara didn't love Mr. Shaw, but she loved her home, and she loved Louisa. Where would Louisa go if Clara didn't do something to keep their home? Clara's father had encouraged her to marry for the right reasons, but suddenly, the right reasons were elusive, and she couldn't think clearly.

What if Mr. Shaw really did care?

No. It wasn't right. She knew it couldn't be. She couldn't marry Mr. Shaw out of fear. *No.*

Earlier, at her bedchamber door, Mr. Shaw had ignored her answer and pressed again. *Come with me,* he'd said. *It's the only way.* Otherwise, she would be adrift with no home and no protection.

Mr. Shaw would fix that.

He had taken a step into her bedchamber.

No! Clara put her hand on his chest to keep him at bay. Even if her thoughts were frenzied, she knew she would not be ensnared to marry because of a compromising situation. Oh, why wouldn't he leave?

Clara pushed him further out, and fortunately, he complied, but only once Mr. Thayne had walked down the hall and seen them. Mr. Thayne's face displayed such an array of emotion in those seconds outside her door. If Mr. Shaw's news hadn't stripped her of hope, she might have found the words to say something to Mr. Thayne, to offer some explanation or beg for help. Instead, she retreated inside her room. She'd wasted no time afterward securing the door and sinking to the floor.

The room still spun around her as she hugged her knees.

Where did Mr. Thayne fit in this world of loss she had fallen into? Would he want her if she was thrown out of her own home, poorer than even she had known? They had never talked of money or inheritances or dowries. They had shared an unforgettable kiss, but they had never discussed marriage.

Except in London when Mr. Thayne had proposed to her out of duty, and she had rejected him.

Maybe Mr. Thayne was right, she sighed. If only she had secured him when she'd had the chance. Perhaps then her current circumstances would not be so awful.

Clara felt herself sinking. She had to make a choice. She already knew what her choice would be, but that didn't make it any easier.

Once again, her life hinged on a single moment.

At least there was one silver lining. Frances was not going to marry such a scoundrel.

Chapter 47

*S*haw sat in the dark on the edge of his bed and rubbed his eyes with the palms of his hands. He was exhausted but didn't want to lie down and risk falling asleep. Who knew that eloping would be such demanding work? Things had been more difficult with Clara than he had anticipated, but he still felt confident he would get what he wanted. He had to.

He eyed his only bag, which still lay in the corner, untouched since he had arrived, and stood to pace around the room. It was nearly time for him to find Clara and sneak out to the carriage he had hired. Shaw had promised the driver extra pay for being quiet, and he sincerely hoped the man followed instructions.

Pulling out his watch, he held it up to his candle to see the time. Four in the morning. *This had better be worth it,* he groaned. His limbs were heavy and slow as he put on his warmest coat, hefted his bag, and stepped into the hallway.

The whole house was dark. His candle cast a mix of strange glows and flickering shadows over everything. Disoriented, he strained to recognize paintings and furniture, anything that told him he was near Clara's bedchamber. He would feel like the biggest dolt in England if he couldn't correctly identify her door after all his trouble.

Luckily, he didn't have to worry. There she stood alone in the dimness of the hallway with two bags at her feet. She wore a dark cloak with the hood pulled up over her head so it hung almost over her entire face. Only her plump lips and small chin could be seen. She wasn't smiling but she didn't frown either. Shaw tried to stay collected, but he had to admit, seeing her there made his blood pump faster. He had expected to do more convincing and urging, yet there she was.

She had given him such pains earlier that evening. It would have been easier to let her read his letter in private, but he couldn't find it. He'd had no choice but to explain it all face to face. At least he still had the statement from Barnes. It had been difficult to watch her cry and beg him to leave her alone, but he couldn't do that. Her distress only made him more adamant. He had explained it repeatedly. It was the only way. Marrying him was the right choice.

"What about Frances?" Clara had asked.

Shaw took a step back. Why Frances would matter, he had no idea, but he explained what he could regarding her situation. Strangely, that seemed to satisfy something in Clara, so Shaw kept pressing her, telling her how much he admired her, how there was no other way to ensure her protection. Marrying him meant she would never have to leave her home, and so on.

When Shaw saw one of the men from dinner approaching, he whispered his last arguments. "Mark my words, Clara, we will be married tomorrow. Wait for my knock. I *will* come for you."

He hoped he had said enough, but he had braced for a struggle. Now, she was there, ready and willing, and he was prepared to play the part of a devoted lover. That was the fun part.

"Darling!" Laying the candle aside, he rushed over and hugged her tightly. When she actually hugged him back, Shaw melted at the unexpected touch. *What a relief!* The arguing now over, and his bride convinced this was the only way, Shaw felt a new wave of strength rush over him. He leaned in for a kiss, but she lowered her head and put a hand on his chest.

"Please, wait till we get to the carriage," she whispered. "I worry we will wake someone. I couldn't bear it if we got caught. Here, take my bags and go first. I need to get one more bag from my room, and then I'll meet you in the carriage."

"As you wish, my darling," Shaw whispered with a bow and a tip of his hat.

He turned around and quietly strode to the front of the house. The great wooden doors were heavy but well-oiled on their hinges. He opened the doors just enough to slip through and then left them slightly ajar so it would be easier for Clara to handle when she came through with her bag. He would show her what a considerate husband he could be.

He tossed the bags over to the driver to secure them and gave the man half his wages for carrying out this part of the plan accordingly. The driver nodded and pocketed the money. The other half was to be given when the job was done.

Shaw climbed in the carriage and waited, hearing only the sounds of the horses snorting and shuffling on the gravel. He tapped his foot on the carriage floor and watched for Clara through the window. It had only been a few minutes since he had left her, but it felt like hours. The freezing air was creeping into his skin, and he realized he did not completely trust her yet. Maybe he shouldn't have left her alone. What if she woke up the entire household to catch him in the act? The driver was poised for just such an emergency, but hopefully, it would not come to that. Not until they were several miles away would Shaw be able to breathe easily.

Just as he was about to go back in after her, he saw her slip through the doors of Brindley Hall like a shadow with her cloak waving in the wind. For the second time that night, relief rolled over Shaw, and, just as quick, a surge of eagerness to see her stowed in the carriage boiled in his stomach. He jumped out to take her bag and help her step in, noting how graceful her every movement was. Maybe he would enjoy being married after all.

Climbing in after her, he secured the door and called to the driver. As the carriage rolled out at the signal, Shaw looked at Clara, still hooded. He leaned over once again to kiss her, but she grabbed his hand and held it tightly in her lap.

"Not yet. Please. I just need a little distance between us and this house."

Shaw thought it charming she was so nervous. "I know exactly what you mean."

He leaned back, closed his eyes, and let Clara hold his hand.

Chapter 48

$\mathcal{A}$s soon as Thayne woke up, he could sense that the house was in a bustle. Floorboards creaked above and below under the pressure of swift feet, and the clinks of teacups on trays sounded in the halls. Had he slept late? He sat up and stretched his arms. He hardly ever slept late unless something especially weighed on his mind, and last night, the arrival of Mr. Shaw had given his worries plenty of weight.

By the time Thayne had caught up with Shaw and Clara after dinner last night, Shaw was at the threshold of her bedchamber standing much too closely and clearly giving her a difficult time about something. Clara looked like she had been crying and was trying to push Shaw away. Her relief at seeing Thayne was unmistakable, but she looked too conflicted to talk. So after Shaw went shuffling away, Thayne wished her a good night and was left to only guess what Shaw might have said to her. Thayne had considered following Shaw and wiping that sneer off his face, but instead, he checked his anger and wandered the halls for as long as he could stay awake to make sure the scoundrel didn't lurk where he wasn't wanted.

Considering how late Thayne had finally retired to bed, it was a wonder he had not slept through the morning entirely. As he dressed, reviewing everything he had observed about Mr. Shaw, he remembered something Martin had told him at Felton Park. Martin had warned him that the insulting, anonymous notes Thayne had received months ago might be from a man named Shaw. Thayne had long since discovered that they were from Mr. Platt, but he tucked away the information, rolled back his shoulders, and determined to stay close to

Clara throughout the day. If he caught Shaw attempting anything dishonorable, he would call him out or, at the very least, break his nose.

Thayne didn't know what to expect as he headed downstairs. With luck, Shaw would already be gone. As he reached the bottom of the staircase, he heard several voices mumbling at once.

"Who would have guessed it?"

"What excitement! So romantic!"

"It's all scandal, if you ask me."

A group of servants instantly quieted when Thayne walked past. Others walked by carrying parcels of various sizes while whispering animatedly.

Thayne found the drawing room in just as much commotion. He scanned the usual group of guests but had trouble taking in the details of who was actually there. Emily and Mabel were running around shouting, "Happy Christmas!" And more servants than usual were drifting in and out with trays laden with drinks and food. Thayne could tell some guests were missing, but in all the chaos, he only took care to confirm that Clara was not there. Though he knew it likely that she had slept late too, he could feel his nerves tightening.

Thayne stood confounded by the whispers until the housekeeper came over and asked if he wanted anything.

"Please, where is Miss Everton?" he asked urgently.

"Haven't you heard, sir? She's gone off this morning."

"Gone off? Where?" Thayne's voice came out louder than he'd meant it to.

The housekeeper was about to respond when Sir Douglas approached and slapped Thayne on the back as usual. "So you've heard the news? We're all in an uproar! To think that Mr. Shaw ran off with that young lady in the wee hours of the morning just like that! Why it makes me think—"

"Shaw? Are you sure?"

"That is what the note said, and they are missing this morning. So all evidence suggests it is so. Why, Thayne, dear boy, you look rather shaken. You appear to be more disappointed than I would have thought."

Unbelievable! thought Thayne. "Please, where did they go? I need to find Clara!" He was already devising a plan.

"Oh, Thayne!" Sir Douglas sounded surprised. "There's no point rushing after her, though I am curious what she has to say to you about all this."

"Where?!" Thayne was growing impatient. Why was Sir Douglas being so insensitive?

"To the Teniford chapel. Only a few miles north of here. It will all be over by the time you get there." Sir Douglas started saying something else, but Thayne had turned and was already bolting for the stables.

Teniford. He knew these parts well. Knight was a reliable horse, and Thayne was a skilled rider. Maybe he could make it in time. Maybe. His heart sank as he thought about it. Thayne had no reason to believe he would reach Clara in time, but he had to try. He could not fathom why she would run off with Mr. Shaw. He suspected Shaw must have somehow deceived or coerced her. She would never go of her own will . . . would she?

Never mind. There was no time for doubts. He would go after Clara no matter what, regardless of how long it took to reach her. He would travel the whole countryside and fight Shaw if he had to. Clara meant the world to him, more so now than ever before! He promised himself anew that he would put every effort into being with Clara.

As Thayne raced toward Teniford, the wind whipped his hair, and the ground rumbled beneath his horse. The speed felt good and strangely made Thayne feel anchored. His thoughts pounded with purpose in unison with his horse's hooves. Clara. Clara. Clara. He would get there in time. He would.

Chapter 49

*S*haw startled awake as the carriage veered. He looked straight in front, steadied himself, and massaged his brow. How long had he slept? The daylight streaming through the cracks in the window flaps pierced his eyes and suggested he had slept hours longer than he had intended. Even though he had been improving his habits for at least a fortnight now, his head still pounded upon waking up and his thoughts were clouded. The rhythmic rumble of the wheels beneath him almost lulled him back to sleep as he rubbed his eyes.

And then it all came back to him.

Eloping. Inheritances. A life of comfort. Proving his father wrong. Keeping what was rightfully his away from Philip. All because he was clever enough to convince Clara to say yes.

Clara!

He turned to the side to see his bride to be. There sat a lovely creature, indeed, but it was not the woman he had meant to carry away. There, with her hood pulled back, sat Elizabeth Watson watching him with an alluring smile and a cocked brow.

Shaw was dumbfounded. Several drips of sweat formed at the top of his forehead as he trembled and cursed himself. He had been in plenty of scrapes before, but being exposed like this was worse than anything he had ever been through.

"Oh, no!" he gasped. "Tell me! I—" He shook his head. He knew how to talk his way out of anything. Why couldn't he get the words out?

"You what?" Elizabeth's grin turned ruthless.

Shaw groaned. "I don't understand."

"Of course you don't!" she said accusingly. She raised her hand and looked at her fingernails. "I never liked being out of the know. Terrible feeling." She leaned back, apparently finished with her speech.

Shaw was astounded. "Is that all you have to say?"

"What else should I say, darling?"

"Darling?" Shaw was growing sick with the carriage's swaying. "Tell me what's going on!"

"Why, I thought you were the one with the plan. We're on our way to be married, are we not?"

Shaw looked her in the eye. "You want to marry me?"

"I'm here, aren't I?" she said sweetly.

"Yes, but *why* are you here? What happened to Clara?"

"First tell me why you came for Clara instead of me. You wrote me a handful of love letters. Did they mean nothing to you?" There was a distinct edge to Elizabeth's voice.

Shaw considered several ways he could answer, some more truthful than others, but there was something about the way Elizabeth pinned him with her stare that suggested he had best not trifle with her.

"All right," he said. "I'll start at the beginning, but you must let me tell you everything."

"I wouldn't have it any other way." She folded her arms and waited.

Shaw drew in a deep breath and braced himself. "My father came to me a few months ago and threatened to cut me off if I did not reform and marry by the end of the year. As I considered which ladies I might pursue, two came to mind, you and Clara. So, I wrote to both of you."

"Hmm. I had a feeling." Elizabeth shook her head and scoffed.

Shaw hated anticipating her reaction, but all he could do was go on. "I had not made a very deep connection with either of you yet. Clara never even replied to my letters, but you did. I must confess, your letters worried me. I sensed in them some urgency on your part, which did not suit me. I prefer to be the one directing things. So, I was hesitant to pursue you. Then I learned that I might be distantly related to Clara. If it were true, I would inherit her estate, which is entailed. I'm not even sure she was aware of it. I thought I had the best chance with her, given our relation, but when I visited her in London, she hardly seemed interested in the news. So, I came up with a plan to convince her to marry me."

"So you could prevent your father from disinheriting you?"

"Indeed," he answered heavily.

Elizabeth frowned. "So you wrote this?" She held up a crumpled piece of paper.

"Is that where my letter went?" Shaw couldn't hide his anger. How had Elizabeth gotten hold of it?

"You are fortunate I found it, you scoundrel!" She folded it back up and secured it somewhere in the folds of her dress. "Is Clara's father really dead?"

"He could be," Shaw answered. "I thought if I were lucky, her father would die before we returned from our elopement."

"What a terrible thing to think!"

"Yes, exactly!" Shaw's voice grew in frustration. "I hated myself for even thinking it. How she would despise me if she discovered my deceit! But I had to do it!" Shaw was almost yelling.

"Because of money? Your inheritance? Your pride?" Elizabeth sneered.

"Yes, all of that!" Shaw rubbed his brow and felt his strength escape with each new confession. It all sounded so much worse out loud than when he had only thought it.

Elizabeth smiled tensely. "That can't be the end of your confession."

"I beg your pardon?" he blurted at her.

She said nothing, but her eyes shot daggers.

His mind reeled. What else did she want him to say? "Look, Elizabeth, I just thought things would be easier with Clara. I still don't understand what you are doing here."

"Fair enough that you should want to know," she said. "I will tell you, but first, I need to know whether you will keep this carriage on course. I still want to be married. You will still retain your inheritance with me as your bride, will you not?"

Shaw had no time to think. "You still want to be married? To me? Or to anyone?"

"Oh, Owen!"

He jolted at hearing her use his Christian name.

"Now is not the time to get sentimental," she said. "We've both made it clear we want to be married. We wouldn't be in this situation if either of us really cared about who we married."

Shaw clutched his stomach. The bouncing carriage combined with Elizabeth's deception made him feel like a ship with a broken helm. The best he could do now was pretend he could still steer. "I'll keep this carriage on course, but it is still your turn to talk. Why do you want to get married?"

Elizabeth made a pouty face and lifted the window flap so she could peer out.

"Come now, Elizabeth! I'll admit in all honesty I'm grateful you found my letter. Imagine if one of the others had found it."

Elizabeth gave a small laugh. "You would have been called out, or at the very least, dragged into the snow and forced to sleep in the stables."

Shaw laughed nervously and agreed.

"Don't laugh just yet." Her eyes turned steely on him. "I haven't decided yet whether I will drag you out myself."

Shaw cleared his throat. He wasn't sure it made sense for her to feel that way, but then again, what did make sense? He was trapped in a carriage with a jealous lady who seemed to be exacting her revenge by eloping with him.

He met her eyes, struggling to understand why she was there and what she thought of him, when, to his surprise, her gaze melted, and she began to sob.

Shaw froze in his seat. Seeing Clara cry had been irritating, but this was much worse. Elizabeth's tears flowed from a place of pain that was raw and deep, a place he recognized because he knew it well.

He slowly reached out and took her hand.

Elizabeth spoke through her tears. "I hate being your second choice! I'm more desperate to marry than you are, but how can I marry you if I believe you have no affection for me? Oh, what have I done!"

Shaw knew he should be sensitive. He should have given her some sort of reassurance, but instead, he had to ask, "Why are you more desperate to marry?"

Elizabeth took a long breath. "I once thought I was in love. I risked everything for him, gave myself to him! I thought we would be married, but he abandoned me! Now I am positively wretched!"

The suffering in her voice was unbearable. Like a wave, it smothered Shaw until the pain of Blaire's betrayal resurfaced. His breathing became heavy, and wanting relief as much as he wanted to give it, he placed a hand on Elizabeth's shoulder.

She flinched and shrugged his hand off.

A look of nausea rolled over her face as she turned away. Was the carriage's swaying making her ill?

"You have no idea what I have been through," she spat. "You understand nothing about love!"

That was an accusation Shaw would not endure. "Oh? And how would you know? I proposed to a girl I adored right before she told me she was marrying someone else!" He leaned forward and allowed his head to sink into his hands. "I suppose that was one of the reasons I resented my father for pushing me toward marriage on his time rather than my own. I hadn't yet healed from the rejection."

After a minute of silence, he looked up and saw Elizabeth staring at him blankly.

She sniffled. "Do you still love her?" Her voice hinted at sympathy.

Shaw was embarrassed by the unsteady laugh that escaped his mouth. "Do I still love her? Yes, and no! I still love the girl I thought she was, but how can I be in love with someone who does not exist?" Shaw could hardly believe his own statement. It was the first time he realized Blaire was not the person he thought she was. He had been holding onto a memory, a hope for something that never existed. He needed to let her go. It was time, whether he was ready or not, and with the decision made, Shaw felt the pain inside loosening. "What about you? Do you still have feelings for this man who abandoned you?"

"No," she whispered. "Like you, I mourn for what once was. I cry for what could have been, and . . ." her voice started shaking, "I worry about the future." She looked down and placed a hand on her slightly rounded belly.

Shaw gasped as he took in the meaning. He couldn't believe she was telling him this.

"You now see why I am even more desperate to marry than you are." Her voice was barely audible.

Shaw nodded. He could see it clearly. Society would shun Elizabeth Watson. Unless she married soon.

Elizabeth sat with the truth exposed, one arm wrapped across her midsection and the other across her chest on the opposite shoulder. Truly, Shaw had always thought her beautiful, but in that moment, her beauty did not blaze with her usual pride. Rather, a tender and fragile air softened her features.

Never before had Shaw wanted so deeply to reach out and comfort someone.

"Yes," he began, "I do see. I see you have been hurt, and I understand your pain. I know how easy it is to give in to passions rather than temper them. When Blaire rejected me, I smothered my heartache with recklessness. I lost half my inheritance to gambling, and I dishonored my family name. And now, I'm reduced to manipulative strategies to get a woman to say yes. Who could live with me now? Who could ever forgive me?" Shaw hadn't meant to sound so pathetic. He had wanted to show Elizabeth understanding. Instead, he drifted back to explaining his own deplorable behavior.

"Forgiveness," she mused. "Society will forgive you. There is always room for a rake. But for a woman like me?" She shook her head as a tear escaped.

Shaw tenderly brushed away the tear, and all sense of loss and panic disappeared. In its place came the distinct desire to make things right. "Ah, but you forget something," he said.

Elizabeth stared widely at him and blinked.

Shaw risked giving her his most rakish grin. "I still want to get married."

Elizabeth leaned closer. "Just like that?"

"Absolutely."

He thought she was about to lean in for a kiss, but then she sat back exasperated. "How shall we ever trust each other? We shall drive each other mad!"

Shaw laughed. "When you put it like that, it sounds fun! We both need this."

Elizabeth rolled her eyes.

"Oh, come now! I don't know! What married couple doesn't drive each other mad sometimes? Elizabeth, it's not as if you have a lot of options right now, but I'm asking you anyway. Will you have me?"

She looked like she was trying to hold back a smile. "You know, I almost think you mean it."

"Of course I mean it! You've got spirit! More than most girls have. I have a feeling, Elizabeth, that you are going to suit me just fine." He reclined to the corner of the carriage with both hands up behind his head.

Elizabeth flashed him a devious smile. "Are you not at all curious whether I think you will suit me?"

Shaw leaned forward and took her hand. "I don't think you would have jumped in this carriage at all if you didn't like the idea of being with me at least a little bit."

Shaw was pleased to see Elizabeth blush. With her hand still in his, he gently pulled her toward him and finally gave her that kiss.

Chapter 50

Clara blinked back the tears that sprang with each stark reminder of where she was. Rafters stretched across arched ceilings. Stained glass windows blossomed against whitewashed walls. Hardwood pews creaked under the weight of guests, and an old clergyman waited to perform his duties. The small bouquet of holly in her hands reminded Clara of the holly bough Mr. Thayne had given her that first morning at the Weltons'. More tears welled up. She closed her eyes and imagined that Mr. Thayne was there to hold her hand and steady her nerves. If only she hadn't felt too shy to ask him to accompany her to a wedding.

She looked over to where her uncle and aunt were sitting, waiting for the ceremony to begin. They kept alternating their smiles between Clara and the bride and groom. Frances was an incredibly beautiful bride. Layers of silk and lace cascaded from her shoulders to her feet while tiny pearls circled her waist, and white silk flowers mingled with her curls. Philip Shaw stood by her side, equally elegant in his black jacket and silver waistcoat, overflowing with pride.

Clara thought about how the couple came to be married that day, Christmas of all days, and how she had been fortunate enough to attend the wedding. It was nothing short of miraculous. At least, that was how Frances had described it.

Somewhere in the middle of Mr. Shaw's horrendous proposal, Clara had learned that Frances and his brother, Philip, were to be married that day at the Teniford chapel. Mr. Shaw seemed to be under the impression that this news would somehow entice Clara to be hastily married herself.

She shuddered to think how he had stood menacingly at the threshold of her bedchamber, insisting that her life in Milton was ruined and that he was her only salvation. Thank goodness Mr. Thayne had come and scared him off! At least Mr. Shaw hadn't come knocking on her door in the middle of the night as he said he would. Clara had spent half the night awake worrying that Mr. Shaw would try to carry her off regardless of her refusals. Such deceit! Eventually she had fallen asleep from exhaustion but not without first shoving the chest of drawers in front of her door. If it weren't for the fact that Frances was getting married that morning, Clara never would have been able to wake up so early.

It was a most fortunate thing she did though, because as soon as she had talked with Rose and William, explaining all that Mr. Shaw had put her through, they were able to ease her mind of her worst fears. Clara's father was not dead. Rose had received a letter from Louisa only the day before describing Mr. Everton's recovery. He was doing quite well.

Once Clara had read the letter with her own eyes, she embraced Rose and William and let her tears flow. She didn't know how long they lasted, only that they cleansed her from the pain of Mr. Shaw's deception. With her heart much relieved, she was able to return to her original purpose. She had to be at Frances's wedding that morning. Frances would certainly want her there. So as soon as they were dressed, Rose and William accompanied Clara to Teniford.

When Clara arrived, the chapel was in a state of commotion. Mrs. Wright could be seen bustling from guest to guest, using big hand gestures to explain something or issue commands. She kept straightening her bonnet and rearranging flowers at the end of the pews. Clara walked in slowly and looked around. The guests who were already seated were whispering to each other in a wind of confusion that flew all the way to the rafters.

Clara was about to sit on a pew in the far back corner when she felt a tug at her shoulders. Turning around, she had only a moment to take in Frances's ecstatic grin before Frances pulled her into the biggest hug she had ever received. Frances then took Clara's hand and pulled her over to a private alcove where they could sit and talk.

"Clara! You're here! I didn't know whether you would receive my invitation in time! Oh, I'm so glad you're here!"

Clara laughed, "So am I! Goodness, Frances, you had me worried! What happened?"

Frances didn't hesitate. "When I sent you that letter, I was so worried about Philip! I thought he had changed his mind or gotten hurt. As it was, he had been feeling guilty about running away with me. He didn't want my parents to view their son-in-law as a scoundrel. He thought it was a selfish thing to do, not to let my parents be at our wedding. Without saying anything to me—and he will pay for that later, I assure you—he travelled to my home and talked with my father. It took a few days, but Philip is so charming! He convinced my father that his intentions were honorable and that he is capable of supporting us. It so happens that his late uncle recently left him a modest estate that will be enough for us to live on. As soon as he learned the details from the solicitor, he went to talk to my father. Philip arrived here just two days ago, bringing with him my father and a common license. Such an amazing gift!

"What's most amusing is that my cousin, Mary Dalton, who was to be married today, ran off and eloped! Apparently, there were last minute objections to the match. Her note said she would not be prevented from being with the man she loved. So, all of the wedding preparations were reappointed for my wedding!" Frances paused, holding her stomach while she laughed. "Oh, Clara, the most amusing thing of all is that my mother . . . my own mother actually said what a good thing it was that I was getting married so it wouldn't all go to waste!" Frances then handed Clara a bouquet of holly and begged her to be a bridesmaid.

"Oh, Frances!" Clara placed her hand on her chest. "Of course! I'm thrilled see you so happy. I actually believed you were engaged to the other Mr. Shaw. To Owen Shaw!"

Frances sat wide-eyed until her laughter broke free again. "Engaged to Owen Shaw? You actually thought . . ." She shook her head and laughed as if it were the most amusing idea.

Clara explained, "Well, your last note was not so clear, and there was the time at Mrs. Chelsea's ball when he singled you out to dance."

"He was only making fun of me. He knew about Philip and me and thought it would be entertaining to provoke my mother. Besides, he asked about you for half the dance." Frances raised a questioning eyebrow at Clara.

"Oh, dear." Clara covered her eyes with her hand and shook her head. "Please, let's never mention it again." Clara then leaned over to adjust a flower in Frances's hair. "Congratulations, dear Frances. You deserve every joy!"

The girls hugged one last time and took their places. Now, as Clara stood and watched Frances and Philip Shaw promise their lives to each other, she wondered what it would take to seal her own happiness. She and Mr. Thayne had only recently become more than friends, and she didn't know how long it would take to become more than that. Time at the Weltons' would eventually run out. Would her time with Mr. Thayne run out too?

Clara tried to ignore her questions and enjoy the present moment. She listened as the clergyman pronounced the final words and watched with a heart full of wishes as Frances and Philip Shaw shared their first kiss as husband and wife. Though the guests had come expecting to see Miss Dalton married that morning, no one seemed disappointed to see Frances instead.

Everyone eagerly rose at the end of the ceremony to line the couple's path to the carriage and give them a proper send off. Frances and Philip ran out the church doors hand in hand as Clara and the guests showered them with dried rose petals and congratulations. Philip wrapped his arm around Frances's waist and kissed her once more before helping her into their carriage. Handkerchiefs waved goodbye and cheers echoed off the church walls. Frances, a glowing new bride, waved farewell one last time.

As the carriage slowly rolled away, a new commotion rose up and fought for attention. A man on a horse at full charge was galloping over, trailing waves of dust clouds as his jacket billowed like a ship's sail. The horse's pummeling hooves competed with the cheers of the crowd until the horse won out and drew all attention to it.

"Stop!" the man yelled frantically. "*Stop*, please! No!"

He sounded so urgent, so loud that the carriage actually stopped for him. Frances and Philip Shaw looked back and waited. The newcomer pulled hard on the reins to slow his horse, and that is when Clara recognized him.

He hadn't noticed her yet. She looked at his face and thought back to their various meetings, the awkwardness at the Chelsea ball, the utter shock at meeting at the Weltons', and even the faint fragments of memories she retained from their very first introduction at the end of last season. All these thoughts whipped through her in a heartbeat, and a rich and hopeful laughter bubbled out. She couldn't help it. Why did their meetings tend to be so dramatic? She had no idea why James Thayne had followed her to Frances's wedding, but it convinced her that he would always come for her.

"James!" she cried, running closer, not caring that the wedding guests were gasping their shock and staring impatiently. Clara smiled brightly as his eyes met hers and then darted in confusion between her and the carriage.

Since his yelling had stopped, and he said nothing else, the carriage pulled away once more, and the wedding guests began to disperse.

Mr. Thayne jumped down from his horse looking out of breath. "Oh, Clara!"

Uncle William ran over and took the reins for Mr. Thayne. Clara thought she heard her uncle mumble something to Mr. Thayne that sounded like encouragement.

Mr. Thayne looked at Clara and buckled over with his hands on his knees.

"James, what is the matter?" Clara asked, truly perplexed. Had something dreadful happened?

"I . . . thought . . . you . . ." Mr. Thayne stepped back to look at her. "I thought you were getting married today. I thought that Shaw fellow had done something to coerce you into it. I didn't know if he had obtained a common license or if he had tricked you into running off to Scotland. I heard you would be here, so I came to . . . to stop you. Or him! Or . . ." He trailed off and shook his head. "I couldn't bear the thought of losing you!"

Clara understood. He had come for her.

To calm his shaking nerves, she took his hand and led him toward the church.

"You are correct that Mr. Shaw tried to coerce me into marrying him. He even lied and told me my father had died. At first, I was heartbroken, but this morning, my aunt Rose showed me a letter she had just received from Louisa regarding my father's mending health. You can't imagine my relief! Mr. Shaw claimed he was to inherit my family's estate, which may have been true, but Louisa's letter actually cleared that matter up as well."

"That horrible—Next time I see him, I'll—" Thayne looked off to the side and pounded a fist to his hand.

"Come sit inside with me. It's freezing out here!"

Clara led Thayne to a pew in the back of the chapel, which was now empty. As they sat down to face each other, Mr. Thayne took Clara's other hand so that both were securely in his. Her heart skipped as she tried to collect her thoughts.

"Louisa told us that the man she had been in love with several years ago recently sent her a letter from India. He regrets they ever argued and has never forgotten her. He is returning to England and wants to see her. Louisa now reveals he is the same cousin who was rumored to be lost in India. This cousin is the one who is to inherit Milton Manor. Before his letter, my father and Louisa didn't know whether another male heir would ever be found. They had been keeping it all a secret from me because my father didn't want me to worry or rush into marriage out of fear.

"Oh, James, I never would have run off with Mr. Shaw! Even if what he said was true. Even if I would have had to give up my home and leave everything behind. That wouldn't matter so long as I could be with you—" Clara stopped, suddenly shy.

He raised her hand to his cheek and held it tight. At first Clara only focused on the way his stubble tickled her skin, but then she remembered something.

"I almost forgot," she said, gently pulling her hands away to retrieve a crumpled letter from her reticule. "This is for you."

Mr. Thayne brushed her fingers with his as he took the paper. Clara could see his eyes move over the lines until his jaw dropped and he looked up. "This is from you. This looks like a reply to my . . ."

"To your last letter," Clara finished. "Louisa sent it to me along with a short note explaining that Mr. Platt's grandmother, Mrs. Hatfield, saw it fall out of his coat when he staggered home after some late night revelry. Mrs. Hatfield sends her apologies and has had her grandson permanently removed from her estate."

Clara's cheeks grew warm as she waited for Mr. Thayne to finish reading. "You see?" she said. "It was a very personal letter."

"My darling Clara!" was all he said as he carefully folded the paper and tucked it into his waistcoat. He reached his hand to her cheek, but as he leaned closer, his eyes paused just above her head.

Clara reached up to check whether a curl had fallen loose, or, *Ah, yes!* She understood. There she had pinned the blue forget-me-nots he had given her in London along with the one he had untangled from her hair after playing with Emily and Mabel. Clara held still as Mr. Thayne's hand brushed the forget-me-knots, then traveled gently down her arm before once again taking her hand in both of his.

Clara lost herself in the warmth of his touch until he dropped to one knee right there in the pew. She sucked in a breath.

"Dear Clara," he sighed. "It was only an hour ago when I thought I had lost you forever. It was an awful moment. Yet even then, I allowed myself to hope there would still be a chance for us. I confess, finding you safe and unharmed feels like a miracle, just as it did when I discovered you were staying at Brindley. Fate has been kind, despite my mistakes, but I won't risk tempting it any longer. I won't wait another minute to ask you . . . what I've asked before but with a truer heart this time and a clearer understanding of who you are." His eyes shone with such ardency that Clara wondered how she ever could have doubted him. "I love you, Clara. I kneel before you and offer myself to you with all my imperfections but with the strongest hope that you will accept me. As for myself, I could never be persuaded to love any differently." Mr. Thayne placed a kiss on her hand and looked up. "Will you marry me, Clara?"

Her breaths came out in happy sputters as tears glistened on her eyelashes. "Yes!"

Mr. Thayne stood up and pulled her in for a kiss. Clara wrapped her arms around his neck and enjoyed the new sensation of running her fingers through his hair as he cradled her face and proceeded to kiss the tears on her cheeks. She relished every touch as his thumb swept off another tear and kissed the tiny mole that sat under her right eye. He wrapped his arms around her waist and let out a deep, contented sigh.

"You have no idea how long I've been wanting to do that."

Clara's laughter chimed with the church bells as she returned his embrace, which eventually turned to another eager kiss. Her smile broke the kiss just long enough to answer, "You have no idea how long I've been wanting you to do that." After another kiss, she looked up to meet his eyes. "And James?"

"Yes?"

"I love you too."

Chapter 51

Dear Mrs. Shaw,

How does that sound to you, dear Frances? I imagine it sounds absolutely musical because that is the way it sounds whenever I am addressed as Mrs. Thayne. Do you think that the giddy rush I feel when I hear it will ever wear off? I know it is still so new, but I am determined to remember that thrill. You would have laughed and laughed if you had heard me accidentally introduce myself to the Felton Park staff as Miss Everton. Mr. Thayne later swept me up in his arms and reminded me with a kiss that I am Mrs. Thayne.

I wish you could have been at our wedding, but I understand you were not up for travelling. I hope all goes well with the birth, and I greatly look forward to meeting your little one in the fall when we come for a visit.

Our wedding was beautiful beyond my expectation. I took your advice and chose the white satin gown with embroidered lace sleeves, and you were absolutely right. Mr. Thayne was speechless. He, of course, looked strikingly handsome in his dark blue suit, which matched well with my bouquet of roses and lilies. The kind, old clergyman spoke the words that finally bonded us together under the same roof my father and mother were married under. Louisa and my father welcomed Mr. Thayne with open arms and expressed their happiness at seeing us united.

It is a day I shall never forget. To the outward observer, our wedding must have looked like any other, but to me and my James, it was the day our worlds changed. I can almost see you smile as I write this because I know you felt it on your wedding day. I saw it on your face. It is truly amazing, isn't it? James Thayne has made me feel like the happiest woman there ever was.

Together, we have overcome so many misunderstandings and obstacles. Much of the time, I think I was just getting in my own way. My dear husband described to me the very moment he committed to giving our relationship every possible effort. Now, we have made that commitment to each other, and we have made it official before heaven and earth. I look forward to this new chapter in our lives. I wish you and your husband every bit of the same joy and felicity I feel with mine.

I forever remain your friend,
Clara Thayne

After Clara signed and sealed the letter, she looked over at her husband who sat on a small sofa in front of a warm fireplace. The light from the fire flickered around the room and everything about the scene beckoned her over. She didn't hesitate to go to him and nestle into his arms. Mr. Thayne tenderly pulled her close and handed her a folded piece of paper.

"What's this?" she asked, taking the paper with one hand and his hand with her other.

He smiled. "A love letter."

Clara loved how he continued to write her letters even after their wedding. She sometimes found a short note from him on her pillow or a letter on her breakfast plate. Once, he even sent her a letter through the post. Whatever the method of delivery, each message expressed his love for her in a new way.

Clara drew imaginary lines on his palm and asked, "Shall I read it now or later?"

As she reclined against his chest, she could hear his heartbeat softly keeping rhythm in contrast to the irregular crackle of fire.

He spoke gently. "Whenever you like, my dear Clara." She felt him shift as a smile hinted across his lips. "On second thought . . ." He took the letter and tossed it on a nearby table. "There's time for letters later."

Clara couldn't tell whether he pulled her in for the kiss or whether she leaned in, but it didn't matter. They were together, and she could reach for him whenever she wanted.

Acknowledgments

To those readers who made it all the way to the acknowledgments page, thank you! It means a lot to me that you would take a chance on me as a new author and read my book. I hope you enjoyed it!

I feel very blessed to have so many people in my life who have supported me on this writing journey. A huge thanks goes to my husband, Jacob. His feedback and ideas were invaluable to me throughout the whole process. No doubt, this book wouldn't be the same without his influence and constant support. I also have to thank my kids. Their innocence and love inspires me and makes me smile every day. They impart so much strength and light just by being themselves, and I can't tell you how much it warms my mommy heart to see them writing their own stories. I'm also grateful to have many friends, neighbors, and family members who read earlier versions of *Dear Clara* and cheered me on, even when I still had a long way to go. I'm thankful for my mom and mother-in-law who always show such enthusiasm for my writing, and I'm grateful for the faith they have in my abilities.

I'm also grateful to God who has blessed me in countless ways. I've felt His sustaining love for me over the years, and I believe I have felt His approval of my choice to make room in my life for writing again. So, so grateful for that.

I'm thankful for the crew at Cedar Fort, including Shawnda Craig who designed this book's beautiful cover, my editors and their helpful feedback, and Angela Johnson, who never tired of my endless questions. Thanks for taking a chance on me! This really is a dream come true!

About the Author

As soon as Shelly Powell was old enough to write, she was crafting stories to share with family and friends. Her earliest works featured princesses and mermaids, which she willingly portrayed on the makeshift stages of home and school.

Although her interests have expanded since then, she still finds writing to be a thrilling process and a unique way to connect with others. Shelly loves happy endings but also believes in happy beginnings. She hopes to write many stories in the years to come.

Shelly enjoys running, yoga, drawing, and spending time with her sweet husband and amazing kids.